Perfectly Fine Christmas

Perfectly Fine Christmas

La Jill Hunt

www.urbanbooks.net

Urban Books, LLC
300 Farmingdale Road, NY-Route 109
Farmingdale, NY 11735

Perfectly Fine Christmas
Copyright © 2021 La Jill Hunt

All rights reserved. No part of this book may be reproduced in any form or by any means without prior consent of the Publisher, except brief quotes used in reviews.

To the extent that the image or images on the cover of this book depict a person or persons, such person or persons are merely models, and are not intended to portray any character or characters featured in the book.

ISBN 13: 978-1-64556-493-5

First Mass Market Printing November 2023
First Trade Paperback Printing November 2021
Printed in the United States of America

10 9 8 7 6 5 4 3 2 1

This is a work of fiction. Any references or similarities to actual events, real people, living or dead, or to real locales are intended to give the novel a sense of reality. Any similarity in other names, characters, places, and incidents is entirely coincidental.

Distributed by Kensington Publishing Corp.
Submit Orders to:
Customer Service
400 Hahn Road
Westminster, MD 21157-4627
Phone: 1-800-733-3000
Fax: 1-800-659-2436

Perfectly Fine Christmas

by

La Jill Hunt

Prologue

Kendall

"Mommy, what's plump?" Kendall asked.

Her mother, who was driving, came to a stop, humming along with Stevie Wonder as he sang "That's What Christmas Means to Me," and then glanced over. "*Plump*? It means, uh . . . 'fuller.' No, wait, it means 'round.' Why?"

"Because in children's church, Mrs. Daniels was giving out parts for the pageant, and I told her I wanted to be either the star of Bethlehem or the angel, but she wouldn't let me," Kendall explained. "She said I had to be a camel."

"A what?"

"A camel," Kendall repeated. She'd been a little disappointed with the role that she'd been given, but she was still excited to be a part of the annual Christmas play with her friends.

For the past two years, she'd been a member of the children's choir, but now that she was seven, she could be a part of the best part of the play each year: the Nativity scene. She'd waited patiently as Mrs. Daniels called the names of the children who had been chosen to play Mary, Joseph, and the Three Wise Men. Those parts were assigned to the older kids, but at that moment there were still several roles available, and Kendall was excited when her name was finally called.

"Kendall Freeman, let's see what we have for you, sweetie." Mrs. Daniels peered over the brim of her glasses as she flipped through the clipboard in her hand. "You sure you don't want to be in the choir? You have such a pretty voice."

"No, ma'am." Kendall shook her head. "I wanna be in the play."

"Okay, then I think I have something that will be good for you. What about a shepherd?"

Kendall scrunched up her nose, as if she smelled something horrible. "A shepherd? No, that's for a boy, Mrs. Daniels. I don't wanna be a shepherd."

"I understand, and you're right. I don't know what I was thinking. I'm sorry. Oh, here we go." Mrs. Daniels used her pen to point to the clipboard. "Kendall Freeman, you will be this year's camel."

"But I want to be either the star or an angel," Kendall said, hoping Mrs. Daniels would scan the list of characters again.

Instead, she gave Kendall a warm smile as she placed her hand on her shoulder. "Not this year,

Kendall. I don't think you'll be able to be either one of those. The costumes for the angel and the star of Bethlehem are being reused from last year, and I don't think they'll work for you."

"Why not?" Kendall whined. They reused the costumes every year; that wasn't anything new.

"Because you're a little on the plump side, and some of the other girls are a better fit. But I know that you're gonna make the best camel we've ever had, and as a matter of fact, I'm gonna talk to Miss Lauren and see if she'll even let you do the closing lines. How does that sound?"

Kendall shrugged, still not understanding why she couldn't have the part she wanted, but grateful for the consolation prize of the extra lines. She took the copy of the play that Mrs. Daniels offered her, along with the rehearsal schedule, then headed back to her seat.

"Why do you always have that doll?" Ciera, one of the girls in her age group, asked when Kendall got back to her seat.

Kendall picked up Missy, her favorite doll, and placed her in her lap. "I don't always have her. My mom won't let me take her to school, but Missy likes church, so I bring her."

"She likes church? How do you know?" Ciera looked at the doll and frowned.

"I don't know." Kendall shrugged. "I just kinda know. She's my best friend, and I like church, so she does too. Don't you and your best friend like the same things?"

Ciera's eyes went from Missy to Kendall, and then she snapped, "I don't have a best friend. And I don't have a doll, either."

"Oh." Kendall didn't know how to respond, so she just smoothed Missy's dress down and went back to listening to Mrs. Daniels call names. She noticed Ciera continuing to stare at her. She finally turned and asked, "You want to hold her?"

"Ciera McNeil," Mrs. Daniels called, and the girl hopped up and went to the front of the room. "You'll be the angel."

Ciera clapped excitedly as she jumped up and down. "Yay! That's what I wanted."

Again, Kendall was disappointed: Ciera had been given the part that she wanted. Then she looked down at Missy and felt a sense of gratitude. *At least I have you, Missy.*

By the time church ended, Kendall was hungry and ready to go. For some reason, the word *plump* still resonated in her head. As she and her mother were on the way to Sunday dinner at their favorite restaurant, Kendall decided to ask what it meant, thinking it was no big deal. She was wrong. Her mother, now visibly upset, turned the car around and drove full speed ahead back to the church.

"Stay in the car. I'll be right back," she told Kendall as she unbuckled her seat belt.

"But . . ." Kendall didn't bother saying anything else, because her mother slammed the car door and marched toward the entrance to the church. Instead, she held Missy, her favorite doll, in her arms as she looked at the stapled papers Mrs. Daniels had given her. "The Birth" was written in bold print on the top page. She was determined not to let Mrs. Daniels down, and so she vowed to be the best camel St. Joseph's Missionary Baptist Church had ever seen.

A few minutes later her mother returned to the car. "Guess what?" she said when she opened the driver's door. Kendall could see that she was still a little agitated but was smiling.

"What?" Kendall asked.

"You're not gonna be the camel," she told her. "You're gonna be the star."

"Huh?"

"You're gonna be the star of Bethlehem in the pageant," her mother said matter-of-factly. "Congratulations."

"But Mrs. Daniels said—"

"Don't worry about what she said. She changed her mind. I promise you're going to be the most beautiful star of Bethlehem anyone has ever seen. But you'd better learn those lines." A huge grin spread across her mother's face as she leaned over and gave Kendall a hug. Kendall nodded excitedly. "I promise I will, Mama. I'm gonna learn all of them, and the songs too, even though I'm not in the choir."

"That's fine too," she said. "And, Kendall, don't ever let anyone tell you what you can't do. Doesn't matter if you're plump or not, you're still amazing, and you can do whatever you want to do. As long as you work hard and strive to be the best, that's all that matters."

Three weeks later, Kendall said all her lines perfectly as the star of Bethlehem and then recited the closing lines of the play. The audience gave her a standing ovation and raved at her gorgeous gold costume with the flashing lights, which her mother had crafted. Kendall was proud of herself, and from the look on her mother's face, she knew that she was proud too.

Her mother rushed over and hugged her tight after the performance was over. "You were amazing, baby! I knew you would be."

"Really, Mama? I didn't forget one word, not one." Kendall grinned.

Her mother nodded. "No, you didn't."

"Where's Missy? And Courtney?" Kendall began looking for her old doll and the new one that she'd gotten from her grandmother for Christmas. Now she had two best friends instead of one.

"They're right here." Her mother held up both dolls. "Now, grab your coat and let's get ready to go."

"But they have refreshments in the back, Mama. Can we please stay?" Kendall begged.

"Fine. For a little while. But I'm gonna need for you to take your friends and put them in the car.

I'm not gonna be responsible for them, and I don't want them to get lost."

Kendall wanted Missy and Courtney to enjoy the after-party festivities, but she figured they could keep each other company for a little while in the car. She held them both tight as she followed her mother into the parking lot. "Hey, guys, you're gonna wait in the car while I get some cake, but I promise I'll be right back. Mama's gonna lock the car door, right, Ma?"

When her mother didn't respond, Kendall realized she was no longer beside her. She turned and saw that she'd walked to the corner where Cierra and her mother were waiting at the bus stop. Kendall watched as they talked for a minute. Suddenly, her mother slipped off her coat and helped Ciera's mother put it on. They hugged, and then her mother walked back over to the car.

"Mama, what did you do? Why did you give Ciera's mama your new coat? Grandma gave you that coat for Christmas," Kendall gasped.

"She did. But I didn't need a new coat, Kendall. I already have plenty of coats. Ciera's mother isn't working right now. She doesn't have a job or a coat, and I have both. It's Christmas, and God gave me the opportunity to be her angel on Earth," her mother explained.

"Angel on Earth?" Kendall frowned.

"Yeah, God blessed me so that I could bless her. That's what angels do. Remember what Ciera said in the play? She brought good tidings of great joy. That's what I just did. Showed her God's love from heaven, here on Earth. That's why we celebrate Christmas, baby." Her mother pulled her close.

Kendall looked down at the two dolls in her arms, then back over at Ciera and her mother. "I'll be right back."

"Kendall, where . . . ?"

Kendall skipped across the parking lot. When she got to Ciera, she pushed Courtney into her arms and said, "Merry Christmas."

Ciera looked shocked. She stared at the doll, then said, "Thank you."

Kendall rushed back to her mother, who welcomed her with open arms. "Kendall, sweetie, you are truly a gift. Look at you. You got to be both the star *and* an angel."

"I did, Mama. I did." Kendall nodded and smiled with joy.

Chapter 1

Kendall

The sky was dark and the usually busy street was void of both traffic and pedestrians when Kendall arrived at Diablo Designs, the high-end boutique where she'd worked as the lead seamstress for the past three years. She was grateful that the weather wasn't as cold as she'd expected it to be, considering the fact that it was five thirty in the morning. The boutique didn't open for hours. Kendall had work to do, and she was excited about getting it done before customers arrived. She carefully balanced the large brown box she had carried from the parking garage on her knee as she unlocked the back door, and then she hurried inside to disarm the security system. The store was eerily quiet, and the shadows of the mannequins throughout the open space were almost frightening. Kendall didn't waste time turning on the lights. She carried the box to the front of the store and set it down in front of the display window that held the seven-foot Christmas tree that she'd assembled two days prior.

"I can't believe we're actually doing this."

Startled, Kendall quickly turned around to see her best friend and coworker, Amber, strolling toward her. The look on her face was identical to the irritated tone of her voice.

"Good morning to you too, sunshine." Kendall smiled.

"Don't 'sunshine' me. The last thing I'm feeling right now is good, especially since it's still dark outside," Amber grumbled. "There was no sign of the sun at all."

"Well, whether the one in the sky is up or not, you will always be my sunshine, and I will always have a good morning for you when I see you. And even though you are grumpy as hell, you still look cute." Kendall beamed and put her arm around Amber's shoulders. "I like your skirt."

Amber glanced down at the denim and leather crafted skirt she wore, which happened to be custom made by Kendall. "Thanks. A friend gave it to me as a bribe to get me to come to work in the wee hours of the morning the day after Thanksgiving."

"I see it worked. Come on now, Amb. I have let you moan and groan enough. It's time for you to perk up and get into the holiday spirit, so we can get this tree decorated," Kendall told her.

"This is about as perky as I'm gonna get. You could've at least waited until after Starbucks opened." Amber sighed.

Kendall nodded. "I promise as soon as they open, I got you. You will have your venti mocha latte, with an extra shot of espresso, extra whipped cream, and a dome top. I'll even throw in an almond biscotti for you to enjoy."

Kendall knew Amber well enough to know that the gorgeous skirt wouldn't be enough to pacify her. She was willing to do whatever she had to do. There was no way she was going to be able to get everything done without a ready, willing, and able assistant. Kendall had a vision, and Amber was going to help bring it to life.

Amber folded her arms. "Oh God. Coffee and a biscotto? Something tells me you're about to be extra as hell this year."

"Not at all. I do, however, have a theme."

"You always have a theme, and it's always over the top, Kendall. Why can't we just put up a nicely decorated tree like all the other businesses on the block?"

"Because we aren't like all the other businesses, Amber. We are Diablo Designs, home of the couture maestro herself, Deena Diablo. We don't do *nice*. We do exquisite. This year we will be displaying a winter wonderland. Snow, icicles, snowflakes, and plenty of bling."

"Fine. What do you wanna do first?" Amber groaned.

"Come on, Am. You already know." Kendall smiled.

"God, no, Kendall. It's too early." Amber's head moved back and forth.

"It's the only way to start." Kendall shrugged as she backed up toward the sales counter. She reached under it and opened the cabinet where the sound system was located, then connected it to her phone's Bluetooth. Seconds later the store was filled with the sound of Chris Brown crooning the lyrics to her all-time favorite Christmas song, "This Christmas." Kendall danced her way back across the store and forced a reluctant Amber to sing and sway along. By the time the song had ended and the next one had begun playing, the two of them were excitedly opening the huge box containing lights, garland, and Kendall's beloved Christmas ornaments. The decorating had begun.

Two hours later, as they were finishing up, Deena, Kendall and Amber's boss, walked into the showroom and stopped in her tracks. "Wow! It's beautiful," she exclaimed as she gazed at the tree. She was wearing a gorgeous black tuxedo-style pantsuit that fit her perfectly. With her height of almost six feet, her slender frame, and her high cheekbones, Deena could easily be a model for the designs she created. Everything about her exuded elegance, and it was apparent even in the way she stood back and gracefully waved her hands toward the display they were in the midst of completing.

Kendall, who was in the middle of draping ivory cloth along the bottom of the raised display area, stood up. "You like it?" she asked.

"I love it, Kendall. Every year I tell you that you've outdone yourself, but this year you truly have. I mean, the tree is gorgeous, but this entire space looks like a . . ."

"Winter wonderland," Kendall and Amber said simultaneously.

"Yes, that's exactly what it is." Deena clapped. "And you two managed to get all of this done before it's time to open. That's incredible."

"We had fun doing it." Kendall nodded with excitement. "It didn't even feel like work, really."

Amber raised an eyebrow. "Yeah, it was a blast. You should've come and helped."

Deena laughed, and her caramel complexion made the red lipstick she wore seem even brighter. "Looks like you two had everything under control. You didn't need my help. Besides, with everything I'm responsible for around here, do you think I have time to have fun?"

Kendall gave a warning look just before her friend was about to make another comment, and Amber went back to hanging lights. Although they both loved their jobs, they had a difference of opinion when it came to their boss. Kendall, who worked as a seamstress in the boutique, adored Deena and appreciated the mentorship she provided. Amber, the boutique's top sales consultant, admired and respected Deena, but she felt that her boss was quite self-serving and micro-aggressive and insensitive at times. Kendall often reminded her that because Deena was one of the most sought-after designers of formal couture, her job kept her so busy that she didn't realize what she said most of the time, and she meant nothing by her comments. Over the years, Kendall had become accustomed to Deena's demeanor a little more than Amber had. The reason for this was that in addition to being her boss, Deena had also been one of her mother's friends.

Deena put her arm around Kendall's shoulders, and they stared at the majestic tree, which was now covered in sparkling crystals, white ornaments, and clear lights. "It's beautiful, Kendall. Actually, it's absolutely stunning."

"Not yet." Kendall shook her head. "Almost, but it's missing one thing."

Within seconds, Amber walked over and placed a glossy stained wooden box in Kendall's hands. Kendall tried not to tremble as she opened it. Inside, buried under soft white satin, was one of her most prized possessions: the tree-topper figurine, an angel, that had been passed down for three generations in her family. She carefully lifted it out of the box and smiled in an effort to avoid tears.

Get it together, Kendall. It's the season of joy, not sorrow.

After she adjusted the wings and the fur-trimmed coat of the precious brown porcelain figurine, Kendall held it out. "Here," she said to Deena. "You do the honors."

"Oh, Kendall, no. You do it. It was her favorite part," Deena replied, sounding as if she was just as close to crying as Kendall.

Kendall nodded. "I know. That's why you should do it."

Deena carefully cradled the angel in her hands, and then she stepped up the ladder beside the tree. She positioned the angel atop the tree so that it was upright and secure, then eased back down the ladder. Then the three women stood back and marveled, taking in the end results of the labor that Kendall and Amber had put in for the past few hours. The tree, in Kendall's eyes, was perfect.

"The angel has been placed atop the Christmas tree. We know what that means," Deena whispered.

"Time for the magic to begin." Amber smiled.

Kendall nodded. "Exactly."

"I wonder what Aunt Nichole is going to task us with this year," Amber mused, staring at the tree topper.

Kendall shrugged. "I don't know, but I'm sure we'll soon find out." Without fail, every year since her death, Nichole's mother, it seemed, sent each of them what they'd come to call "angel assignments." These assignments weren't as simple as serving meals at the local shelter or organizing the successful toy drive they held each year in the boutique. No, they usually involved unusual circumstances that seemed to come out of nowhere. For instance, one year Deena paid the hotel bill for a traveling family of four whose car had broken down in front of the store. Another year Amber treated one of their clients' entire fourth grade class to a presentation of *The Nutcracker* after the funding from the school fell through. Kendall lost count of how many times she had paid tabs at restaurants or grocery stores because someone didn't have enough money.

"She's right." Deena laughed. "We never have to wait too long once the angel is in place. That thing is like a bat signal for the Christmas holidays." Deena's tone went from pleasant to direct as she shifted gears. "We need to get in place for the busy day ahead, and the two of you need to get changed. Doors open in fifteen minutes. I hope there's a cup of coffee waiting for me, since you two have some."

Kendall glanced at the two cups of Starbucks that she had had delivered as soon as the app allowed her to order. "Of course. Yours is waiting for you in your office."

Deena smiled. "Good. I can't be upset about your drinking coffee on the showroom floor if I'm doing the same, right?" She walked away, then suddenly stopped and turned back. "Great job on the display, ladies, but let's get these leftover decorations put away and let's play more fitting music," she added. "The holiday songs are fine, but find something a little less urban. Staff meeting in ten minutes, so get to it."

"I swear, I love that woman, but she gets on my nerves," Amber hissed when Deena was out of earshot. "She should've been the one bringing coffee to us, instead of asking if there was some for her. And what the heck does 'less urban' mean? Since when are the Jackson 5 considered urban? Has she forgotten that she's black too?"

"Deena knows that, Amber. The problem is she's bourgeois," Kendall said as they packed up the remaining Christmas decorations. "She also looks at how everything will affect her bottom line. Look at the caliber of our clientele. They're just as *siddity* as she is, and so is everyone else who works here. You and I are the only cool kids."

"You stay defending her, but I get it." Amber sighed and picked up the box with the decorations. "I hope when you start your own fashion line, you don't become 'less urban' and you keep it real, meaning black."

"Girl, you are hilarious, and you know my starting my own line ain't happening anytime soon. I keep telling you that I'm not even close to being ready," Kendall commented as she picked up the two now empty coffee cups.

"As far as I can see, you are ready. Your designs are incredible. The same people who pay Deena top dollar will pay you," Amber continued, as if they hadn't had this conversation dozens of times already. "You and I both know people are trying to get you to make stuff now."

Kendall could admit that she did have amazing design ideas, and her sewing skills were impeccable. But starting a designer clothing line would take a lot more than artwork and a sewing machine. She knew her dream would happen one day. Until that time came, she was grateful to have a job in her field and to work for a high-end designer who paid her well and gave her the opportunity to do what she loved. And despite the fact that she had been approached about sewing projects outside the boutique, the noncompete agreement Deena had required her to sign prevented her from doing so.

"I love the way you believe in me, Am. That's why you're my bestie. I promise, when I start my own label, I'll charge you only half of the retail cost for the garments." Kendall nudged her and pointed to Amber's skirt. "Now, hurry up, so we can change out of this 'urban attire' and get back out there for Insight."

After they had cleaned up from the morning activities and had changed into their work attire, Kendall and Amber rushed back onto the floor so they wouldn't miss the morning meeting, which Deena referred to as "Insight." Like their boss, the entire staff wore all black. It was a requirement for everyone. Although Kendall spent most of the day in the alterations room, she was still expected to observe the rule, because there were times when she was called to assist clients. She didn't mind the dress code. Black wasn't her favorite color choice, but it was easy to put together black pieces. Plus, the color was slimming. Not that she felt the need to look thinner.

Kendall was quite comfortable in her curvaceous, size twenty, larger-than-average body, despite being the only plus-size employee at Diablo Designs. Her wide hips, ample DDD breasts, thick waist, and vivacious derriere worked to her advantage. Because nothing at Diablo's went beyond a size twelve, Kendall was exempt from having to wear certain signature pieces, the cost of which would have been deducted from her paycheck. Amber, who wore a size ten, wasn't so lucky.

Deena smiled at all the staff members gathered around. "I hope you all had a fantastic Thanksgiving, are well rested and recharged for today. Special thanks to Kendall and Amber for the beautiful window display to welcome our clients and get them in the spirit to buy gifts." Deena gazed at each of her employees. "In addition to fulfilling the seasonal needs of our regular customers and Christmas brides, the holidays also mean the start of something else, right?"

They all nodded and shouted in unison, "Holiday ball season!"

Chapter 2

Niya

"Niya, please sit up and put that away. The dining-room table is no place for a cell phone."

Niya quickly slid her cell phone into her pocket and sat straight in her chair without even looking at her grandmother, who'd given her the instructions. Instead, she focused on her food, picking at the rubbery turkey bacon beside the eggs and toast. She didn't mind the eggs but would've preferred regular bacon and some jelly on the dry bread instead of the pat of margarine. Deciding to make the best of her breakfast situation, Niya placed the meat and eggs on the toast and was in the process of folding it when once again, she was scolded.

"That is not the proper way to eat. I didn't prepare a plate for you to eat a poorly constructed sandwich like it came from a cheap fast-food drive-through. Why would you do that?" her grandmother said.

Again, Niya quickly straightened up. She dropped her sandwich onto her plate and stared at it. At this point, it was as if she couldn't do anything right, not even eat breakfast. Grandma Claudia constantly picked at every little thing. Niya didn't make her bed properly, because the sheet wasn't ever tucked in tight enough. Her clothes weren't hung up correctly, because the hangers should all be facing the same direction. Not that this should have mattered, considering the fact that she had commented that Niya's clothes were unappealing.

What does that even mean? Who am I supposed to appeal to in a T-shirt, jeans, and sneakers? Niya had wondered at the time.

Being at her grandmother's house was exhausting, tiresome, and lonely. She missed her mom. It had been two weeks since the car accident that had robbed Niya of the one person who loved her no matter how she looked or the manner in which she chose to eat her breakfast. The last fourteen days felt like a continual, endless nightmare, and it all started when Mrs. Hester, the guidance counselor at her school, had come and got her out of her AP English class and had escorted her to the main office. Mrs. Hester, who was usually full of chatter, had been oddly silent. Something about her energy had seemed off.

"Am I in trouble?" Niya had asked as they walked down the vacant hallway. She knew that she wasn't, considering the fact that other than to her two best friends, she barely talked to anyone in school.

"No, sweetheart." Mrs. Hester put her arm around Niya's shoulder. "Not at all."

"Is this about the field trip to the planetarium?" Niya asked. "I told Mr. Hawkins that I'd rather do a written assignment instead of going. I've been to the planetarium, like, four times since third grade, and I really think it would be a pointless trip," she explained. She also dreaded the thought of being on a crowded school bus with her rambunctious classmates for forty-five minutes, riding to a place where the only thing most of them planned on doing was fool around in the darkness instead of learning about constellations. Granted, Niya had no desire to learn about the stars, either, but she definitely wasn't interested in getting groped by any of her classmates.

"This isn't about the field trip." Mrs. Hester sighed.

Niya's anxiety increased when they arrived at the main office. As soon as she entered the glass-encased area, everyone immediately stopped what they were doing and stared.

"Niya, sweetie."

Niya was so focused on the stares that she didn't even realize Ms. Monica, her best friend Jada's mom, was there and had spoken to her until she was pulled into a tight hug.

"Miss Monica, what are you doing here? Where's Jada?" Niya frowned, noticing the tears in Miss Monica's eyes.

"Jada's in class," Mrs. Hester told Niya. "Come into my office, so we can talk." Mrs. Hester guided them past the administrative area, into the guidance counselor's suite, and then into her private office. She sat down at her desk, and Miss Monica took one of the chairs on the other side. "Sit down, Niya."

Niya sat, now afraid about what was happening. "Is something wrong with Jada? Is she sick?"

"No, baby, Jada's not sick," Miss Monica assured her as she shook her head and placed her hand on Niya's arm. Niya noticed her glance at Mrs. Hester before she continued. "Jada's fine. But we need to tell you something."

"What? What is it? You're scaring me, Miss Monica." Niya's heart raced even faster as she looked her in the eyes.

Miss Monica took a deep breath but became choked up when she tried to speak. Mrs. Hester walked over, gave her a tissue, and then knelt beside Niya. In that moment, Niya knew why she'd been brought to the office, why Miss Monica was there, and why everyone had been staring at her.

"My mom?" Niya whispered.

Mrs. Hester nodded. "Yes. There was an accident."

Niya's breathing was so hard that she saw the rise and fall of her own chest. "Accident? Where is she? Is she okay? Can you take me to her, Miss Monica?"

"Baby, she . . . she . . . is . . ." Miss Monica choked up again.

Niya jumped from her seat, nearly knocking down Mrs. Hester. "I have to get to her."

Mrs. Hester shook her head. "Niya. She's gone."

Niya's body began to shake. "You're lying," she responded, her voice trembling.

It can't be true. Somebody has made a mistake. My mom is at work. She's picking me up from Jada's house, and we're going to the Chinese buffet, like we do every Thursday night. Afterward, we're heading home and getting there just in time to curl up on the couch, under her favorite blanket, and watch Grey's Anatomy.

Ms. Monica stood and put her arms around Niya. "I'm so sorry. It's gonna be okay."

"We're here for you, Niya." Mrs. Hester rubbed her back.

"Don't." Niya quickly moved away from both of them. The last thing she wanted was to be touched, comforted, or held. She wanted her mother.

Niya would quickly learn that wanting and having were two very different things. There was nothing she could do to have her mother ever again. Before she could process that nightmare, a funeral was held, the casket holding her mother's body was lowered into the grave, and Niya was packed up and moved in with her grandmother, whom she barely knew.

"May I be excused?" Niya said now, her voice barely above a whisper. Niya didn't understand the purpose of asking permission to leave the table once she had finished with her meal. The whole thing seemed cold and formal, much like her new home and its owner.

Her grandmother looked at her, then tilted her head. "You're finished?"

Niya nodded. "Yes, ma'am."

"Yes, you may," Grandma Claudia said with a brief nod.

Niya slid her chair back, stood, and quickly reached for her plate, which held the same amount of food as when she had sat down. The only difference was the toast, which was now bent from the makeshift sandwich that hadn't made it to her mouth.

"We have plans this morning. I expect you to be ready to leave in thirty minutes," her grandmother declared.

"Plans?" Niya paused.

"Yes. I have some shopping to do, and you need to get out of the house. You haven't been out since your arrival. It will be good for you," her grandmother told her. "Besides, the Christmas preparations for the house will start today, and the noise will be unbearable."

She's gotta be kidding. No way. I'm not going anywhere with her, Niya thought.

Just as she was about to voice her objection, Niya heard movements coming from the hallway, then the opening of the front door. She didn't say another word as she walked out of the dining room. She went into the kitchen, scraped her food into the garbage, then shoved the plate into the dishwasher. Niya tried her best not to make any excess noise or bring any attention to herself as she hustled out the back door. She prayed, *Please don't be gone. Please don't be gone.*

"Uncle Reese!" she called out as she rounded the side of the house. When she spotted the sleek motorcycle heading down the driveway, her heart raced and she stopped, knowing there was no way she could chase him and catch up once he pulled out of the driveway. She was already out of breath. The all too familiar feeling of a knot forming in her throat caught her attention, and she tried to swallow it down, knowing that tears would soon follow. As she watched the wheels of the bike roll, her heart sank.

It's too late.

Suddenly, just as he got to the end of the driveway, instead of pulling off, he stopped the bike. It was as if Uncle Reese had sensed her watching. He planted his feet on the pavement, then turned his torso and looked in her direction. Niya quickly waved and ran at record speed across the yard.

"I thought I heard someone calling me," he said when she reached his side. He smiled, turned off the engine, and flipped the eye cover of his helmet up so he could look at her.

"Where are you going?" Niya asked.

"I need to go into work, grab my schedule, and talk to my boss. You know I go back to work Monday, so I gotta make sure everything's straight," Uncle Reese said.

"Can't you do that later? Do you have to go now?" Niya's voice cracked.

"Yeah, I gotta go take care of it now. What's wrong?" He frowned. "You all right? Did something happen?"

"Not really, but . . ." Niya shrugged instead of completing her sentence. Yes, something happened, Uncle Reese. My mother died! she thought. She wanted to remind him of this in case he had forgotten.

"Niya, what's going on?" Uncle Reese placed his hands on her shoulders and looked her in the eyes.

"Grandma Claudia, she . . ." Niya shrugged again.

Uncle Reese removed his helmet and groaned. "Oh God. What did she do now? Just tell me."

"She says that I've been "cooped up" inside, and she's making me go shopping and run errands with her," Niya announced. "I don't want to go, Uncle Reese. Please stay so I can hang here with you," she pleaded.

Uncle Reese gave her a sympathetic smile. "Listen, I get it, and I understand why you don't wanna go. But I can't save you on this one."

"Please, Uncle Reese. I can't deal." Niya shook her head.

"Yes, you can." Uncle Reese nodded. "She's right about your needing to get out of the house. It's time. We've all gotta get back to . . . normal."

Normal? How? Nothing about my life is normal anymore.

Again, she wondered if Uncle Reese had forgotten that she was grieving the loss of her mother. And she now lived in a strange house, one that she didn't feel like leaving just yet.

"I'm not ready," Niya whispered and then looked down at the ground so Uncle Reese couldn't see the tears that threatened to fall from her eyes.

"Yes, you can. You're gonna be fine. I promise. Getting out, even though you'll be with her, is good for you. You have to leave the house, anyway, on Monday, right?" He raised an eyebrow at her.

"Don't remind me." Niya shook her head. The thought of going to school on Monday gave her as much anxiety as the idea of running errands with her grandmother. She didn't want to do either one.

"Trust me, I know my mother. She won't be out for long. Especially with them here." He motioned toward the front of the house.

Niya turned to see two vans and a large delivery truck with the name Carmichael's Nursery on the side. A couple of men were adjusting ladders against the house, while others were unloading plastic buckets.

"What are they doing?" Niya asked.

"Decorating. Who do you think makes this place look like it belongs on the Strip in Vegas?" Uncle Reese laughed.

"They're the ones who hang the lights?" Niya asked, watching a young guy who looked her age carrying a box with silver tinsel hanging out of the top. In the past Niya and her mother had visited her grandmother's home only once a year: on Christmas Day. Each year, as they drove away, Niya would turn around and stare at the family mansion, lit up like a gigantic gingerbread house. All the other homes in the neighborhood had Christmas lights as well, but the Fine mansion, which sat at the back of the cul-de-sac and also happened to be the largest, was the brightest of them all. People would come for miles just to see it."

What? Did you think your grandma climbed up there and decorated it herself ?" Uncle Reese laughed.

"I never thought about it, honestly," Niya mumbled.

"Well, I gotta get outa here, kiddo." He went to put the helmet back on. "Have fun with Grandma."

Niya glared at him. "Not funny, Uncle Reese."

"I'm just trying to make you smile, Niya-Boo. You know you're my favorite niece."

"I'm your *only* niece, Uncle Reese." Niya gave him a blank stare. "Will you be here when we come back home?"

Instead of answering her question, Uncle Reese looked away for a second, then back at her. His lack of a verbal response made Niya uneasy.

"Oh my God! You're not coming back?" Niya gasped.

"Niya, I haven't been to my condo in weeks," he said.

"But you promised . . . ," Niya whined.

"I promised I'd stay here with you until you got settled. You knew it wasn't permanent. Don't act like that," Uncle Reese said as Niya folded her arms and turned to walk away.

"How am I supposed to act? I wish someone would please tell me. According to you, I'm wrong for being upset right now, and we both know how *she* feels. I don't eat right, dress right, breathe right. Why did she bring me here in the first place? I could've stayed with my friend Jada and her family. At least they wanted me." Niya's bottom lip quivered as she brushed away the tears.

Uncle Reese climbed off his bike, walked over to Niya, and gathered her in his arms. His presence was the only reason Niya was able to tolerate being in the house. She knew his being there was only temporary, but she hadn't expected him to leave so soon. She was less lonely with him there. It was like having a friend in the house. They laughed and talked, hung out and watched TV. They were there for each other, because truth be told, neither of them was comfortable around her grandmother. Grandma Claudia seemed to be as dissatisfied with him as she was with Niya. If Uncle Reese cared about that, he certainly didn't show it. He acted as if Grandma Claudia's constant comments about him were entertainment rather than criticism.

"Niya, we are your family, and we love you." His voice was tender.

"You tolerate me. That's not love. My mother loved me. Jada and her mom love me." Niya sniffled. "They told both of you that I could stay with them. They wanted me at their home."

"You're my niece, my sister's only child. Here is the only place I want you to be."

"You don't, and neither does she. But it's cool. At least you can leave. I'm stuck living here with someone who isn't kind to me. She doesn't even like me. She treats me like a guest, not family. The only time she talks to me is while we're eating, and then it's to correct something I've done wrong," Niya told him.

"Grandma Claudia just has an odd way of showing her love, that's all. She can be uptight and frigid, but her intentions are in the right place. She just has a funny way of showing it, that's all. Believe me, she does," he said. "You'll grow to see it."

"Niya! What are you doing out here?" Grandma Claudia's voice caused both of them to turn around. "You should be getting dressed. I told you we have places to go."

"She was saying goodbye to me, that's all," Uncle Reese yelled back. "She's coming in now."

Grandma Claudia folded her arms and shook her head, then began talking to the men working on the house. "Please be careful not to mess up my flower beds. Move that ladder over to the left. I don't want it to disrupt the bushes."

"Yes, Mrs. Fine," one of the men answered and obliged.

"Niya! Now!" Grandma Claudia yelled before returning inside.

Niya glanced at her uncle and said, "Bye, Uncle Reese."

"Hey, I love you. It's gonna be okay. Who knows? You may actually have fun." He gave her a weak smile.

"I doubt it." Niya turned and stepped away.

"I tell you what. How about we swap promises? If you'll promise to at least try to have a good time, then I promise to order pizza for dinner tonight." Uncle Reese grinned.

Niya rushed over to her uncle and gave him a hug. "Deal."

Chapter 3

Reese

"Well, well, well, look who decided to show up for a shift. Vacation over," Herb yelled as Reese walked into the ambulance bay of the rescue station. Rick and Emmi, two other coworkers, appeared on the other side of the ambulance.

"Wow. Vacation?" Reese responded to Herb's dry humor.

"Don't be a jerk, Herb," Emmi scolded before she approached Reese and gave him a hug. "How are you? Good to see you back."

"I'm good, Em. Just checking in today. I'll be back in full swing on Monday, though," Reese said.

"That's good, man. You were definitely missed." Rick shook Reese's hand. "Everything cool with your family?"

"Come on now. You know the answer to that question." Reese gave Rick, his best friend since elementary school and now his roommate, a knowing look.

"Ah, man, you know what I mean." Rick shrugged. "Maybe that wasn't the right choice of words."

"How's Niya?" Emmi asked. "Is she adjusting?"

"It's hard to say, honestly. Niya's always been a quiet kid. She hasn't really said much, other than the fact that she'd rather be living with her best friend's family than with my mother," Reese explained.

"Can't say I blame her," Rick said. "Your mom is kind of . . . abrasive."

"Exactly. Nina was definitely more of a nurturer. Although my mom means well, that's not who she is. I think that's why my sister didn't bring Niya around a lot." Reesc sighed.

"Let's not forget that your mom hated Niya's dad before he passed away," Herb volunteered. "That probably had a lot to do with it as well."

They all turned and stared at him.

Emmi's head moved back and forth. "That really didn't need to be said, Herb. Please, go finish taking inventory."

"I'm just saying." Herb shrugged and then scurried back to what he was doing.

"There's a lot going on, and I feel bad for Niya," Reese told them. "She thinks we don't realize everything she's dealing with. And that's not the case."

"At least she has you, though, bro." Rick patted him on the shoulder.

"Yes, and you guys have a great relationship," Emmi offered.

"True, but as much as I love Niya, I *cannot* move into that house. I've been staying there since the funeral, but now it's time for me to get back to work and into my own space," Reese continued. "My plan was for that to happen today, but she damn near had a meltdown before I left the house."

"Aw, poor baby. You've gotta give her some time." Emmi sighed.

"Yeah, I know, which is why I promised to go back tonight, even though I have a date. Someone isn't gonna be happy when I cancel it." Reese didn't miss the slight eye roll Emmi gave him. "What?"

"If someone doesn't understand the need for you to spend time with your niece, then that's their problem, not yours," Emmi commented.

"I didn't say Lynnette wouldn't understand, Em. I said she won't be too happy," Reese responded.

"Now you know how Emmi is. The last thing she wants to hear about is another woman," Rick teased. "Her jealous streak is showing."

As soon as Rick made the joke, Reese knew it wasn't going to be received as funny. Emmi never hid the fact that she didn't like who Reese was dating. She had no romantic interest in Reese. Her response was a result of their brother-sister-like relationship; she didn't feel as if any woman he selected was good enough. Emmi found flaws in one way or another.

"Me? Jealous? Of who? Not *her*. Believe me, there is no reason for it, sweetie," Emmi snapped at Reese.

Reese held his hands up, as if he was surrendering. "Why you yelling at me?"

Rick shrugged. "Look, I gotta agree with Em on this one, Reese. Niya needs you right now. She's the priority. Your girl ain't gonna like it, but it is what it is. You already know the crib ain't going nowhere. Just give a brother a heads-up before you come home."

"Why do I need to give you notice before I come to the spot I pay for each month?" Reese asked.

It had been over a week since he'd stopped by the condo they shared to pick up his mail and more clothes. The place hadn't been as clean as it usually was when he was there, but nothing had seemed too out of sorts. Rick was known to throw a party not only without giving a reason but also without consulting Reese beforehand. Reese was sure he'd been enjoying having the place to himself.

"I just wanna make sure it's in tip-top shape, that's all. You know how upset you get when there's a bowl and spoon in the sink," Rick teased.

"Just make sure the dishes are washed every day and you won't have to worry about when I come back," Reese told him.

"Fine! Is this a social call, or are you here to check in?" Captain Yates yelled from the doorway of the station.

Reese waved at him. "I was just on my way to see you, sir."

"Then come on in and let these folks get back to what they are supposed to be doing," Captain Yates barked. "Herb seems to be the only one working."

They all turned and looked at Herb, who was now suddenly hard at work, with a clipboard in hand, instead of leaning against the rig, eavesdropping on their conversation.

"Yes, sir," Reese said. "A'ight, y'all, we'll catch up later. Emmi, as always, thanks for the advice. Rick, wash those damn dishes and replace my juice."

Reese hugged both of them before going inside. He missed his work family, even Herb. They had been truly supportive of him after the loss of his sister. Captain Yates had checked on him just as much as Emmi and Rick, and he'd made the three-hour drive to attend Nina's funeral. His boss's presence there had spoken volumes. Working together the past seven years had made them a tight-knit group. The long shifts, the small shared living and working quarters, and just the level of teamwork their job required had resulted in the special bond.

Captain Yates nodded when Reese entered his office. "Good to see you, Fine. Everything all right with your family?"

"For the most part. My niece is getting settled, and my mother seems to be getting back into her routine." Reese sat in the chair closest to the door.

"And what about you? How are you feeling?" The captain looked him in the eye.

"I'm good. Ready to come back and do my thing." Reese shrugged. "I've missed it."

"Understood, and we're anticipating your return. I just want to make sure you're ready," Captain Yates said.

"I am. I've been keeping up with my working out and running daily—"

"That's not what I'm talking about, Fine. Your physical fitness has never been a problem. I'm more concerned about your suffering a traumatic loss, a major one. I don't want you to feel like you have to rush back. This job is just as much mental as it is physical."

Reese nodded. "I know, Captain. I assure you, I'm ready."

"All right. We'll see you on Monday, at six a.m.," Captain Yates said. "That's where we'll keep you until the New Year."

Reese frowned. "Morning shift? That's it? Captain, I can go back to my regular schedule."

"Let's see how it goes. Trust me on this one, Fine."

Reese had no choice but to trust Captain Yates, who'd been his supervisor for six of the seven years he'd been at the rescue station. Reese had been hired and had started as an EMT. Now he was a paramedic who held the position of sergeant, thanks to Captain Yates's mentorship. As much as

Reese looked forward to getting back in his regular routine of working nonstop, he knew his boss was not going to allow it, despite it being the busiest season of the year.

"First shift it is," Reese agreed. "I'll be here bright and early."

"See you Monday, Fine," Captain Yates told him as they shook hands before Reese exited the office.

After saying his goodbyes to Emmi, Rick, and the rest of the crew, Reese was about to place his helmet on his head and climb back on his motorcycle when a sleek silver Lexus pulled up and parked directly in front of him. He watched with a smile as Lynnette Graham, the sexy driver, stepped out. It had been a few days since he'd seen her. As she walked toward him, he took in the small, beautiful woman headed in his direction.

"Let me find out you're stalking me," Reese said.

"I mean, at this point that seems like the only way I'm going to see you." Lynnette's sarcastic response didn't surprise him. She'd been quite vocal about her dissatisfaction with his recent lack of attention.

"Aw, don't be like that." Reese reached out, took her arm, and pulled her to him, then rested his hands on her slender hips. The soft scent of Rose Prick, her favorite Tom Ford perfume, drifted into his nostrils.

Lynnette wrapped her arms around his neck and stared at him with her beautiful brown eyes. "Would you prefer that I not miss you, Reese?"

"Of course I want you to miss me. I miss you too, Lynnette," he told her.

"Good. I hope you are ready to show me just how much later on tonight, after dinner, because I am ready." She seductively licked her lips.

Reese didn't respond immediately, because he was trying to think of the right words to say so that Lynnette wouldn't be too reactive. Lynnette must have interpreted his pause as an indication of what he was preparing to say, because she spoke before he did.

"You can't be serious. Again, Reese?" she snapped as her arms dropped to her sides. She tried to turn and walk off, but his tightened grip prevented her from moving.

"I know, but listen, Niya is still a little uncomfortable at the house without me being there."

"That's why you need to leave." Lynnette sighed. "I'm not trying to sound mean, but if you allow her to start guilt-tripping you into staying and you're always there, she'll never adjust. She's gonna have to just deal with it."

Reese understood what Lynnette was saying, as well as the frustration she felt. They hadn't been intimate in a while. He was certain that she needed some bedroom time just as much as he did. The idea of one of their marathon sessions crossed his mind. As much as he wanted to spend time with Lynnette, it would have to wait. His priority right now was Niya and her well-being.

"Trust me, I'm just as frustrated as you are. But I'm not going to abandon my niece. She's mourning and adjusting. It's gonna take a little while longer," Reese responded, attempting to be diplomatic about the situation.

"How much longer, Reese?"

"Not much, I promise. And we can definitely go to dinner tomorrow night. That I can do. We can go to Tampico's." Reese's arms encircled her, and he gave her a pleading look. Thinking the invitation to her favorite restaurant wouldn't be enough, he decided to sweeten the deal. "Maybe we can hit up a couple of your fave designer stores before we go eat."

Lynnette didn't respond immediately, but the tightness of her lips softened, and her eyebrows, which had been raised, slowly lowered. Both were positive signs.

"I wanna spend time with you, Lynn. I miss you. You know that." Reese pulled her closer.

"And what about Niya?"

"What about her?"

"Won't she be *scared* at the house with your mother?"

The way Lynnette asked the question, Reese couldn't tell if she was being sarcastic or concerned.

"Scared?" he repeated to impel her to clarify exactly what she meant.

"I mean, isn't that why you said you have to stay there? Because she doesn't want to be alone with your mother?" Lynnette's eyebrows went back to their raised position.

"Not scared. Uncomfortable. My mother isn't the most welcoming person in the world. It's more than just that. Like I said, she's been through a lot. But we'll be out only a few hours, and she'll be fine." Reese sighed.

"Well, dinner and shopping are cool with me, I guess. But I'm not trying to be on a time limit. I'm a grown-ass woman. I don't have a curfew, so if that's gonna be a problem—"

Reese cut Lynnette's words off by covering her mouth with his. The kiss was enough to halt her complaint, but the familiar rise of Reese's nature signaled that if he didn't stop now, he would quickly arrive at the point of no return. The way Lynnette's hands were rubbing his back, and the way she was moaning lightly, indicated that she wasn't far from getting there herself. Reese pressed his forehead against hers.

"Dinner tomorrow?" he whispered.

Lynnette, still breathless, nodded.

After placing his helmet on his head, Reese climbed back on his bike and drove off. He smiled at the thought of Lynnette still standing there, with a satisfied smile on her face.

She tries to play hard core, but I know exactly how to get her to melt.

Chapter 4

Kendall

"Kendall, you've done it again. It's perfect," Mrs. Tucker said as she admired herself in the mirror. The silver gown, which had seemed two sizes too big at the top and a size too small in the hips when she purchased it two weeks ago, now fit like a glove.

Instead of suggesting another dress, Deena had assured Mrs. Tucker that if she paid the hefty price on the tag, Kendall would make the minor adjustments and simple alterations needed, and the gown would be ready in days. Despite there having been nothing minor or simple about the total reconstruction of the gown, Kendall had worked her magic, and it had resulted in the smile on Mrs. Tucker's face.

"It looks amazing," Amber said as she admired Kendall's handiwork from the doorway.

"I can't wait for them to announce Simon and me at the ball." Mrs. Tucker turned and looked at Amber. "You're sure no one else has this gown, right? You double-checked?"

Amber nodded. "I did. You will be the only one at the Rotary Holiday Ball in this design. I triple checked." One of the reasons their clients preferred shopping at Diablo's Designs was that in addition to the exclusivity of Deena's label, they were assured that they would not arrive at prestigious balls wearing the same dress. Each dress was catalogued according to the ball where it would be worn to avoid such a situation happening.

"Good. I can imagine the reaction people are going to have when they see me in this. I'm so much smaller than last year, you know?" Mrs. Tucker smoothed her hands along the metallic-sequined fabric hugging her body.

Kendall nodded and said, "You are definitely a different size than last year. I'll bag it up and bring it to the front for you."

"Thank you again, Kendall," Mrs. Tucker said as she slipped out of the gown.

After carefully collecting the fabric in her arms, Kendall carried the gown back into the alterations room and placed it on one of the custom satin hangers with the Diablo Designs logo. She admired her work one final time before she placed it in one of their signature bags.

Another one done, she thought, then turned around and saw the racks of gowns that remained.

Deena was right: ball season was in full effect. The number of orders seemed endless, between dresses for holiday events and the debutante balls. Instead of being overwhelmed by the amount of work that needed to be done within the next few weeks, Kendall was excited. She loved the balls, and even though she hadn't attended one in years, being a part of the preparation brought her a sense of contentment.

There was nothing like looking at the pictures posted on social media of ladies all glammed up in the Deena Diablo dresses that she had helped create. Ball season also gave her another reason to love Christmas. In addition to the already high holiday spirits, the anticipation and excitement of the balls brought even more energy to the already busy boutique. And even though she had plenty of alteration work, it was the one time of year when she spent time on the showroom floor with everyone else.

"All bagged up and ready to go," Kendall said as she delivered Mrs. Tucker's gown to the register. She paused and looked around the crowded store. "Where's Mrs. Tucker?"

"To the left, to the left." Her coworker Luigi motioned with his hand as he rang up a woman who seemed to be so mesmerized by his black, shoulder-length, curly hair, dark olive skin, and perfect teeth that she didn't even realize he was waiting for her to insert her credit card into the machine. “I think she’s looking at another gown for the First Noel.”

“What? Why?” Kendall frowned. “She has already bought three gowns, two of which I still have to alter.”

“I know. But based on how she has Amber cornered over there near the new arrivals rack, it looks like she’ll be getting a fourth.” Luigi shrugged as he stretched his already long neck to get a better look at what he was reporting.

“Amber won’t let that happen.” Kendall shook her head, confident that her best friend would tell Mrs. Tucker that buying another gown would be pointless, because there wouldn’t bc time for the proper alterations.

“She won’t be able to do that, but Deena might,” Luigi smirked. “She’s headed over there now.”

Kendall hung the bag on the rack behind the register and hastily made her way across the store. Any other time, she wouldn’t be concerned, but Deena had been known to make special allowances for high-paying clients like Mrs. Tucker and to overpromise in an effort to make the sale. Kendall needed to make sure that didn’t happen today.

Deena smiled as Kendall walked up. “We were just talking about you.”

“Oh really?” Forcing a pleasant smile on her face to mask her concern, Kendall waited to hear what had been said instead of reacting too quickly.

"Yes, I told Deena that my gown fits so perfectly that it almost looks like a brand-new design." Mrs. Tucker smiled. "Deena, this young lady is somewhat of a magician with a sewing machine."

"I agree," Amber said. "It's almost custom designed for you now, Mrs. Tucker."

"Well, that's why Kendall is our lead seamstress. She makes sure all the Diablo Designs fit our clients perfectly." Deena winked at Kendall.

"My granddaughter Lexi is very excited about her First Noel gown. I see some of the other debs are here today." Mrs. Tucker pointed at a few teenage girls gathered on the other side of the boutique. "I'm glad we've already selected her gown."

"It's that time of year," Deena agreed.

"Oh my. Look, is that Claudia Fine?" Mrs. Tucker said, her voice lower now. "It is."

The woman in question walked over.

"Claudia, so good to see you," Mrs. Tucker greeted.

"Wonderful to see you too, Patricia."

Kendall turned her head to see to whom Mrs. Tucker was speaking. A beautiful woman who looked more like she was headed to a formal luncheon than shopping on Black Friday stood on the other side of Mrs. Tucker. Everything about her screamed regality: from her black pantsuit, leather heels, and matching clutch to the tight chignon bun at the back of her head and her fierce red lipstick.

"I see you're like everyone else in the city. Getting some shopping done," Mrs. Tucker observed.

Claudia nodded. "A little."

Mrs. Tucker continued her questioning, as if she were interviewing Claudia for the society page of the newspaper. "I understand your granddaughter is living with you. She's sixteen, right? Will she be following the Fine family tradition and participating in the First Noel Ball this year?"

Claudia shook her head. "She is with me, but no, she won't be a participant."

"Oh, I guess not, considering everything that's happened. My condolences to you and your family." Mrs. Tucker gave an apologetic look. "Maybe next year. The First Noel Society has been known to make exceptions for age, and you do sit on the board."

"Thank you, Patricia. It has been a tradition for years. However, in the grand scheme of things, I don't think she'll be the one to continue it for several reasons. The society has a reputation to uphold. I love my granddaughter, but I also recognize that she doesn't have the—how can I say it?—je ne sais quoi needed for such an esteemed event." Claudia sighed.

"Oh, I see." Mrs. Tucker nodded. "It isn't for everyone, but . . ."

"It certainly isn't, and especially not for young ladies who haven't been raised in a conducive environment and received the proper training to be a deb," Claudia explained. "And she recently lost her mother, remember. Beyond that, I firmly believe, just because you have the pedigree doesn't mean you're fit to wear the crown."

"Well, I mean, surely . . . ," Mrs. Tucker began, as if she didn't know quite how to respond. "Certain exceptions can be made, considering the circumstances. You know I'm on the board, and I'd have no problem making sure the application is approved. There's still time if—"

"We won't be seeking any exceptions," Claudia interrupted gently. "No need for that."

Kendall suddenly became self-conscious and felt as if she was eavesdropping on a conversation that she shouldn't be privy to hear, but there didn't seem to be the right moment for her to excuse herself.

"Well, welcome to Diablo's. How can we help you today?" Amber smiled.

"I'm looking for Deena Diablo, actually," Claudia answered.

"This is Deena." Mrs. Tucker immediately touched Deena's arm. "Deena, this is *Claudia Fine*." The way Mrs. Tucker said the name indicated how important she felt the other woman was.

"Of the Fine Foundation?" Amber asked.

"Yes," Mrs. Tucker said.

"Pleased to meet you, Mrs. Fine." Deena extended her hand, and Claudia shook it. "What can I do for you?"

"Well, I placed an order online a few weeks ago, but I realized instead of delivery, it's scheduled for pickup. So I'm here to pick it up," Claudia said.

"No problem. Come with me. I can help you with that," Deena said, taking her by the arm.

"Niya, I'll be back in a few moments," Claudia called as she and Deena began to walk away.

Kendall's eyes shifted, and she noticed a young lady in a black hoodie and jeans leaning against the far wall. She seemed to be so consumed with the cell phone in her hand that she barely looked up. Kendall looked over at Amber, who gave a simple shrug.

Claudia stopped in her tracks, gave a deflated sigh, then looked back at Mrs. Tucker. "Like I said, je ne sais quoi." Then she and Deena headed across the boutique.

Hold up. Wait. This can't be the granddaughter, Kendall thought. *There's no way they stood there and talked about her like that, as if she wasn't standing nearby.* If anything, the entire conversation they'd had moments before demonstrated a lack of class and demeanor, she decided.

Without hesitating, Kendall walked over to the girl and said, "Hi there. Niya, is it?"

"Yeah." Niya barely nodded.

"We actually have a lounge area where you can sit and wait for your grandmother if you'd like," Kendall offered.

"I'm good," Niya said, giving Kendall a bothered look as she stuffed her phone into the pocket of her oversized sweatshirt.

"Are you sure? There are some young ladies your age sitting over there. You don't have to be over here all alone," Kendall told her, pointing to the open area in the center of the store, where several teen girls had assembled. Some were waiting to try on dresses, and others were waiting while their mothers shopped.

"I said I'm good. Hopefully, we won't have to be here that long." She sighed and looked down at the floor.

"Kendall, you're needed for a fitting," Luigi announced over the sound of Bing Crosby's non-urban voice singing "White Christmas."

Had it not been one of the busiest days of the year and had she not already had a ton of work, Kendall would've stayed and talked with Niya until Claudia returned. But now wasn't a good time. It was obvious that the young lady was uninterested in moving, so Kendall gave up.

There's definitely something about her. Despite her nonchalant demeanor, this girl is special. I know it, she mused silently as she headed to the alterations room.

***

"Oh my God, I'm tired. Maybe instead of going home, we should just sleep here. There's no point in leaving, anyway," Amber said as she flopped dramatically onto the large cutting table.

Kendall looked up from the dress she was hemming and checked her watch. She'd been so busy that she hadn't even realized how much time had passed. "Is the floor clear?"

"Floor is clear and clean, and the chaos is over for the day." Amber placed her hand across her forehead.

"I can't believe it's this late." Kendall yawned. "Today has been a day, that's for sure."

"It has," Amber agreed. "We still hitting the mall?"

Traditionally on this day of the year, the two besties would be ready to walk out the door the moment the boutique closed and join the rest of the Black Friday shoppers. It wouldn't matter to them that they'd missed the doorbusters or early morning bargains. The only thing that would matter was that it was the first shopping day of the holiday season and they would participate. But this year Kendall didn't have that same sense of urgency. Something was bothering her, and she couldn't understand what it was.

"Uh, I don't know. I'm not really feeling it this evening," Kendall said.

"What? Why not? We always grab our Black Friday bargains, then go to dinner, so we don't have to eat leftovers," Amber whined. "And I'm starving."

Kendall began pondering whether she had enough energy to indulge Amber in their usual tradition. It had already been a long day, and they had to work again tomorrow.

Just then, Deena strolled into the large, open work space where Kendall spent most of her workdays. It held various sewing and serger machines, racks of material, and shelves filled with thread, buttons, lace, and anything else any great seamstress could possibly need to get any sewing job done. "Good. You're still here, Kendall. I need a huge favor."

"Uh-oh," Kendall said with a faux sigh.

"Can you drop this off to Claudia Fine for me on your way home?" Deena asked, holding up a small plastic bag. "I would take it myself, but I'm meeting some friends for dinner."

"What is it?" Kendall asked, curious about the contents of the bag that Deena held.

"Her glasses. She left them at the register," Deena answered. "She called, and I told her you live in that direction, so I figured you wouldn't mind dropping them off for her."

"Why can't she just come get them herself?" Amber asked. "Or just wait till the morning?"

The annoyance in the glance Deena gave Amber was obvious. "Well, maybe they're for reading and she needs them."

"It's fine. I can take them." The words came from Kendall's mouth so fast that they nearly took her by surprise. Driving fifteen minutes out of her way wasn't something she would usually agree to, but she felt inclined for some reason.

"Really?" Deena and Amber said at the same time.

Kendall nodded and stood. "Sure. I mean, I do drive that way to get home. This could be my first angel assignment of the season."

"That's exactly what I was thinking." Deena placed the bag in Kendall's hand. "Also, can you please lock up? Everyone else is gone."

Deena wasted no time hurrying out the room as quickly as she had entered it.

"Guess that'll be your second angel assignment," Amber murmured.

Kendall ignored Amber as she grabbed her denim jacket, along with her purse. "It's no big deal, Amber. Deena has plans, and she's right. It is on the way home."

"But what about *our* plans?" Amber asked.

"We can grab something after I drop off the glasses." Kendall put her arm around Amber's shoulders as they walked toward the exit. She hit the security code as she grabbed her keys.

"I can't believe she suckered you into doing this. The only reason she even asked is that it's Claudia Fine. Deena's about as scared of her as you are of Deena. I don't get it," Amber said.

"I'm not scared of anyone. I wish you'd stop insinuating that." Kendall closed the door with a little more force than she had intended, causing Amber's eyes to widen. Kendall gave her an apologetic shrug. "I'm just saying, you know that's not true. I agreed because it's no big deal. If it was, I would've said something."

Amber remained quiet as Kendall locked the door, and she didn't speak until they got to Kendall's car.

"You want me to pick up food from Magnolia's and bring it over? We can watch *This Christmas* and start working on plans for the party," she finally said.

Kendall nodded. "Apology accepted."

"Whatever," Amber retorted. "You might not be scared, but you aren't slick, either."

"What are you talking about?" Kendall asked.

"The holiday lights at the Fine mansion. Don't act like that's not part of the reason why you don't mind going over there."

Kendall couldn't help but smile. Her best friend knew her well. It wasn't her main reason for agreeing to take Claudia her glasses, but seeing the incredible light display was an added incentive for doing the good deed. But beyond the opportunity to do her first angel assignment of delivering the glasses and to see the holiday lights was also something more: the unshakeable feeling that this was something she was *supposed* to do for some unknown reason.

Chapter 5

Niya

"Uncle Reese, where are you?" Niya said into the phone, making sure her voice remained low, as she glanced back toward the kitchen.

"I'm on my way back to the house. What's wrong?" Reese responded. "I stopped at the store to grab something."

Niya didn't enjoy sounding like a needy toddler, but it was getting late, and based on the aromatic smells coming from the kitchen, her grandmother was in the middle of preparing a dinner that Niya had no plan to eat.

"She's in the kitchen, cooking, I think. I thought we were having pizza," Niya told him, now wondering if her uncle had changed his mind. The last thing she wanted to endure was another meal alone with her grandmother.

"Yes, we are. I already ordered it. Just go in there . . ."

"Go in where? I'm not going in that kitchen, Uncle Reese. You need to tell her," Niya replied as her head shifted back and forth. Just as her mouth opened so that she could continue her objection, the doorbell chimed. Niya froze. It wasn't that late, but the sun had long set. She definitely wasn't expecting anyone, and although this was now her home, she didn't feel comfortable answering the door. Confused, she whispered into the phone, "Uncle Reese, someone's at the door."

"It's probably the pizza I ordered. Go ahead and open it. I already paid and gave a tip," Reese told her.

"You want me to open the door? I can't do that. She'll be upset." Niya swallowed the nervous lump in her throat. "She doesn't know about the pizza. She'll probably think I ordered it."

"Jesus, Niya, it's just pizza. I'll call and tell her I ordered it, if it'll make you feel better. It's fine. Now, what will make her upset is if someone keeps ringing her doorbell. Go to the door, and I'll call her right now and tell her," he said.

"Are you sure?" Niya asked just as the bell chimed again.

"I'm positive. Go ahead. I'll be home in a few minutes. I promise."

"Okay, Uncle Reese. Please hurry up," Niya told him.

"I will. I'm calling her now," he said before the call ended.

The sound of her grandmother's cell ringing gave Niya a little relief as she headed toward the front entrance, praying that she made it there before the bell rang again. Trusting her uncle's instructions, she quickly turned the lock and opened the massive door without verifying who was on the other side. She was surprised when instead of a pizza delivery driver, she saw someone else on the doorstep.

"Oh." Niya's eyes widened with surprise.

"Hi there, Niya."

Niya stared at the woman standing in the doorway. There was something about the way the bright Christmas lights surrounding the front porch illuminated her from behind that made her look like an angel. Niya recognized her from the boutique that she and her grandmother had gone to earlier in the day. The beautiful woman had been friendly and had attempted to make conversation, but after the comments that had been made about her, Niya had been embarrassed and in no mood to engage. Now, here they were face-to-face.

Niya nodded slowly. "Uh, hi."

"Remember me? I work at Diablo's. You and your grandmother came in earlier today." Her smile was warm and inviting, and she had the whitest teeth Niya had ever seen. "I'm Kendall."

"I remember," Niya said. "Uh, come in."

Niya stepped aside so that Kendall could enter. Her eyes followed Kendall as she walked past, and Niya took in everything she could about what had to be the coolest dressed woman she'd ever seen. She'd been so busy trying not to be seen earlier to really pay attention, but now she couldn't stop looking at Kendall. Everything about her screamed high fashion: her outfit, her hair, her makeup, even the soft perfume she wore. As they wandered into the living room, Niya's eyes went from the chunky-heeled boots on Kendall's feet to her big, curly hair. What stood out the most was the jacket she had on. It was denim, but it had colorful patches and words painted all along the sleeves and on the back: *beautiful*, *sassy*, *inspired*, *artist*, *peace*, *love*, *pride*, and other positive affirmations. It was one of the most incredible things Niya had ever seen.

"Your home is beautiful," Kendall said, glancing around the massive living room.

"Thanks, but it's not really my home," Niya said nonchalantly as she continued admiring the artwork on the jacket.

Kendall shrugged. "Oh, I'm sorry. I thought you lived with your grandmother."

"I mean, I do, but it's not my home. Not here with her," Niya revealed.

Kendall stared at her for a second, then said, "I get it. It probably doesn't feel quite like it yet. It takes a minute to adjust. It took me almost a year after I lost my mom for the house I moved into to feel like home." Kendall's voice was just as warm as the look she gave Niya.

For the first time since the funeral, Niya felt as if someone understood. So many people had offered condolences and prayers that she'd become numb to them. Kendall's words were sincere, and Niya could sense the distant ache that came with them.

"Niya, I hope you don't think you're eating pizza in my living room. You need to take it—" Her grandmother stopped in mid-sentence when she entered the room and saw Niya talking to Kendall.

"Hi, Mrs. Fine," Kendall greeted her. "I was just telling Niya how beautiful your house is."

"Oh, I wasn't expecting someone to be visiting at this hour, especially someone uninvited."

Niya slowly sucked in air as she tensed up. The chill in her grandmother's voice was enough to cause the temperature in the room to drop several degrees. Niya had quickly become accustomed to the icy demeanor of Claudia Fine, and now she felt nervous for Kendall.

"I apologize. I thought Deena spoke to you about me coming by," Kendall replied. Niya was surprised that Kendall didn't seem intimidated or affected at all. As she spoke, she maintained the same warmth and friendliness that she'd displayed with Niya.

Kendall reached into her pocket and took out a plastic bag. "You left these at the boutique, and Deena asked me to bring them to you."

Claudia paused for a moment before taking the bag from her.

"They're your glasses," Kendall told her. "I'm sure you need them. Personally, I wear contacts, but when I don't, it's stressful when I can't find my glasses. A sister needs to be able to see at all times."

Niya laughed at Kendall's joke, unlike Claudia, who remained stoic as she opened the bag and removed the eyeglasses that were inside it.

"Thank you for bringing them. I did call Deena and confirmed that my glasses had been found, but I wasn't aware that she was having them delivered. How much do I owe you for your services?" she asked.

"Oh my, nothing. It's no problem at all. I'm glad to be able to do it, and it gave me a chance to chat with Miss Niya here," Kendall replied.

"Well, I'll make sure to give Deena a call and thank her for having you do this, and I'll let her know it was appreciated." Claudia nodded, then as abruptly as she had entered the room, she exited, without saying goodbye.

For someone who constantly comments about proper decorum and etiquette, she certainly doesn't apply the rules to herself, Niya thought.

"You're so beautiful, like your grandmother," Kendall said, then pointed. "And your mother. That's her, right?"

Niya glanced at the large framed photo on the wall: a picture of her mother, smiling and looking regal in a white gown, crown, and sash as she held what seemed to be dozens of roses. "Yes, that's her. She was crowned queen of the First Noel Ball."

Niya watched Kendall as she walked over and peered closely at the picture.

"That's my grandmother in the other picture. She was the first queen ever to be crowned," Niya said.

"It's crazy how it's always the same crown and sash, even decades later. Some things never change." Kendall laughed. "I still have mine."

Niya's eyes widened. "Huh?"

Kendall turned around. "My crown and sash from the ball. Man, it seems like yesterday."

"You were a First Noel queen?" Niya anxiously waited for her answer.

"Not a queen, but I was a deb. I got a crown and sash for being Miss Congeniality. My escort was Baron Hughes. Jeez, we had a blast." Kendall laughed again. "He was so fine back then. Now, not so much."

"I can't believe you were a deb. That's crazy," Niya said with disbelief.

"Why not? I loved being a deb." Kendall walked back over to where Niya stood.

"Because . . ." Niya tried to think of an answer that wasn't insulting. "I mean . . ."

The confused look on Kendall's face as she waited for an answer made Niya feel even worse. Niya's eyes went back to the photos of her mother and grandmother. They looked so similar that it was scary. Both had the same smooth skin, deepened tan tone, high cheekbones, slender build, and silky hair. As she'd done so many times before, Niya looked for some trace of similarity between herself and the two women but couldn't find any. Her own skin was much darker, her face was rounder, and her hair, although curly, was much kinkier. In addition to all those contrasts, the most obvious was the fact that Niya was nowhere near slender. She'd always been a bigger girl. To hear that Kendall had been a First Noel Debutante was surprising, because it was obvious that Niya and Kendall shared more similarities than Niya and her mother and grandmother.

"Oh, I guess you were smaller back then," Niya commented.

"Nope, not really." Kendall shrugged. "I was a couple of pounds lighter, but not much. Wait, are you saying that curvy girls can't be debs? Because that's not the case at all. I was one of the best debs to ever do it. I think all beautiful young ladies such as yourself should do it."

Niya shook her head. "No, that's not for me. I can't."

"Why not you? I would think that of all people, *you* should be the main person who'd want to do it. From what I can see, being a queen is in your bloodline. It's a part of the legacy you come from." Kendall pointed at the pictures on the wall.

"I'm not like them." Niya's turned to face Kendall. "Or you."

Kendall frowned. "I don't understand. What do you mean?"

Ding. Dong.

The doorbell's chimes rescued Niya from having to explain something that she didn't even understand herself.

"That's probably the pizza," Niya quickly said, and then she walked to the front door. This time, she checked to make sure who was at the door before opening it, just in case.

Thankfully, standing on the other side was a guy in a red shirt and hat, carrying a large cardboard box with the name Tito's on the top. "Delivery for Fine," he said when Niya opened the door.

"Thank you." Niya took the box from him.

"No problem. Hope you enjoy." He smiled, but Niya couldn't help but notice that he was looking past her at Kendall. She quickly closed the door.

"Well, let me get outa here," Kendall told her.

"You're leaving?" Niya asked as she turned around, hoping that she didn't sound disappointed.

"Yeah. I gotta get home. My best friend is probably waiting outside my house right now, mad because I'm not there. But it was nice hanging out with you. You're pretty dope, Niya."

Niya blinked, trying to ascertain if Kendall was being overly nice because she felt sorry for her. As far as she could tell, Kendall seemed to be genuine.

"Thanks for stopping by," Niya told her.

"See you next time, Niya. And be inspired." Kendall pointed to the word on her sleeve as she reached for the door handle.

"That's gotta be the coolest jacket ever. Where'd you get it?" Niya said.

"I made it." Kendall shrugged and smoothed down the front.

"Wow? Really?"

"I did." Kendall nodded, and then, without hesitating, she slipped it off her shoulders and held it out.

Niya stared for a second, unsure of what to do.

"Take it," Kendall instructed. "Put the box down and see how this fits."

Niya placed the pizza box on the side table and took the soft fabric from Kendall's hand. Within seconds, she was wearing the jacket, and it looked as if it had been custom made just for her.

"Perfect fit. It looks good on you." Kendall smiled.

"You think you can make one for me like this?" Niya asked before she chickened out.

"Nah. My designs are kinda one of a kind." Kendall sighed. "This one is custom."

"Oh," Niya responded.

"You can have it, though, if you think you can handle it," Kendall told her.

A wide grin spread across Niya's face, and she asked, "Handle it? How much does it cost?"

Between her checking and savings accounts, Niya had only about two hundred dollars, which probably wasn't enough for the custom-designed jacket. It didn't matter how much it was going to cost; she was willing to pay. It was worth it.

"It doesn't cost any money. But if you're gonna wear it, you're gonna have to own it. And by that, I mean own every word that's written on it. You have to believe them too. That's what makes it so special. This jacket is powerful. People can see those words on you even when you're *not* wearing it," Kendall told her.

Niya looked at the words on the sleeves again. "I can handle it."

"The words on the back too?" Kendall asked her.

"I got it," Niya said.

Kendall stood back and stared. "I have to admit, it might look better on you than on me."

"I doubt that, but I'll take the compliment," Niya told her.

"Ah, ah, ah. I told you, you've gotta be able to handle it. That means the flattery that come along with it too. And believe me, you're gonna get lots of comments," Kendall said.

Niya was certain that what Kendall had just said wasn't going to happen, but she was willing to say whatever it took to convince Kendall that she could be trusted with the jacket. "Okay, I can deal with the compliments."

"Then it's yours." Kendall gave her a hug and opened the front door. She stepped onto the porch, then turned around. "And for the record, Niya, I think you'd make a great deb, and I'm sure if your mom was here, she'd say the same thing."

Niya watched as Kendall strolled to her car, which was parked in the circular driveway. Again, the bright lights seemed to illuminate her, and she looked like an angel who'd suddenly appeared out of nowhere. Kendall waved as she drove off, and Niya was still watching the taillights of her car when she heard the sound of a motorcycle in the distance. A few moments later, a bright single headlight pulled into the driveway. Uncle Reese was finally home.

He quickly parked and pulled off his helmet. "What's up, niece?" he asked as he walked up the walkway. "Nice jacket. It looks good on you."

Niya looked down at the jacket she was wearing and smiled. "Thanks."

Chapter 6

Reese

"I thought you said your being here at the house was to help Niya, Reese."

Startled by his mother's voice coming from behind him, Reese almost dropped the top of the trash can that he was holding. He quickly turned around. "Jesus, you scared me."

"I hope it's not because you were doing something you had no business doing." Claudia folded her arms and gave him an accusatory look.

"If you consider throwing an empty pizza box and soda cans away *something*, then yeah, I was." Reese quickly turned back around to the trash can in case she could see him cutting his eyes at her. Not that he was trying to avoid his mother, but he had made sure that he and Niya ate dinner and watched television in the den until almost midnight, well after her usual bedtime. His mother's accusatory tone was just as annoying as her creeping up from behind.

"It is. And your allowing her to indulge in pizza and soda as a way to help her is something too, and not helpful at all. It's actually quite harmful."

Reese shook his head as he turned to face her. "I know you probably do see it as some kind of harmful deed rather than quality time, but believe me, it's not. And I know my being here with Niya isn't something you even agree with."

"That's not true. This is your home as well, and you're always welcome here," she told him.

Reese almost laughed, because the words she had spoken definitely didn't reflect the way he felt whenever he was at the house. He couldn't remember the last time he had felt welcome in the home he'd grown up in. Once Nina, who was almost eight years older, had left for college, home had become a little less enjoyable, but it had still been tolerable. But after the death of his father when Reese was in college, home had become a glacial place of distant memories of times before. He had soon realized that what his sister had always said about their father was true: he was the sun that warmed their lives. After he had gone, things had become very dark, and the house had no longer seemed like home.

After the birth of his niece that same year his father passed, he would come by the house only when Nina made her obligatory brief visits once or twice a year, he wouldn't even last a day.

Eventually, Nina's visits to their childhood home became less frequent, and so he would make the three-hour drive to visit her and Niya whenever his schedule permitted. He couldn't recall if his mother had ever been to his sister's house. Then again, he doubted if Nina had ever invited her. He definitely hadn't ever extended an invitation for her to visit his apartment. He knew better.

"Niya's more comfortable when I'm here," he commented.

"That's because you indulge her with whatever she wants. You're spoiling her, the way her mother did. That's why she's the way she is now."

"How is she? Sad, grieving, lonely? Behaving like a sixteen-year-old kid who just lost her mom and had her entire life turned upside down and is living with a grandmother she barely knows? I'm not having this conversation with you. There's not even a need for discussion." Reese sighed. "You act like you don't even care that she's hurting."

"I do care, which is why I'm attempting to have this discussion about her well-being. Emotional well-being is connected to dietary intake, Reese. You have a medical background and are well aware of this," Claudia stated.

"Please don't do that," Reese pleaded.

Claudia frowned. "Do what?"

"Act like your concern is more about her mental health, when we both know that's not what this is about at all. If it was, you would've been with her in therapy for the past three sessions. You weren't," Reese replied. "I don't want to be here any more than you want me here. I'm here because she needs me. You don't want us to eat pizza here at your house, fine. We'll eat it somewhere else." He attempted to pass her, but she grabbed him by the arm. His eyes went from her hand on his arm to her face. It was the first time she'd touched him since Nina's funeral, where they had shared an awkward hug.

He loved his mother. He had discovered early on that although she wasn't physically affectionate, she loved him in her own way. There was an unspoken understanding between them that allowed him to know that she would go to the ends of the earth for him, but it would be on her terms, and there was no need to speak about it. Knowing that meant nothing in this moment, though, and her putting her hand on him only made an already tense situation worse.

"Reese." As she said his name, she quickly moved her hand. "The girl is unhealthy and overweight. She walks around with her head down and barely talks to anyone. You should've seen how she cowered in the corners of the stores while we were shopping. She didn't even want to try anything on."

He looked at her. "Do me a favor, please. Just give both Niya and me some space for a few more days. She starts school on Monday, and hopefully, that will help. She'll be busy with her own life, I'll go back to mine, and you can return to doing whatever it is that you do in yours."

"You don't think I want her to make a new life here? She's my granddaughter, for God's sake. She is family. I only want the best for her," Claudia hissed.

"Then you might wanna start acting like it. And you can start by caring more about how she feels than about what she eats or how much she weighs." Reese walked away before his mother could say anything else.

"I mean, maybe your mother is right," Lynnette said the following evening. She'd been occupying herself by taking selfies from the moment they'd gotten into the car. As promised, he'd picked her up, and now they were heading to the mall for a bit of shopping before their dinner reservation, which he'd made.

As he drove, he shared more of the conversation he and his mother had had about his niece.

"From what I can tell, your niece isn't very outgoing, and maybe that does have something to do with her weight."

"I don't know of too many people who are outgoing after losing a parent, Lynnette. I remember your telling me that when Denver passed away a couple of years ago, you could barely get out of bed for a week," Reese reminded her.

Lynnette looked at him as if he was disturbed. "Denver was my *baby.*"

"Denver was your cat. He wasn't even a person. But you get my point," Reese said.

"I guess," Lynnette answered, relenting, and sat back in her seat. "I'm just saying, I don't think your mother meant any harm. You know as well as I do that fat people are usually sad and angry and don't have a lot of friends. They're bullied in school and constantly picked on. No one wants their child to go through that, especially after losing a parent."

"Hold up. Niya's a good kid, and she has friends. They're just back where she used to live. I'm sure she's not going to have a problem making friends here," Reese replied, defending his niece.

"Maybe if she was in elementary or middle school. High school is brutal, even for pretty girls like me. Girls are mean. You know that," Lynnette told him. "It wasn't that long ago that you were in high school."

"It's been long enough. I'm sure Niya's gonna be fine," Reese insisted. "She's smart, funny . . ."

"That should help. Most bigger kids are funny," Lynnette pointed out. "They cover their pain with humor."

"You're not helping this situation." Reese glanced at her from the corner of his eye as he pulled into the crowded parking lot. People and cars were everywhere. He slowly guided his sleek Acura down the rows, hoping to spot someone walking to their car just in time.

"Oh, wait. That guy looks like he's leaving." Lynnette pointed to an older guy carrying a shopping bag in one hand and a Starbucks cup in the other. Reese waited a few moments and tried to gauge which car the guy was heading toward. As luck would have it, the guy took out a set of keys and aimed it in Reese's direction. The headlights of a late-model Buick in the next row flashed, and Reese hurried toward it. By the time he made it to where the car was parked, the man was putting his bag in his trunk and taking a sip of his coffee.

"Perfect timing." Reese smiled.

"And it's a good spot too." Lynnette pointed to the nearby mall entrance.

Reese turned on his signal and patiently waited for the man to get into his car. Finally, the guy got behind the wheel, but instead of backing up in the opposite direction, the tail end of his car headed toward Reese and then remained there.

"What the . . . ?" Reese frowned.

"Why is he stopped like this?" Lynnette stretched her neck toward the windshield, as if it would help her get a closer look.

"Oh, hell naw," Reese snapped as he realized what was happening. Another car, coming from the opposite direction, pulled into the space he was waiting for. Once the car was fully in, the old man honked his horn and waved as he pulled off.

"You gotta be kidding me!" Lynnette gasped. "They stole our spot."

"They did." Reese shook his head in disbelief. He was about to drive off in search of another one, but Lynnette stopped him.

"No, wait. We aren't gonna let them get away with this!" she told him.

"It's cool. We'll just find another one."

"Like hell. That's *our* spot. They gonna have to move! Roll the window down," Lynnette demanded.

"I'm not doing that. It's fine, Lynnette," Reese said.

"Reese, what the hell? It's not fine."

Before he could stop her, she opened her door and stepped out of the car.

"Excuse me! That's our space! You need to move!" Lynnette yelled in the direction of the other car.

Reese turned his head and watched as a woman and her passenger stepped out of the car in question and stared at Lynnette like she was crazy, and for good reason.

"I don't know what you're talking about, or who you think you're talking to!" the passenger yelled.

"I'm talking to *you*! Now move your car!" Lynnette screamed back.

"Lynnette, get back in the car. What the hell is wrong with you?" He tried to reach across the seat and grab her to pull her back inside.

"I'm not moving anything," the woman stated matter-of-factly. Unlike the passenger, she was calm and seemed almost amused. She pointed. "You're the one who needs to move. You're holding up traffic."

Reese turned his attention to his rearview mirror and saw the line of cars that was now waiting behind him. "Lynnette, people are behind us."

"You better listen to your boo and keep it moving," the passenger taunted. "Or if you're feeling froggy, close the door."

The beeping car behind them caused Lynnette to finally get back into the car. Reese didn't waste any time pulling off.

"What is wrong with you?" he muttered.

"You think I was gonna just let them take our spot and not say anything? Two fat roly-polies who could barely get out of the car? I don't think so," Lynnette huffed. "You should've got out and made them move."

Reese looked over at her, totally surprised by her rowdy behavior. She was usually cool, calm, and classy, unless she didn't get her way, and even then, she never really popped off the way she had. This was a side of her he'd never seen before. And as amusing as the thought of her getting into a rumble with two women over a parking space was, it was also a little disturbing and too much. Even more so because she felt as if he hadn't done enough.

"You're tripping," he said.

"No, *they* were tripping," Lynnette said, her attitude still quite noticeable.

"If you say so, but that was a bit much. And see, there wasn't even a need for it," Reese said as he stopped the car and turned on his blinker. "We ended up getting a spot even closer to the one they took."

Lynnette seemed to relax a little as he pulled into the space almost directly in front of the entrance. "It's still the principle."

"Relax. We got a good spot, and we're about to go and browse these stores for a few, then get some good food." He reached over and grabbed her hand after he had parked.

"Browse?" Lynnette gave him a questionable stare.

"Unless you plan to buy me something, of course." He grinned and leaned in for a kiss.

"Now you're tripping just as hard as those two fat chicks." Lynnette playfully pushed him away, then quickly pulled him back to her and kissed him softly.

After a few seconds, he opened his eyes and said, "You know you couldn't beat them, right? We both know you can't fight."

"I wasn't worried at all. You don't have to fight when you're pretty. Someone always fights for you." She grinned. "You wouldn't have let them touch me."

Reese opened his car door and stepped out. As he walked around the back of the car to open the passenger door, he noticed the two girls approaching the entrance. They were both pretty, and although one was larger than the other, they weren't nearly as big as Lynnette had made them out to be. The two ladies looked over at him and noticed him staring. Reese tensed, hoping that they weren't about to continue the scene in the parking lot.

"Merry Christmas," they shouted in unison and waved. They laughed as they headed inside. Reese continued watching until they disappeared through the revolving glass doors. He didn't even realize he was smiling until he heard Lynnette's voice.

"What are you smiling at?" she asked as she walked over. "And why didn't you come and open my door?"

"Oh, my bad. Someone just wished me a Merry Christmas, that's all," he told her as he took her hand in his. "I guess some people are in the Christmas spirit already."

"I guess." Lynnette shrugged. "Well, come on, because I'm already in the shopping spirit, and I know exactly what I want."

Chapter 7

Kendall

"How you doing, Kendall?"

The deep baritone voice caused Kendall to almost drop the ream of fabric she was carrying. She took a deep breath, then smiled as she slowly turned around.

"I'm good, Simon. How about you?" Kendall's eyes took in all six feet, three inches of the bald, bearded milk-chocolate man in the perfectly pressed FedEx uniform as he wheeled the cart of stacked boxes into her work space. She'd been so busy that she hadn't even realized that it was late in the afternoon, the time when Simon would arrive with the store's deliveries for the day.

"I'm good." He came to a halt. "Did you have a good Thanksgiving?" he asked.

"I did. What about you?" Kendall replied.

"It was cool. Plenty of good food, liquor, music, and drunk relatives," Simon said as he unloaded the stacked boxes from his cart. "I even had to break up a fight."

"Sounds like quite an event," Kendall commented.

"It was. Had I not been at my mother's house, I would've thought I was at the club." He chuckled. His laugh was just as sexy as his smile.

"I can imagine," Kendall told him.

"I meant to tell you, that display window out front this year is fire. I drove past here last night and had to stop and stare. It looks even better at night. You are talented."

"Thanks, but it wasn't just me. Amber helped," Kendall told him.

"Maybe, but she's the one who told me the vision was yours and she was the muscle."

"Muscle? Really?" Kendall raised an eyebrow and folded her arms.

"Yep, that's what she said. And she also said you paid her with a cold, weak latte," Simon continued. "I find that hard to believe, though, and I'm sure she was exaggerating."

"Good. I'm glad you recognize her untruths." Kendall shook her head and smiled.

"Of course. We all know Amber can be extra. I also know you're better than that. The latte was probably lukewarm." Simon chuckled, and Kendall playfully hit his arm.

"Oh." Deena, who happened to walk into the room at that moment, stopped and stared at them. "Simon, I have some other packages that need to go in my office when you're done in here."

"No problem, Ms. Deena. I can grab them." Simon dropped Kendall's wrist, which he had grabbed moments earlier.

"Thank you," Deena said with a flirtatious wink.

It was a well-known fact that almost everyone in the boutique was captivated by Simon and found him attractive: Deena and most of the sales team members, including Claude, the only male employee, took notice of Simon every time he came into the store. The only people he didn't seem to have an effect on were Kendall and Amber, who ironically was too busy trying to set him up with Kendall to be interested.

The three of them stood in an awkward silence until Kendall finally spoke. "Well, the only boxes for me are right there."

"Oh, let me grab those first. Then I'll come back and meet you in your office, Ms. Diablo," Simon said to Deena.

"Sounds good." Deena turned and walked out of the room.

"You'd better hurry, before she comes looking for you," Kendall teased when Deena was gone.

"You're not funny," Simon sighed as he picked up the two boxes Kendall had pointed to earlier.

"I am. That's why you're laughing." She reached for her shears to begin cutting the fabric on the table.

"Well, how about you come and hang out for some laughs later? I told Amber that after work a couple of friends and I are going to happy hour at Mangeaux's," Simon said.

"That's the new spot down on Fairway, right? I heard about it," Kendall replied.

"Yep. Tonight they have a live band. You guys should come and hang."

"I'll consider it. Depends on how I feel when I get out of here. As you can see, I have a lot to accomplish." Kendall motioned toward the rack of ball gowns and dresses she had to alter.

"Well, if you're up to it, the invitation stands," Simon said as he rolled the cart toward the door. "Enjoy the rest of your day."

"You too, Simon." Kendall smiled. She couldn't remember the last time she'd hung out at a bar. She usually spent what limited free time she could find shopping or working on her own designs, though on occasion, she did enjoy dinner dates, wine festivals, or weekend girls' trips with Amber. Bars weren't usually her thing, but the thought of hanging with Simon did sound like fun. She looked over at the full rack of alterations that still needed to be done.

It's ball season. There's no time for fun.

"Kendall, you have a call on line three. Kendall, you have a call on line three," Amber announced over a loudspeaker.

Kendall put down the cutting shears, then glanced down at her cell phone, which was lying on the table nearby. There weren't any missed calls.

"Kendall, line three please. Kendall, line three," Amber announced again.

After walking over to her cluttered desk, Kendall shuffled through the pile of papers and swatches of material until she found the store phone. People who weren't customers rarely called her at work. And even then, Deena had informed everyone at the boutique to handle whatever they called for so that Kendall could continue working undisturbed. Whoever was calling had to be important.

"This is Kendall," she said into the receiver.

"Hi, Miss Kendall. It's Niya," a tiny voice said, so low that Kendall could barely hear the words.

"Niya?" Kendall turned up the volume and then pressed the phone closer to her ear.

"Niya Fine, Claudia Fine's granddaughter."

"I know who you are, Niya. I just couldn't really hear you. How are you? What's going on?" Kendall leaned against the desk, curious as to what had prompted the phone call. She wondered if it had something to do with the jacket she'd given the girl a few days prior. *Maybe I left something in the pocket*, she thought.

"Um, I was wondering if you could maybe come over later this evening," Niya told her.

"This evening? Is anything wrong?" Kendall frowned.

"No, I just need to talk to you about something. It's really important," Niya said.

Kendall glanced over at Amber, who had strolled into the work space, undoubtedly to be nosy.

"Uh . . ." Kendall didn't know what to say. "Hold on for one sec, Niya."

"Okay," Niya responded.

"What does she want?" Amber whispered once Kendall had pushed the HOLD button.

"She says she needs to talk to me, and it's important." Kendall shrugged.

"Important? What in the world?" Amber's face wore the same confused look as Kendall's. "Ask her what it's about. See if she can just tell you over the phone."

Taking her friend's suggestion, Kendall took the call off hold and said, "I'm back, Niya. Sorry about that."

"No, I'm sorry. I know you're really busy, and this is a bad idea, anyway. It's okay. Don't worry about it," Niya quickly said. "I didn't mean to bother you . . ."

"No, you're fine, Niya. You're not a bother," Kendall told her. "We can talk about whatever it is. I get off at six tonight, and I'll come straight there. Will that work?"

"What? What about happy . . . ?" Amber's whispers were hushed by the hand that Kendall held up.

"Six is perfect. Thank you so much, Miss Kendall. I appreciate you. See you at six." Niya's soft, somber voice was now excited and appreciative.

"See you then," Kendall said before hanging up the phone.

"Are you kidding?" Amber asked. "You're kidding, right?"

"Don't be like that," Kendall sighed.

"Kendall, Simon told me he invited you to Mangeaux's."

"He did. He invited you too. But I didn't tell him I'd go. It's not like he's expecting me to show up." Kendall shrugged.

"But you should show up. That's my point," Amber pointed out. "You always talk about wanting to meet a nice dude, but you don't ever wanna meet a nice dude. Simon is a nice dude."

"He is a nice dude. And you're right. I do want to meet someone. The right one. And I will when the time is right," Kendall told her.

She knew Amber was trying to be helpful and had her best interests at heart. This was a conversation they'd engaged in countless times. Amber was adamant that Kendall needed to be more aggressive when it came to her love life. Kendall was confident that love would happen when the time was right. She'd never had a problem dating, but over the past couple of years, she'd become bored with it, so she'd eased up. This had given her more time to focus on designing, which was her passion. Bringing her visions to life and creating had become more enjoyable and appealing than monotonous phone calls and dry dinner convos with someone who ended up not being worth her time. Instead of looking for love, Kendall had decided to let love find her: the right person at the right time.

"Simon is the right one, and now is the right time," Amber insisted. "I feel it, Kendall. This is your season for love. I told you I had a dream that you were designing your wedding gown and you put it in a garment bag, and then we went to the hotel to get ready for your wedding. It's happening. You know my dreams are always accurate."

"You believe that, huh?" Kendall smiled.

Amber nodded. "I do. I really do."

"Good. Then it'll happen whether I go to happy hour tonight or not," Kendall said. She was amused by the frustrated look Amber then gave her. "Amber, this girl needs me for something."

"You already gave her my . . . I mean, your jacket. She probably wants another one, that's all. And here you go, giving up a date with a perfectly fine, sexy, funny, gainfully employed man to go over there." Amber tossed her hands up in the air.

"If I didn't know any better, I'd think you want Simon," Kendall teased. "Maybe you should be the one to go to Mangeaux's, not me." She smiled at Amber.

Amber frowned, then gave Kendall an evil grin. "Now, you know if I wanted Simon, I would have him. I ain't like you."

Kendall's smile faded. "There you go with that again. I'm not scared of anything or anybody. You always take stuff to the extreme."

"I didn't say you were scared, Kendall. At least, not this time. That's you." Amber winked, then left the room before Kendall could say anything else.

Kendall took her time as she approached the Fine mansion in her car. When she'd visited a week ago to deliver Claudia Fine's glasses, she'd briefly admired the holiday lights along the driveway and elsewhere on the property. This time, she took them all in.

When she reached the top of the driveway, she rolled to a stop and gazed at the house, which was bedecked in dazzling lights and other festive garb. The decorations made the glorious house seem even more magical than it already was. The entire frame of the home was outlined in white and ivory bulbs, while the columns on the wrap-around front porch were encircled in red, green, and silver. A spotlight beamed on a beautiful nativity scene on the lawn, one complete with Mary, Joseph, Jesus in a manger, all the animals, the three Wise Men, and the angel. The entire display was harmonious and something to behold. After a few minutes, she returned her gaze to the driveway, drove forward, and parked. She got out of the car and went to the front door. Niya opened it before Kendall had a chance to knock.

"You're here," Niya exclaimed.

"I am," Kendall said. "I see you're still enjoying the jacket."

Grinning, Niya looked down briefly at the jacket she wore. "I wear it every day. You're right. It's magic. That's why I need to talk to you." She welcomed Kendall inside and led her into the living room, where they'd talked before.

Amber is right, Kendall thought. *She wants me to make another jacket. That's what this is about. I should've listened to Amber and gone to happy hour.*

"That's great, Niya. But we could've talked about that on the phone," Kendall told her.

"No, there's something else too," Niya said.

"Niya, was that the door?" Claudia Fine said as she walked into the living room. She looked surprised to see Kendall standing in her home.

"Yes, ma'am. It was."

Kendall noticed the change in Niya's demeanor. Her energy and voice level dropped, and her body tensed. It was obvious that she was anxious.

"How are you, Mrs. Fine?" Kendall beamed, hoping to increase the vibratory level in the room. "It's nice to see you again."

"Hello. What are you doing here? I haven't been to Diablo's, so I'm sure I didn't leave anything there." Claudia looked Kendall up and down. "Did Deena send you here for something?"

"Oh, no, ma'am, you didn't. And no, she didn't, either." Kendall remained cheerful, although it was challenging to do so.

Niya spoke up. "I asked her to stop by. I told her I wanted to talk to her."

"That's why I'm here." Kendall stepped beside Niya and put her arm on her shoulder. "To talk to Niya."

"Talk about what?" Claudia asked. "Niya, you barely know this woman. What could you possibly want to discuss with her?"

With that, Kendall became as tense as Niya. She had yet to learn what Niya needed to talk about, but she wanted the girl to feel safe and supported when she did, even if it was something as simple as asking for another jacket. And based on how things felt right now, that wasn't going to happen as long as Claudia was present.

"Mrs. Fine, Niya and I had a nice chat last time I was here. And I told her she could call me anytime. It's no problem," Kendall told her.

Claudia peered at Kendall. "You're the one who gave her this graffiti coat, which she insists on wearing every day, aren't you?"

Kendall hesitated, then, with confidence, said, "Yes, ma'am. It's one of my original designs."

"Well, my granddaughter isn't a charity case, and we don't usually accept handouts, so I have no problem compensating you . . ."

Kendall shook her head. "No, Mrs. Fine, that's not necessary. If you could just give Niya and me a little alone time to chat, that's all. I'm sure we won't be long."

Claudia's eyes went from Kendall to Niya. "Niya, I don't know what this is about, but . . ."

Kendall felt Niya's body become even more tense. Then the young girl inhaled and took a step toward her grandmother.

"I'll tell you," Niya said.

"Niya, you—" Kendall began, trying to intervene, but Niya interrupted her.

"I've decided to be a deb," Niya announced. Then, with a little more conviction, she added, "That's what I want to talk to her about."

"What do you mean?" Claudia's face was a mixture of confusion and disbelief.

"I mean, I submitted my application to the First Noel Society to participate in the ball this year." Niya turned and smiled at Kendall. "I'm gonna do it."

Chapter 8

Niya

Niya's original plan was to talk to Kendall about her decision to participate in the ball before telling her grandmother. After all, it was kind of Kendall's idea and suggestion. Until the night Kendall came to their house, Niya had never even considered it. The First Noel Ball was something her mother had always told her about. It was like a favorite bedtime story. She would curl beside Niya and snuggle her chin against the top of her head and talk about learning to waltz with her friends and their escorts, finding the perfect gown, and wearing her precious pearls, a gift from her mother. Niya would close her eyes and listen to the soothing sound of her mother's voice and imagine her mother, looking young and beautiful like in her framed picture, smiling and dancing with her father in the middle of the ballroom floor. She'd fall asleep smiling, thinking the ball was a part of some mystical place and time reserved for the two of them.

Hearing Kendall, someone who looked more like her, speak of her debutante experience was different. Her story was reminiscent of the ones her mother had told, yet it was somehow enlightening. Until that moment, Niya had never imagined or considered being a debutante herself. Despite the legacy of Claudia being crowned queen and then herself, Nina had never broached the topic of her daughter becoming a deb, at least not with Niya. Kendall's suggestion that Niya do it in honor of her mother was all she had thought about since their chance meeting. She had been so caught up in thinking about becoming a debutante that she had forgotten to be nervous on her first day at her new school. It was as if the possibility of being a part of something that her mother had been a part of was all that mattered.

Before she knew it, Niya had Googled the director of the First Noel Society and then had contacted her, asking to be considered. As she fired off the email, Niya had told herself that her chances of being given the opportunity were almost nonexistent, especially since the application deadline was months earlier. *At least I have tried*, she thought after hitting the SEND button. *Even if they say no, I know Mommy would be proud of me.* The last thing she had expected to receive three days after submitting her application was a response welcoming her, along with a list of requirements and a schedule of events she'd be expected to attend beginning the same weekend.

Staring at the iPad screen, Niya's heart had begun racing, and she'd looked around at the students sitting nearby, making sure they couldn't hear the rhythmic pounding in her chest, which seemed deafening. Feelings of shock, excitement, and nervousness all happened simultaneously. Then fear set in as the reality of what she had done sunk in. In the huge leap of faith that she'd taken, she hadn't considered what her grandmother would say. There was no way she'd be able to participate without telling her, but she didn't want to say anything without at least having some kind of plan in place. Niya scrolled down the list of items she'd need.

"This was a bad idea."

"Miss Fine, did you say something?" said Mrs. Donahue, her AP English teacher, and Niya realized that she'd spoken the words out loud and not in her head.

Embarrassed, Niya quickly whispered, "May I be excused? I don't feel well."

Mrs. Donahue nodded and held out a lanyard holding a bright orange plastic card that served as a hall pass. Without hesitating, Niya tucked her iPad into her bag, then picked it up.

"Thanks," she mumbled, taking the lanyard. Then she scurried out of the classroom and into the hallway. She raced to the closest bathroom and into the first empty stall, then leaned against the door and tried to think.

How am I going to do this? What was I thinking? I don't have anyone to even help me do this. This is for girls who have a mom. And I don't have one. My mother's gone, my best friend is miles away, and my grandmother doesn't even like me. The only person who loves me is a man—Uncle Reese. Feeling overwhelmed, she closed her eyes and began to pray. Tears formed in her eyes as she swallowed the lump in her throat that had become all too familiar. *Please God, help me. I can't do this alone. I need someone. I need my mommy.*

Tap. Tap. Tap.

Someone had knocked on the stall door. Then a small voice asked, "Are you okay?"

Niya remained quiet as she tried to pull herself together, grabbing some tissue and dabbing her eyes.

Tap. Tap. Tap.

"Hello?"

"Uh, yeah, I'm fine," Niya finally answered, hoping that the person would leave her alone to wallow in her misery.

"Are you sure?" the voice asked. "I'm gonna wait out here until you come out to make sure, just so you know."

"I'm sure. I'm fine," Niya replied. "You can leave."

"I know I can, but I'm not going to," the voice told her.

Niya took a deep breath and finally opened the door. She stepped out and saw that it was one of her classmates, Jira Phillips. Even though she'd been at Collingswood High School for less than a week, Niya had quickly learned three things about Jira: she was very pretty, popular, and smart, the trifecta of high school objectives. Jira gave her a semi-smile with her perfect teeth. Her catlike eyes were a mixture of hazel and green, and her wavy hair cascaded down her back despite having been pulled into a ponytail. Even though she was standing in the middle of the bathroom, she looked like she'd just stepped off the set of a Pantene hair products commercial.

"I'm good. Thanks." Niya walked over to the sink and washed her hands, choosing not to look at her reflection in the mirror, because she knew it would make her feel worse than she already did.

"Okay, cool." Jira nodded.

"You don't have to wait. I'm fine. Thanks." Niya gave her a side glance.

Jira waited a few more seconds, then, before turning toward the door, she said, "I've been meaning to tell you that jacket is fire."

Niya looked around for a moment, searching for someone else, then realized Jira was talking to her. "Oh, thanks. I appreciate it."

"You mind telling me where you got it?" she asked.

"Um, a friend of mine designed it. It's an original piece." Niya nervously looked down at the jacket, and the words seemed to jump out at her: *bold*, *unique*, *amazing*. She'd had the jacket for a few days, but it was as if every time she looked at it, she noticed new words.

"That's so dope. It's like you're wearing a piece of art for the world to see. That's really cool, Niya." Jira opened the door and walked out.

Niya didn't move for a few seconds. Her mind was a whirlwind of thoughts and emotions. First, she was shocked at the fact that Jira Phillips knew her name. How? She'd been in school for only a week. Somehow, the most popular girl in school knew her name. Niya wondered if it was because her classmates had been teasing her behind her back. Even though she hadn't heard any jokes herself, she could imagine the names they'd called her. She'd heard them all before: fat, big, sloppy, heavy, black, burnt, smoky. Being teased about her weight and her skin tone wasn't anything new, and she'd become numb to the pain of verbal bullying from her peers over the years. She was a bigger, darker girl, and bullying came with the territory, and so she had been expecting it, especially since she was new. What she hadn't expected was the compliment from Jira and her nice, pleasant demeanor, and now she wondered why Jira had acted that way.

Was she trying to be funny? Wait, she probably feels sorry for me, because she heard about my mom. Or can it really be that she likes my jacket and thinks I'm cool?

Niya glanced at her reflection in the mirror.

This jacket is powerful. If you're gonna wear it, you're gonna have to own it.

"Wait, the jacket. Kendall's jacket," Niya gasped. "Kendall!"

Without hesitation, Niya grabbed her phone from her bag, Googled the Diablo Designs boutique, and dialed the number. Kendall agreeing to come to the house gave her the confidence she needed and was confirmation that she might really be able to handle what she'd gotten herself into. Now all she had to do was convince her to help.

"I think that's wonderful, Niya. Congratulations." Kendall hugged her from the side as they stood in the living room.

"How is that even possible? The young ladies go through a screening process, and the selections have already been made. The chosen participants are being announced . . ."

"Saturday, at the luncheon. I know," Niya remarked, finishing her grandmother's sentence. "I have to be there at eleven."

"This is ridiculous. I don't know if this is some kind of joke or prank, but it's not funny," Claudia declared.

"It's not a joke. I didn't think they'd say yes." Niya shrugged.

"You didn't *think*? Then why'd you submit an application? How were you even allowed to submit one? This makes no sense." Claudia closed her eyes and shook her head.

"I submitted it through the website and sent an email. The director emailed me back this afternoon and said I'd been selected," Niya explained.

"Do you even understand what a debutante is, Niya? Never mind. It's clear that you don't. It takes time, preparation, planning, none of which you've done. *None.* How do you even expect to be able to do this? Do you know all that's involved?" Claudia finally opened her eyes and glared at Niya.

The confidence Niya had gained earlier was now gone. Instead of feeling as if she had decided to do something bold and powerful in honor of her mother, she felt embarrassed and ashamed.

"I'm sure the ball committee took all of that into consideration. You said yourself that they are meticulous about the selections, and I'm not sure what Niya said in her email, but obviously they were moved by it. I think they made a great selection, and granted, it will take a lot of work, but she's going to make a beautiful deb," Kendall stated. "Her mother and grandmother both did. It's part of her heritage and probably part of why she was selected."

Niya caught the slight wink Kendall gave her from the corner of her eye. She was grateful that she'd made the call and that Kendall was there for support, because there was no way the conversation would be able to continue had she been by herself. Kendall had her back, and she needed it. Still, she was worried that it may not have been enough, because her grandmother was not letting up. Her mother had warned her about Claudia Fine's fits of displeasure, but now she was witnessing it for herself, and it was even scarier than she had imagined.

"That's my point. This is nepotism at its finest, and I don't agree with it at all. Granddaughter or not, the society has rules, regulations, and guidelines in place for a reason. Niya, you shouldn't even want to be selected based on your last name. It should be something that is earned." Claudia raised an eyebrow.

"Now, Mrs. Fine, I mean no disrespect, but we both know being selected has a lot to do with the applicant's pedigree," Kendall volunteered.

Niya watched as her grandmother opened her mouth to speak, then quickly closed it, pursing her lips instead of giving a verbal response. *Oh snap. Kendall won round one.* The heaviness in

Niya's chest lifted slightly at this minor victory, and despite wanting to turn and give Kendall a high five, she remained in place and waited. The room was quiet. It was as if each of them was waiting for the other to speak next. Niya felt as if she'd said enough, so she remained silent in order to allow Kendall to continue doing a good job at being her voice of reason.

Claudia finally spoke. "You really have no idea what you've gotten yourself into, do you? Do you even have an appropriate suit for the luncheon or the other events? Hat, gloves, shoes? What about your hair?"

The familiar lump made its way to Niya's throat, accompanied by the hot tears in her eyes. Her grandmother was right; she had none of those items. She hadn't even thought about them. Her only thought had been being a part of the ball, like her mother. The reality of what she'd truly done set in.

Niya wiped the tears that were now rolling down her cheeks. "I . . . I don't . . ."

Kendall spoke up. "I can help her with all of that. She'll be ready for tomorrow. No problem."

"That's just one event. What about all the others?" Claudia's questions were now directed at Kendall, whose demeanor, unlike Niya's, hadn't changed at all.

"She'll be ready for those too. All of them," Kendall said, as if they were talking about Niya bringing a dish to weekly neighborhood potlucks instead of participating in formal events that all would be captured on film, which meant she needed to be camera ready every time.

"Oh really? Look, we don't know one another at all, and you don't know my granddaughter. Your being here as some sort of morale is endearing but not needed. This is a private family matter, and Niya had no business even involving you. Hence, another example of her not having the judgment required of the First Noel participants." Claudia exhaled. "Thank you for your time, but I think it's time for you to leave."

Niya felt defeated. It was over, and it seemed as if her grandmother had truly won the war. She turned and faced Kendall. "Thank you. I'm sorry I had you come all the way over here and got you involved."

"Don't apologize, Niya. You did nothing wrong. You did exactly what your heart led you to do, and you never apologize for honoring your heart. That's what being fearless means." Kendall pointed to the word *fearless* on the front of Niya's jacket. "I'm proud of you. Your mom is too. I know it."

Niya smiled. "Yeah, she probably is."

"I'm not certain about that. My daughter was very smart and quite analytical. She thought things through before doing them. I'm sure Niya didn't even consider the fact that she had no one to even present her at the ball. Her grandfather has passed as well as her father," Claudia pointed out.

It was Niya's turn to raise an eyebrow at her grandmother. "I did consider that."

Claudia looked surprised and amused. "Oh really? And who did you come up with?"

At that moment, the universe decided to step in and lend her a hand. Niya was excused from having to give an answer.

"Hey, what's going on?"

The voice caused all three ladies to turn around and focused their attention on her uncle as he entered the living room, looking like a superhero in his black leather jacket, his helmet tucked under his arm. His timing could not have been more perfect. Niya's grin was wide, and she eased out from under Kendall's arm, which was still holding her shoulder protectively, and strolled over to greet him before he got within earshot.

"Uncle Reese, you're home early," Niya said.

Reese frowned slightly, then leaned over and whispered, "What's going on? You sent me a text and told me I needed to be home by seven for something important."

"This is important," Niya whispered back. "And I need you, please."

"Who's that?" Reese's eyes landed on Kendall as he placed his helmet on the small table near the living-room door. He purposely avoided looking at his mother because he could sense the displeasure on her face at his putting the protective headgear on her precious marble piece, which served as decor, not storage, as she'd stated more times than he could count.

"That's my friend Miss Kendall. She's here to help too," Niya told him.

"Help with what? Niya, what the heck is going on?" Reese murmured. "And talk fast, because based on your grandmother's face, whatever it is, she's not happy about it at all."

Niya took Reese's free hand and guided him to where she'd been standing moments earlier. She looked at her grandmother and said, "He'll do it."

Claudia's eyes widened. For the second time that evening, she was eerily silent. Niya held her breath and waited, along with her uncle and Kendall, who both seemed to be just as anxious for Claudia's response to Niya's announcement.

"Him? You're kidding, right?" Claudia's voice was barely above a whisper.

"No, ma'am. You will, won't you, Uncle Reese?" Niya turned and gave him a pleading look. He looked down at her, his face full of confusion. Niya's heart began to pound.

Reese looked at his mother. "Yep, I sure will."

Claudia then did something none of them expected. She laughed.

Chapter 9

Reese

Reese had no idea what was happening or what he'd agreed to do. He couldn't remember the last time he'd seen his mother so amused. She was laughing so hard that she was crying. However, she was the only one laughing in the room. Niya and the other woman seemed to be just as put off as he was. He quickly learned what he'd agreed to.

"What's so funny?" Reese asked.

His mother finally stopped chuckling long enough to say, "The fact that you're standing there agreeing to be a part of this nonsense. It's not funny. It's quite hilarious." She looked at her granddaughter. "Niya, your uncle didn't even show up at the ball the year he agreed to be an escort, and that young lady was his longtime girlfriend. Well, at least she was until he stood her up on one of the biggest nights of her life."

Reese's face flushed with embarrassment and anger. The memory of that night was one he'd resolutely banished, and having his mother share it with his niece and a total stranger made him uncomfortable. As much as he hated to admit it, his mother had a point. The First Noel Ball would be the last place he'd ever go. He was going to have to tell Niya that.

"Wow," Kendall said.

Reese turned his attention to her. "Kendall, is it?"

She smiled and extended her hand. "Yes, Kendall."

"Reese. Nice to meet you," Reese told her, then turned back to Niya. "So, the First Noel Ball, huh?"

Niya's eyes lit up in a way that he hadn't seen since before the funeral.

"Yep. Got the acceptance email this afternoon. I'm officially gonna be a deb, like Mom and . . ." Niya lowered her eyes for a second, then looked up and said, "Kendall. She was a First Noel Deb."

Reese nodded. "Okay, okay, well, uh—"

"You were a deb?" The accusatory tone of Claudia's voice interrupted his thoughts.

"I was. About eleven years ago. I loved it. I'm sure Niya will too." Kendall smiled. There was something familiar about her, but Reese couldn't exactly pinpoint what it was. In his line of work, he'd encountered hundreds of people every week, so he'd become accustomed to running into someone he'd met while on a call.

"I don't think she will," Claudia said.

Reese turned and asked, "Why not? Why wouldn't she?"

"Because this nonsense isn't happening. I won't allow this fiasco to tarnish our family name in the community or the legacy of my daughter. I'm calling the executive director and putting a stop to it," Claudia told him.

The hurt look on Niya's face was crushing. She had been through so much and deserved to have something to enjoy and look forward to. As crazy as it sounded, even if it was the dreaded ball that he despised. Reese knew that he had to do something. He couldn't allow his mother to take this away from Niya.

"Mother, don't," Reese said.

Claudia frowned. "Don't what?"

Reese faced his mother. "Don't call anyone."

"I don't take instructions from anyone, Reese, including you." Claudia looked him up and down.

"Niya, can you maybe go upstairs and give us a moment to talk?" Kendall asked.

"Sure," Niya said. Just before heading up the stairs, she turned around briefly. Her eyes met Reese's, and she placed her hands together as if she was praying and mouthed the words, "Please, Uncle Reese."

Reese exhaled. Supporting his niece was one thing; having his mother as his adversary was another. He'd experienced her wrath more times than he'd wanted, and he had no desire to become embroiled in any situation that would result in their relationship becoming any more strained than it already was. Were Nina still alive, she'd know exactly how to deal with this situation. She was stronger and had a lot more fortitude than he had ever had with their mother. And although their mother-daughter relationship had been just as strained as his relationship with his mother, somehow, his sister had managed always to find a soft spot, something he had yet to locate. At this point, he no longer cared. The only thing that mattered was Niya.

"Wait, why don't we sit down?" Reese suggested. He had no idea how long they'd been standing there and talking before he arrived, but Kendall still had on her coat. He hoped that taking a seat might lessen the tension, if that was even possible.

Kendall shrugged, and they both turned to his mother, who hesitated before finally saying, "This is all pointless."

They followed her over to the sofa and chairs arranged in the center of the posh living room, which looked like it was straight out of *Better Homes and Garden*. They had barely sat down before she began stating all the reasons why Niya's participation in the ball was ridiculous and damn near impossible. As he listened, he had to agree somewhat with what she was saying.

"Niya is probably so excited at the idea that she doesn't truly understand what she's gotten herself into," Reese murmured.

"Exactly," Claudia responded with a satisfied nod.

"With all due respect, may I speak?" Kendall asked.

"You may," Claudia told her.

"I know Niya springing this on everyone is a lot. And you're probably right about her not realizing everything involved. But I think that's why she reached out to me . . . well, to all of us. So that we can help her do this," Kendall stated. "And I think we can. It will take a team effort, but it's not impossible."

Reese was impressed by the assurance of her tone. Undoubtedly, whoever this woman was, she was confident. It was kind of refreshing. Most people had the tendency to shrink whenever they spoke with Claudia Fine. This woman didn't seem intimidated at all. She seemed quite the opposite: she was bold.

"That's my point. I'm not willing to help," Claudia told her. "It's the holiday season, and I have my own personal obligations to take care of. I don't have time to be involved."

"That's fine. No pun intended, of course," Kendall told her. "What about you?"

Reese realized the question was directed at him. "Me?"

"Yes. Are you willing to be on board and make this happen for Niya?" She stared at him as she waited for his response.

Something about her made him know that she would be fine with his answer whether it was yes or no. It was as if she was asking out of respect, not necessity. That made him even more curious about who she was.

"Uh, well . . ."

"The only thing Reese is willing to be on board is that motorcycle of his," Claudia quipped.

Reese cut his eyes at his mother, then glanced back at Kendall. "Look, I'm willing to help out."

"Help out with what, Reese? What can you possibly do to help? You're just now returning to work, and you barely have time to spend with her."

"I can make time," Reese said. "It's for Niya."

"Niya doesn't have a proper wardrobe or shoes or accessories."

"I'll personally make sure all of that is taken care of. That won't be a problem," Kendall assured her. She glanced over at Reese. "I'm sure you can help out with transportation, right? And, of course, you'll agree to stand in for her father, like she asked. That's the biggest thing."

"The biggest thing is a gown, which she doesn't have, either," Claudia pointed out.

Reese might not have known everything about the First Noel Ball, but he did know that having a gown was the most important thing. When his sister was a debutante, her gown was ordered almost a year in advance, well before she even applied. It seemed as if procuring a gown for Niya was going to be impossible.

"I'll take care of that too," Kendall volunteered.

"Huh?" Reese was surprised at how easy she was making this seem.

"I'm a seamstress, and a good one. And I have a lot of connects for most of the other stuff she'll need. I'm telling you this can happen. I have full confidence in Niya, and she really wants to do this. If she didn't, she never would've submitted the application or called me. She needs this."

Claudia stood. "She needs time to adjust to everything she's dealing with. The poor girl barely holds her head up and doesn't even look people in the eye when she talks to them. She doesn't have the social skills of the other girls, who've been preparing for this event their entire lives. Now you're telling me she can handle being a debutante in one of the biggest social societies in the state? You're setting her up for failure, and I want no part of it." Claudia walked out of the room.

Reese waited until she was gone to speak. "You really think Niya is ready for all of this? It's a lot."

Kendall nodded. "I believe she is."

"She was already kind of introverted before her mom passed, and now she's really isolated. Being here probably doesn't help, but I don't want her to be pressured by anyone or anything else. My mother's choice of words wasn't the best, but what she was trying to say is that Niya is fragile."

"That's exactly why she needs to do this. Niya is stronger than you guys think. This is an opportunity for her to thrive and flourish," Kendall explained. "That's part of what being a debutante is about. I truly believe doing this will allow her to bloom where she's planted."

"And what if she doesn't bloom?" Reese raised an eyebrow.

"That's a possibility too." Kendall shrugged. "But in my experience, a seed planted in good soil and watered daily usually grows, right? From what I've heard, the Fine soil is about some of the best around. All we have to do is water her."

The intense energy of Kendall's stare drew him in. He could sense her faith in Niya and what she was trying to accomplish, and her enthusiasm was infectious. There was something about her that instantly made him want to be a part of making it happen. She may not have convinced his mother, but she definitely had his support.

"Where do we start?" Reese asked and then gave Kendall a semi-smile.

"We start with convincing your mother not to make that phone call. You handle that, and I'll get started on everything else," Kendall told him.

"I'll take care of that," Reese agreed.

"Team Niya," she exclaimed.

Reese reached for the perfectly manicured hand that Kendall extended to him. "Team Niya."

Convincing his mother to allow them to put their plan into action wasn't easy, but somehow, he did it. She promised not to undermine Niya's participation in any way, but she also made it clear that she wouldn't be a part of what she predicted would be "an even bigger fiasco than my son's failure to appear at the ball years before." Instead of becoming angry, Reese decided to accept his mother's negativity as motivation to prove her wrong. *This isn't about her or me. It's about Niya*, he reminded himself before saying something just as disrespectful in response. Her decision not to support Niya was actually a blessing, he decided, because it meant that they wouldn't have to deal with her.

The next hurdle Reese had to jump over was Captain Yates. After convincing his supervisor that he was ready to return to his full-time schedule, he now had to amend his request. There was no way he was going to be able to work double shifts until after the ball. Due to the fact that he was Niya's only source of transportation and he had to stand in for her father, his time was going to be limited. As it turned out, Captain Yates was much more supportive than his mother and even mentioned that he and his wife already had tickets to the event.

"Seeing you dancing in a monkey suit gives me something to look forward to at the ball, Fine. I'm gonna make sure I take lots of pictures to show everyone," Captain Yates teased.

After dealing with his mother and his boss, Reese began to think Kendall was right: helping Niya achieve success was easier than he had anticipated. Until he broke the news to Lynnette.

"You're doing what?" she squealed, causing the other diners in the restaurant to stare at them. He'd invited her to lunch, telling her he had some news to share, and she'd gladly accepted.

Reese lowered his voice. "I'm presenting Niya at the First Noel Ball."

"How? Wait, why? When did all of this happen?" Lynnette sat back in her chair.

Reese forced his eyes away from the smooth cleavage that was now visible from her blouse being pulled by her folded arms. "It literally just happened yesterday. I was just as surprised by all of this as you are."

"I thought you said your niece was adjusting, was antisocial, and was not talking to people. Now you're telling me that she's about to be a debutante, Reese? That makes no sense whatsoever." Lynnette shook her head.

"She *is* adjusting, and this is gonna help her become more socially involved. Kendall says that it'll help her . . ."

"Who the hell is Kendall?" Lynnette demanded.

"She's a girl, well, a woman, who's helping Niya with this, and me. She works at Diablo's as a seamstress," Reese explained.

"A seamstress? Why isn't your mother helping?"

"Because she doesn't even want Niya to participate. It's a long story, Lynnette, but I promised Niya I would do this for her." Reese reached across the table and took Lynnette's hand.

"You also promised me that we would get back to normal. Now you're sitting here telling me you'll have even less time to spend with me during the holidays. I understand your family just went through a crisis, Reese, but I'm starting to feel like I'm not a priority. Maybe we need to . . ."

"We don't need to do anything, Lynnette. You are a priority and have been for the past two years," Reese assured her.

"I was, but now I'm not so sure." Lynnette's eyes lowered to her hand that he was holding. "Two years is a decent amount of time. I told you when we started dating that I'm not getting any younger, and I don't want to invest any more energy into something or someone who isn't going in the same direction that I am heading. I have a career, financial stability, and I'm secure in what I want. And I thought you were too."

Reese felt her finger flinch under his palm. He knew exactly what she was referring to. It wasn't the first time that Lynnette had hinted at her expectation of a ring. She was right. She was everything she'd named and more, and before Nina passed, he'd been considering proposing. It was actually one of the things he'd planned on talking to his sister about during Thanksgiving. Now she was gone, and he had no idea what to do and no one to talk about it with. At this point, proposing was the last thing on his mind, but he didn't want to lose Lynnette, either.

"Baby, you are the most valuable asset in my life right now. I'm not going to lose you or what we have, I promise. I love you." Reese squeezed her hand as he looked into her eyes.

"I love you too, Reese, but . . . ," Lynnette began.

"But nothing. I will make time to spend with you. We'll figure it out. And I'm going to need you to be right there with me at the ball, so I can show you off for all the world to see," Reese said. Then he thought of something he knew she would love. "There's something else I'm thinking about doing too."

"What?" Lynnette's voice was dry, and she sounded uninterested.

"Looking for a new place after the first of the year."

"A house?" Lynnette asked.

"Yeah, it's time, don't you think?" He shrugged.

Lynnette's eyes widened. "Are you serious?"

"I am. After the past couple of months—plus what I'm about to deal with over the next few weeks with Niya—I'm sure I'm gonna need to treat myself." He sighed, thinking that having her help him pick out a house was easier than choosing an engagement ring and equally as satisfying for both of them.

Based on the way Lynnette squealed in delight, he was right. Now all he had to do was learn how to waltz—something he'd failed to do almost twenty years ago.

Chapter 10

Kendall

"Have you eaten? Never mind. I already know the answer to that question," Amber said, walking over to the workstation where Kendall was sitting and handing her a white paper bag. The aroma of steak and cheese drifted into Kendall's nostrils, alerting her about the bag's contents without her opening it.

"OMG, Philly egg rolls." Kendall closed her eyes and inhaled. "You do love me."

"I do." Amber nodded. "Which is why, instead of pointing out how ridiculous all of this is, I'm just going to make sure you're well nourished instead, so you don't pass out."

"You are doing much more than that, Amber, and I appreciate it," Kendall said as she opened the bag and took out one of the egg rolls. It was late, and the store had been closed for hours, but Kendall was still hard at work. She had been going nonstop for the past week and had no plans to stop. It was already the busiest time of year for her. Between addressing the massive amount of seamstress work she had to do during the day and putting in the extra hours at night to get things ready for Niya, she barely had a free moment to sleep, let alone eat.

"Look, I know you really want to help this girl, but, Kendall, this is a lot to take on. You're burning the candle at both ends, and you barely had a wick to begin with," Amber pointed out.

"I'm fine, Amber. You act like I've never pulled all-nighters before. This was routine stuff when I was in design school, remember?" Kendall told her.

"But you're not a stressed-out student trying to impress a teacher and get a good grade. You're a college graduate with nothing to prove to anyone, so I don't even understand why you're doing this. You don't even know this girl." Amber hopped on the cutting table.

Kendall had considered not sharing what she'd taken on, but she'd known that she would need her friend's help. Just as Kendall had expected, Amber's reaction had not been too receptive, especially considering the fact that it meant that Kendall's already limited availability to hang out, shop, and socialize with her friend would be even less. She hadn't been too pleased, but she had stepped up and had gone above and beyond to help. Amber was well connected to other area boutiques and had used her resources to make sure Niya had all the shoes, accessories, and jewelry she'd need. Kendall had altered a beautiful suit she already owned and had never worn so that it fit Niya perfectly, and on the day of the luncheon, the girl had looked just as perfect as all the other debutantes.

But there was still a lot of work to do, and a short time in which to do it. The last thing she needed was Amber complaining, even if she meant well.

Kendall finished the egg roll and took a napkin out of the bag. "Since when are random acts of kindness reserved for people we know?" she asked as she wiped her hands.

"This isn't a random *act*, Kendall. This is a whole random *series*." Amber shook her head. "How long do you plan on staying here?"

"I'm almost finished. I just wanted to get this corset foundation for Niya's gown done. I'm gonna stop and let her try it as a fitting tomorrow morning, right before I come in to work on it some more." Kendall wiped her hands on the napkin once more before carefully removing the white bodice she'd spend the past two hours constructing and holding it up.

"Tomorrow? We're supposed to get a jump start on the party stuff," Amber reminded her.

Kendall winced. She'd totally forgotten that she and Amber were in charge of the staff holiday party, which was being held in a few weeks. Deena had given them a modest budget, along with instructions to make it as memorable as the year before. They hadn't hesitated to accept the challenge. After putting their artistic heads together and thinking outside the box, they had decided to have a "Holiday Hoedown" and had secured a venue, a local country-western bar. The idea was quirky and creative, and the party was sure to be lots of fun. But there was still a lot of work to be done. They had to order food, secure a deejay, get the final decorations, and come up with games and prizes. Kendall had been looking forward to it, but now it didn't seem as important as everything else she had going on.

"Oh, yeah," Kendall told her. "What time do you want to do that?"

Amber shrugged. "I guess we can go after your fitting with Niya."

"It won't take that long, I promise," Kendall assured her. "I tell you what. I won't even work on the gown. Tomorrow I'm all yours, Ambi Bambi."

Kendall pulled Amber off the table and hugged her playfully.

Amber laughed and told her, "Good, because you know we gotta make sure this is the absolute best party ever."

"It will be. You know how we do," Kendall assured her. "This isn't gonna be a party. It's gonna be an entire turn-up event."

The next morning, as soon as she arrived at the Fine mansion, Kendall could tell that something was off. Niya opened the front door and barely said hello. The grin and hug that Kendall had come to expect weren't offered. Kendall followed Niya inside, but instead of going into the living room, they continued farther into the house and headed into another large open space, which looked like a cross between a sitting room and a library. Endless shelves of books lined the walls, and there was a large mounted television. A sofa and two chaise lounge chairs seemed out of place and were randomly pushed to the side of the room, along with a Versailles desk and matching chair.

"This is a cool room," Kendall commented.

"Thanks," Niya mumbled.

"Oh, here. Here's the gown. I can lace it up once you have it on." She passed Niya the bag. "I just wanna make sure it holds your girls up and feels comfortable, if that's even possible with a corset."

Niya hesitated for a moment before taking it. "It doesn't matter how it fits. I'm gonna look stupid, anyway."

"What?" Kendall frowned.

"Nothing," Niya said and rushed out of the room before Kendall could stop her. Just as she was about to go after her, Reese walked in.

"Oh, hey, Kendall," he said, looking as irritated as Niya. She'd become accustomed to seeing him in his EMT uniform each time they ran into each other. Seeing him so relaxed in a white T-shirt, Nike sweatpants, and Air Max shoes was odd. The first time she saw him, she'd had the odd feeling that they'd met before, and even though she'd tried, she hadn't been able to place where or when.

"Hey, Reese. Can you explain what's going on? Why does everyone seem aggravated? Did your mom say something again?" Kendall asked.

"No, this time it's not on her. It's on me," he sighed. "Well, on both of us."

"What did both of you do?"

"Unfortunately, we both have left feet," Reese confessed.

Kendall tried to hold her composure, but between the bashful way Reese said this and the look on his face, she couldn't stop the giggle that escaped.

"Wow, and here I thought we were on the same team." Reese shook his head and plopped down on the sofa, visibly upset.

Kendall walked over and sat beside him. "Uncle Reese, you're right. We are on the same team. I'm sorry. I thought you were joking. Okay, let's start over. Now explain what's going on."

Reese glanced over at her. "I told you, neither one of us can dance. First rehearsal yesterday afternoon was a complete disaster, and today it's even worse. Her feet hurt, my feet hurt, and the only steps we've gotten correct are stepping on each other's toes."

Kendall giggled once more, and again, she quickly apologized. "Sorry."

"I'm glad you find our rhythmic shortcomings so amusing."

"I don't," Kendall told him. "What's amusing is the way you're talking about it. But I'm okay now, so continue."

Reese leaned forward and stared at the floor. "This stupid waltz. I don't understand why they're still doing this same wack dance, anyway. After fifty years, you'd think they'd at least find some better music to make it easier to learn."

Kendall's next giggle was stopped by the warning look Reese gave her. She paused, then said, "Are you really whining and pouting? You sound like a fifth grader, you know that, right?"

"I'm not whining or pouting. I'm stating facts," he retorted. "We've been at this for hours and can't get it right. I'm frustrated. Niya's frustrated. At this point we're both ready to quit."

"That's not happening. So you may as well get that thought out of your head. Where's the remote?" Kendall stood. Reese pointed to the television remote on the edge of the desk. After picking it up, she aimed it toward the TV screen and typed in the name of one of her favorite Babyface songs. As the intro music began to play, she reached for Reese's hand. "Come on. Stand up."

He looked at her like she was crazy. "What? This isn't the song we're supposed to dance to."

"How about you stop worrying about what song this is? Now get up." Kendall rolled her eyes, grabbed his hand, then pulled him to his feet. He exhaled loudly as he followed her instructions. They stood in the middle of the room, and she positioned his hand in hers, stared at him, then gave him an encouraging smile. "Relax. You can do this. Just follow the beat with the steps you already know. That's it. Ready?"

Reese took a deep breath and then took a step, right on Kendall's foot. He immediately became frustrated and went to drop his arms, but she stopped him and nodded again. They started over, and this time, they completed a full box step before his foot came to rest on top of hers.

"I'm sorry," he said, apologizing. "I . . ."

"You're doing fine," Kendall reassured him. "Let's start again. Relax and have fun this time. Loosen up. It's a waltz, but you can give it a little swag. Stop being stiff."

Kendall shimmied her shoulders and encouraged him to do the same. Reese smiled and mimicked her shimmy. They laughed and began again, and this time they continued the steps until the song finally ended. Kendall clapped excitedly, and they gave one another a high five.

"Okay, that was kinda a'ight." Reese nodded. His energy was higher, and his attitude had improved drastically. "Let's try it again."

"You sure you're up for it?" Kendall teased.

"I am," he told her, reaching for the remote and starting the song over. This time he took the lead, and although there were a few missteps, he didn't become frustrated or stop.

His newfound confidence made Kendall smile. She began to enjoy the dance as much as he did. As they moved in sync, she took notice of his broad shoulders, strong brow line, and perfect teeth. He bore a strong resemblance to his mother. Both had the same complexion of toasted almond, wavy black hair, and small, pouty lips. But whereas Claudia Fine was noticeably beautiful, Reese's attractiveness was subtle. Or maybe it wasn't. *Maybe I just didn't notice until now,* she thought.

"Better," she said when the song ended again. "See? I told you it was okay."

Reese nodded. "This is crazy. It's gotta be the song."

"Not really. Once you've mastered the steps, you can do them to any song. It's just easier to learn them to something familiar instead of the traditional Chopin," Kendall pointed out.

"It also helps when the teacher is cool too." Reese's eyes met hers, and she held his stare for what seemed like a moment too long.

Kendall finally looked away. "Like I said, you already knew the steps. I probably need to go check on Niya. She's probably been ready for me to make sure the top of her gown fits right."

"I appreciate you doing all of this, Kendall. I still can't believe you're making her gown. Are you sure you don't want me to just order her one? I checked on Amazon Prime, and I can have one delivered in two days."

Kendall's mouth dropped open. It was his turn to giggle, and she quickly told him, "You play too much, Reese."

As she walked out, she could still hear him laughing. Even though she had no idea where she was going, she continued down the hallway in the direction that she'd seen Niya go, and called out her name. "Niya, where are you?"

"In here." Niya's voice came from behind a closed door a few feet away.

Kendall knocked on the door, and Niya let her into the large bathroom. Much like the rest of the house, it looked like something in an interior decorator magazine. Kendall took a few seconds to admire the decor, then turned her attention to Niya. The young girl was a sight to see with the fancy corset covering the top of her body and a pair of oversized jeans on the bottom.

"What took you so long?" Niya asked as Kendall began touching the foundation that would eventually become the bodice of the gown. "I thought you had left."

"I was helping Uncle Reese with the waltz steps," Kendall said. "Looks good from the front. How does it feel? Turn around."

"I guess it's okay. I hope it doesn't fall off." Niya turned her back to Kendall, who then began pulling the satin ribbon to tighten the corset.

"Trust me, it won't," Kendall said, pulling as hard as she could.

"Whoa, wait! Too tight. I can't breathe," Niya groaned.

Kendall laughed and loosened the ribbon a little. "Better?"

"Much." Niya nodded. "Wait, did you say you were helping Uncle Reese waltz?"

"I did. He's got it pretty much down pat."

"He does? That fast? How?" Niya stared at Kendall in the large bathroom mirror.

"This looks perfect. Take it off so you can come and see for yourself," Kendall told her and smiled. "Meet you in the study."

A few minutes later, Kendall and Reese were in the middle of practicing when Niya walked in the room. Kendall stopped, then motioned for Niya to take her place.

Niya shook her head. “This isn’t the song we are dancing to.”

“Don’t worry about that,” Reese said. “Worry about the steps, not the music. We got this. Come on.”

Kendall stood back and watched Reese lead Niya in the dance. Much like her uncle, Niya stumbled at first, but she quickly recovered, and before long, they were in sync and enjoying themselves.

Kendall clapped when they finished. “That was awesome.”

“I can’t believe this. We’ve been practicing over and over for hours and couldn’t get it,” Niya told her.

“We got it now, though.” Reese hugged Niya.

“Yes, you do!” Kendall said. Suddenly, there was movement right outside the doorway. She glanced over and could’ve sworn she saw a shadow passing by.

“Thank you, Kendall. You always come in and save the day. You’re like our personal superhero,” Niya said.

“Nah, I’m just a part of Team Niya, that’s all. I’m just doing my part, like Uncle Reese is doing his,” Kendall said. “You guys keep practicing. Use whatever song you want. Just do the same steps.”

“We will,” Reese and Niya chorused, both of them nodding.

They were escorting Kendall to the front door when Niya stopped in her tracks at the entrance to the foyer.

"Wait, my gown top!" She snapped her fingers. "I forgot it in the bathroom."

"Go get it. That was my purpose for coming here." Kendall laughed.

Niya scurried back down the hallway. While she waited, Kendall looked around her. From her vantage point, her eyes took in the living room, the spiral staircase, the foyer.

"What's wrong?" Reese asked.

"Huh?" Kendall realized she was frowning. "Oh, nothing."

"Something's wrong. What is it?"

Kendall paused for a moment. "Can I ask you a question?"

"Sure."

"I'm just curious. The outside of your house is decorated to perfection for the holidays, but there's nothing in here. I guess I expected the interior to be a little more festive. But it's not," she told him. "You guys don't even have a tree up."

"We haven't had a Christmas tree in years, not since my father died. He would pick the tree every year. That was his thing. Mom handled the outside, and he handled the inside. When he passed, the inside was no longer important, I guess. My mother cares only about how the house looks on the outside," Reese explained.

Niya's voice came from behind them. "Mommy and I would put up the tree together every year. And we would sing old-school Christmas songs, like ones by Luther Vandross."

Kendall laughed. "I love Luther Vandross Christmas songs, but I don't think he's considered old school."

"Me either," Reese agreed. "But Luther was Dad's favorite, too, while he put up the tree and hung our Christmas stockings."

"Well, maybe this year, you two can keep the tradition and put up a tree together," Kendall suggested.

Reese was quiet and seemed to be lost in thought for a minute. Kendall thought she had said something wrong, until he said, "That's not a bad idea. Not a bad idea at all. We should put up a tree."

"I don't know." Niya paused for a moment. "You think that's okay?"

"I don't see why not," Reese answered.

"I guess," Niya murmured. Kendall could sense her uncertainty.

Reese turned to Kendall. "Wanna come and help us pick one out?"

"Yes, Kendall, come with us," Niya pleaded.

Kendall hesitated.

Before she could answer, Reese spoke. "She's coming. Go grab your jacket. I'll pull my car around and meet you both out front."

Niya and Reese rushed off, leaving Kendall in the foyer, alone. She sensed that she was being watched. She looked up at the top of the staircase and directly into the eyes of Claudia Fine, who was standing on the upstairs landing. They stared at each other for a second.

"Good afternoon, Mrs. Fine," Kendall offered.

"Indeed it is," the woman answered before walking away.

Moments later, Niya returned, wearing the jacket Kendall had given her, and they walked out the front door. As soon as they stepped out onto the wraparound porch, a sleek black Acura pulled up, driven by Reese.

It's him. The jerk from the mall parking lot, the one with the psycho woman who screamed at us. The memories of the funny moment came flooding back, and Kendall realized why Reese had seemed so familiar. The woman he was with had tried to fight Amber over a parking space. *Amber*. She checked her watch. *I need to call Amber and tell her I'm running late*, Kendall told herself.

Reese hopped out of the car and walked around to open the door for Kendall and Niya. "Ready?"

"Definitely," Kendall said, then got in the back passenger seat. As she pulled the seat belt across her body, she glanced at Reese in amusement as he got in the car. "I hope we find a good parking space."

He nodded. "Me too."

Chapter 11

Niya

Niya was full of mixed emotions as they arrived at Carmichael's Nursery. She loved Christmas, and so had her mother. It seemed unreal that the holiday season was happening and her mother wasn't here to celebrate. As odd as the absence of indoor decorations at her grandmother's house seemed, she had been relieved by this in a way. The gaudy Christmas lights on the outside were enough of a reminder that the holiday was happening without her mother; having to look at a tree constantly might be too much. But her uncle Reese was excited, and she didn't want to be a killjoy, so she went along with it.

"Are you okay, Niya?" Kendall asked as they walked toward the festive tree lot, which was buzzing with customers. Everyone seemed so happy as they meandered around the large space. Christmas carols played through speakers hanging above on light poles that were wrapped in tinsel and lights. Niya tried not to stare jealously at the various mothers holding hands with their children.

"Yeah, I'm cool." Niya nodded, holding back tears. *This is a bad idea*, she thought. *Maybe I can fake feeling sick and go wait in the car*. Just as she was about to announce that she had a sudden headache, she felt the warmth of someone's hand clasping hers. She looked over at Kendall.

"I'm here." Kendall smiled. "I got you."

Niya's fingers tightened, and she nodded. The sting of sadness was still there, but the loneliness faded, along with the heaviness, she had felt just moments before. Kendall's hand was exactly what she needed, and having this woman beside her helped Niya relax.

"Well, there are plenty to choose from." Reese, who was steps ahead of them, turned around. "What kind of tree should we get, Ni-Ni?"

It had been a long time since she'd heard the nickname that he'd given her. He hadn't called her that even once after she'd moved in. For the most part, he'd been so concerned about how she felt and how she was doing that they really hadn't had any fun. There had been so much somberness. She missed the fun uncle Reese, and so it was good to see him enjoying himself.

"You pick," Niya told him.

"If I pick, I'm gonna pick the biggest one we can find, and I don't think your grandmother would want that." Reese shook his head.

Niya shrugged casually. "I say go for it. She's not gonna want any kind of tree we pick, anyway. She barely wants us at the house, and now we got the nerve to be bringing a tree. She's gonna be frowning at us harder, if that's even possible."

The shocked look on her uncle's face let her know that her statement had caught him off guard, and she wondered if she'd been too honest. After all, it was his mother that she was referring to.

"Niya," he said as a grin spread across his face, "you're right."

Kendall, who was now chuckling, grabbed Niya's arm. "Niya, you're so funny."

Seeing them so tickled by her statement made Niya smile, and seconds later, she joined in the snickering. It felt good to laugh. But a minute later, she caught a glimpse of a familiar boy standing a few feet away, and she quickly tried to regain her composure. It was Gavin, one of her classmates. For a second, they looked at one another. Then he smiled and waved at her. Niya nervously waved back.

"Who's that?" Kendall's whispering in her ear startled her and caused her to jump.

"Jeez, why are you sneaking up on me like that?" Niya realized she'd been holding her breath, and exhaled.

"How can I sneak up on you when I've been standing beside you this entire time?" Kendall laughed. "Who's the cutie?"

"That's Gavin. We're in AP Lit together. I mean, not together, but we're in the same class."

"That does mean together. But I get what you mean," Kendall told her.

"Oh, crap. He's walking over here. Why is he walking over here?" Niya whispered as she watched Gavin head in their direction. "Wait. Is he walking over here?"

Kendall nodded. "Yeah, he's walking over here. Relax, and be yourself. Own it."

Niya shifted her weight from one leg to the other. Suddenly, the warm jacket she had on didn't seem to be enough, and she was freezing. She considered escaping and running after Reese, who had set off to look at the trees, but it was too late.

Gavin smiled as he walked up to her. "Hey, Niya."

"Hey, Ga—" Niya's voice cracked, and she cleared her throat. "Hey, Gavin."

"I knew that was you. I recognized your jacket." Gavin pointed to the jacket Niya wore.

Niya looked down. "Yeah, it's kind of noticeable, huh?"

"It is. Jira and I were talking about you the other day," he said.

"Really?" Niya resisted the urge to ask what had been said. She could only imagine why she would be the topic of a conversation between him and the most popular girl in school, a girl with whom she'd had only one conversation, the one in the bathroom.

"Yeah, she told me you were selected to be a First Noel deb. That's dope." Gavin nodded. "Congratulations. It sounds like a lot of fun. A lot of work, but still fun."

"Thanks," Niya told him. How she'd forgotten that Jira was a fellow debutante was beyond her. At the first meeting, which was held immediately after the luncheon, Jira had been selected group president. She hadn't wasted any time stepping into her position: right away she had explained what a privilege it was and had assigned the other debs certain duties, which they would have to fulfill over the course of the next month. While Niya had been slightly overwhelmed, Jira had been fired up and ready to conquer every line item on the detailed agenda. "Jira is our fearless leader."

"I can imagine. Taking charge is something she's always been good at. She's a leader, so I'm sure you're in good hands." Gavin paused, then added, "Jira is good people and enjoys helping everyone."

Gavin looked Niya up and down, and she became self-conscious about her outfit choice. The last thing she looked like was a debutante. In fact, she looked more like someone who worked at the tree lot. Instead of changing out of her oversized sweats and her favorite, well-worn sneakers and into something nicer, Niya had followed Reese's instructions and had merely grabbed her jacket, then headed out the door. She glanced over at Kendall, who was pretending not to watch them. She was looking as amazing as always in her jeans, long-sleeved T-shirt, and black riding boots, her outfit casual yet chic. There was no reason for Niya not to look equally as nice, especially since Kendall had not only helped her go through the clothes she'd brought to her grandmother's home but had also pretty much given her a new wardrobe to choose from.

Just then, Reese walked over and announced, "I think I found the perfect one. Don't worry. It's not too big, but we're definitely gonna need to get it delivered."

"I can help you take care of that," Gavin told him.

"You work here, Gavin?" Niya asked.

"Wait, I know you, don't I?" Reese said. "You helped decorate our house."

Gavin proudly pointed to the Carmichael's logo on his shirt, which Niya hadn't noticed. "Yes, I do, and I did. My grandfather has owned this nursery for three decades. That's also how long he's been decorating the Fine mansion. It's one of his bragging rights. We have to hear about it every year, as if I don't go out and help him."

Niya gasped, as if she'd just discovered a formula to cure the common cold. "Gavin Carmichael."

Gavin nodded. "That's me."

"Well, Gavin Carmichael, can you hook a brotha up with a deal on this tree since you and Niya are such good friends?"

Niya cringed as she watched her uncle put his arm around Gavin's neck as they walked off into the rows of trees. She turned and saw that Kendall was still standing nearby, watching.

"He seems nice, Niya. And he's cute."

Niya acted nonchalant. "I guess."

"I like him. You should ask him to be your escort to the ball," Kendall said, as if she was suggesting a menu item at Chick-fil-A instead of something so important.

"What? Are you crazy? I can't do that." Niya shook her head so hard that she almost became dizzy.

"Why not? He knows about the ball, and he seemed kind of interested. Wait, he isn't escorting anyone else, is he? He mentioned your other friend. What's her name? Gina?"

"Jira, and she's not my friend. I don't really know her like that, either."

"Seems like she knows you if she mentioned you to him." Kendall shrugged. "I mean, you're gonna have to ask *somebody*. Why not him? Do you have someone else you're considering?"

Niya didn't. She'd mentioned that she didn't have an escort yet to Mrs. Knight, the First Noel Society's director, and she'd said she would help Niya find a suitable one, so Niya had decided to let her handle it. Allowing Mrs. Knight to do it seemed so much easier, and it would save her the pressure of doing what Kendall was suggesting at that moment.

"Nope. Mrs. Knight is taking care of it," Niya said.

"You'd rather have her pair you with a stranger instead of you choosing someone you know? You do realize your escort is the person you'll be spending a lot of time with, right? Practicing, social gatherings, community service. But if you're that confident about her choice, instead of that handsome, friendly, smart young man that you see every day in class, then that's fine too." Kendall sighed and turned to walk away.

Niya thought for a second, then said, "I mean, I get what you're saying, but how? I can't just ask him."

Kendall turned back around. "Why not? You're making this way harder than it is."

"Have you ever asked a guy out before?"

"Yeah. Guys aren't some scary monsters that you have to be afraid of, Niya. Wait, I got you. Come on." Kendall pulled Niya down a row of trees and over to where Reese and Gavin were finalizing the tree purchase.

"I'll make sure it's delivered within the hour, Mr. Fine," Gavin said. "I'll be right back with your receipt."

"Cool." Reese greeted Niya and Kendall, then pointed to the large spruce beside him. "This is a nice one, huh? My dad loved a spruce. You like it?"

Niya nodded. "It's nice."

"It is," Kendall agreed. "Reese, I've been meaning to ask you something. If you're not busy the Saturday after next, my job is having a holiday gathering, and I need a plus one. It's gonna be fun. You down?"

Reese stopped admiring the tree long enough to look at Kendall. He hesitated for a second. Niya, shocked that Kendall had been bold enough to ask him out, held her breath and waited for the excuse she expected from her uncle about why he couldn't attend. She prayed that whatever he said wouldn't be too embarrassing. She'd seen the women Reese dated, and although she was a beautiful woman, she knew that Kendall wasn't his type. He always went for the slim model chicks who, oddly enough, resembled his mother: fair skin, long hair, perfect smile.

"Next Saturday?" Reese asked.

"Saturday after next," Kendall replied, clarifying the matter.

"Sure. I don't have anything planned." Uncle Reese shrugged, then said, "I forgot we need a tree stand. I'll be right back."

When he had left, Kendall turned to Niya and said, “See? That wasn’t hard at all. All you have to do is ask. The worse he can say is no, but you’ll never know if you don’t ask.”

“But . . .” Niya shook her head. She was about to give Kendall another reason why she couldn’t when Kendall grabbed her shoulders and looked her in the eye.

“You can do this. You’re *fearless*, remember?” Kendall pointed to the word on the jacket, then spun Niya around and gave her a push that nearly sent her bump into Gavin, who’d just returned.

“Whoa. I’m sorry.” He reached out and steadied Niya.

“No, that was my fault.” Niya blushed. Her heart was racing so fast that she was certain that her blood pressure was sky high. “My uncle went to grab a tree stand.”

“Okay, cool.” Gavin nodded. “I meant to tell you that when you pointed out that Hester Prynne was involved in an entanglement long before Will, Jada, and August Alsina, I was cracking up. The fact that Mrs. Donahue agreed made it even funnier. It definitely made people want to read *The Scarlet Letter*.”

Niya smiled. She didn’t think anyone had paid attention to the comment she made while she was turning in her English paper. “Wow. Thanks. You should read it. It’s a guaranteed A.”

Gavin laughed. "I'd be ashamed if I couldn't tell anyone about it. You know the entire town would be dying to find out."

His ability to crack corny jokes about the classic novel the same way she did put Niya at ease. Kendall was right: he was handsome, funny, and nice. Before she lost her nerve, Niya blurted out, "Gavin, I still need an escort to the debutante ball. I think it would be cool for you to do it, if you don't mind."

Gavin's eyes widened. His only response was, "Me?"

Niya immediately felt embarrassed and uncomfortable. She tried to think of a way out of it. "I mean . . . You know what? I didn't mean . . . I'm sorry."

"You're sorry for asking me?" Gavin looked confused.

"Yeah, it was just a thought. You don't have to answer. I understand," Niya told him.

"Oh, okay." He seemed deflated. "It's cool."

"What's cool?" It was Niya's turn to be confused.

"Why you would change your mind about asking. I know we just met and everything, but the First Noel Ball is a huge deal, and I'm sure you'd rather have someone you know escort you. So, I get it," Gavin told her.

"Wait, so you *want* to be my escort? You don't mind?"

"No, I wouldn't mind at all. I'd have to clear it with my grandfather, because, you know, I work the lot most evenings and weekends, but I'm sure he'll be cool with it."

"Wow. Thanks, Gavin." Niya was shocked that he wanted to do it.

"Wanna hear something crazy?"

"Sure." Niya wanted to point out that whatever he was about to say couldn't be any crazier than her asking him to be her escort, but she didn't.

"Our company sponsors the ball every year, but my grandfather never attends. Now this will give him a real reason to go. I'm sure he'll be excited," Gavin told her.

"I'm excited too." Niya smiled.

"I guess I should give you my number, huh? And I should get yours." Gavin took out his cell phone.

"Oh, we probably need to do that," Niya said, reaching into her jacket pocket for her phone so they could exchange numbers.

"I'll call you later tonight so we can talk." Gavin grinned. "I mean, so I can tell you what my grandfather says."

"Sounds great," Niya told him.

"A'ight, I got the tree stand," Reese yelled. "Let's head home so we can be ready to decorate that bad boy when it arrives. Come on, Ni-Ni!"

"Oh my God, Reese. Stop yelling," Kendall chastised. "Niya, we'll wait for you in the car."

Niya turned and nodded at Kendall, who was pulling Reese toward the parking lot by the sleeve of his coat. The two of them were a hilarious sight, and although Niya was slightly embarrassed, this was the happiest she'd been in months.

"Last one," Niya said hours later, as she hung the ornament on the tree, which they'd spent all evening decorating. Reese had gone into the attic and located the boxes containing the family ornaments, and they'd taken turns hanging them, along with the strings of lights they'd picked up on the way home from Carmichael's. They'd even turned on the surround sound and listened to Luther Vandross's album *This Is Christmas*.

When the last ornament had been hung, Reese hugged her. "Dad would definitely be proud."

"Mommy would be too," Niya told him. When they started decorating the tree, she'd felt somewhat guilty for having fun and enjoying the moment without her mother being there, but as she listened to her uncle Reese share stories of their Christmases while growing up, Niya had relaxed. They'd laughed and sung, and it was as if she had felt her mother's presence there with them.

"There's one thing left." Kendall carefully held up the porcelain angel tree topper that Niya's mother had told Niya about but that she'd never seen until now. “My mother always says the angel is the most important part of the tree, because it reminds us of the true meaning of Christmas.”

“Is that Great-grandma’s angel?” Niya whispered.

“Yep, that’s it. Technically, it’s your Great-great-grandma’s angel. It was passed down from my mother’s grandmother, my great-grandmother,” Reese told them.

“Wow. It’s real old school,” Niya commented.

“I guess you could call it that,” Kendall said, passing the angel to Niya. “You want to put it on?”

Niya looked up at that moment and saw that her grandmother was watching from the upstairs landing. She quickly answered, “No, I couldn’t. It’s too precious. I’d probably drop it.”

Kendall looked up at the landing and, her voice raised, said, “Mrs. Fine, would you like to join us and do the honors?”

Niya’s grandmother seemed surprised by the invitation.

Reese beckoned his mother. “Mom, you want to?”

“No, thank you. It’s late and time for me to retire to bed,” Claudia told them before turning away.

Niya looked at her uncle. “It’s only, like, nine o’clock. Who goes to bed that early?”

Kendall’s head snapped. “Nine o’clock? Is it really that late?”

"Actually, it's nine thirty," Reese told her. "You got a hot date you forgot about?"

"Something like that," Kendall said. "I can't believe I've been here that long. I gotta get out of here."

"You can't leave before we finish." Niya pointed to the angel Kendall was still holding.

Kendall passed the angel to Reese, who stretched his arm and tried as best he could to pull the very top of the tree toward him. Unfortunately, it didn't work. The tree was too tall and he couldn't place the angel on top.

"I guess we'll have to get a ladder or something and finish another time," Reese said, placing the angel back in the box. He turned to Kendall. "Thanks again, for everything. Once again, you saved the day. The dance lessons, tree trimming . . . What can't you do?"

"What can I say? I'm a jill-of-all-trades. Today was definitely fun, though. Thanks for letting me hang out." Kendall smiled. "Don't forget to practice, both of you."

"We will," Niya and Reese said simultaneously.

While Reese cleaned up, Niya retrieved the bodice of her gown and then walked Kendall to the front door. "Thanks again, Kendall, for everything. Oh, and Gavin texted me."

"Really? Does that mean you have your escort?" Kendall asked with excitement.

Niya nodded. “I do. His grandfather says he can take all the time he needs to participate.”

Kendall hugged Niya. “See, I told you. And sounds like he’s just as excited about the ball as you are. I’m so proud of you facing your fears.”

“He is. I couldn’t have done it without you,” Niya said.

Kendall stepped out the door and waved. Niya watched her walk to her car and climb in, and after Kendall drove off, she walked back into the living room. She stared at the tree again. Reese turned the lights off and stood beside her.

“How you feeling?” he asked.

Niya looked at him and smiled. “I know this is gonna sound weird, but I’m starting to feel like this is home.”

Chapter 12

Reese

"You left for the day?"

Reese had just parked in front of the men's store when Rick's FaceTime call came through. "No, just a couple of hours. I'll be back. I got an appointment to get fitted for this tux. Lynnette is meeting me here."

"I hope she knows this tux is for the ball and nothing else. You did make that clear, right?" Rick raised an eyebrow at him.

"Of course she knows that, Rick. You're trying to be funny." Reese rolled his eyes.

"I'm being serious. From what I've been hearing, the two of you are about to be engaged and to buy a house."

Reese had no idea how Rick knew about his considering becoming a homeowner. He certainly hadn't mentioned it to anyone other than Lynnette, mainly because it was still a consideration, and he certainly hadn't said anything about getting engaged. Both of those were serious life events that he would definitely need to take time to think about, research, and plan. But it was the holiday season, and there was no time for him to do any of that. When he wasn't working, he was doing something in preparation for the ball he would be participating in.

"You heard wrong," Reese told him.

"That's good to know. I get the moving into your own crib, but as your best friend and future best man, I hope that you'd give me plenty of notice about a wedding, so I'll have time to plan the most epic bachelor party ever." Rick laughed.

"You'll definitely be the first to know when the time comes, but it won't be anytime soon. After dealing with all this stuff with Niya, I think a wedding is nowhere in my future." Reese sighed. "I told Kendall the other night that I don't see how she does it all."

"Ah, Kendall. I've been hearing that name more than Lynnette's these days. What's up with that?"

"Nothing's up with it. I told you, she's really stepped up and taken the reins with Niya, man. She's cool people, and she's helped out a lot. Heck, more than a lot," Reese explained.

"Is she cute?" Rick asked.

Reese remained silent. An image of Kendall popped into his head: her smile, her laugh, her quirky sense of style, which he'd come to expect, but most of all, her infectious spirit and the good vibes she brought. There was an aura about her that made him feel good.

"Well, is she?" Rick repeated.

"She's good people."

"That's cool, but is she cute?" Rick gave him a knowing look.

"Yeah, she's cute."

"A'ight, then hook a brother up. Make it happen."

Reese shook his head. "I don't know about all that."

"What? Why not? Come on, Reese. You got a girl, damn near a fiancée. You can't hold on to both of them. That's just selfish."

"I ain't trying to hold on to Kendall. Like I said, she's good people," Reese told him.

"Uh-oh. What's up with her? You said she's good people twice."

"There's nothing wrong with her, man. She's cool, and her personality is really dope."

Reese knew exactly what Rick was referring to, and for some reason, he wished to avoid the subject at hand. Any other time, he wouldn't hesitate to give a detailed description of a woman: height, skin tone, facial features, and, of course, the other female assets men were interested in knowing. But he held off sharing that information about Kendall. She was beautiful. Her skin was a darker shade of brown, smooth and flawless; she had deep-set eyes that were bright and full of happiness, even when she was serious. Her lips were full and pouty, and when she smiled, it was magical. Then there was her voice: low and husky, but powerful. That was one of the reasons Reese enjoyed listening to her speak. Kendall was stylish and fun, and her personality was magnetic.

He understood why Niya had been drawn to her. He also knew that as important as all those traits were, that wasn't what Rick was interested in hearing. And Reese just didn't feel comfortable telling him that Kendall was what they referred to as a "big girl." She was much more than that, but Rick wouldn't care, so he decided not to say anything. He opted to keep the facts about her to himself, including how he'd surprisingly found her full breasts, curvy hips, and voluptuous body quite appealing. Not only because he knew his friend would have plenty of jokes about it, but also because he already had a woman, Lynnette.

Rick peered at Reese for a second, then groaned. "Aw, man, you're either lying or holding out. It's cool, though. I'll find out for myself at the ball. I can't wait."

Reese's cell phone beeped. He put his FaceTime call on hold and saw Kendall's name on the screen. He returned to the FaceTime call, looked at Rick, and said, "I gotta take this."

"Which one is it calling? Lynnette or Kendall?" Rick teased just before Reese hung up to answer the other line.

"Hey there. Is this a bad time?" Kendall asked when he clicked over.

"Not at all. I'm sitting here in my car, about to go in for my fitting," Reese told her.

"Oh, wow. I forgot all about that. You remember exactly what you're required to wear, right?"

"Required?"

"Yes, required. Don't be funny," Kendall warned him playfully. "Remember, white dinner jacket, black tuxedo pants, black shoes, and white gloves."

"I know, I know. You and Niya have been telling me over and over again, and it's on the list they emailed me. I got it."

"Good. I'm just making sure. Well, I want to know if you could bring Niya by the boutique after you picked her up from her service project. I need to do a quick measurement."

"I would, but I'm not picking her up. She's riding with her *escort*." Reese purposely emphasized the word *escort*.

"Awww, that's cute. She's with Gavin," Kendall squealed. "Isn't he adorable?"

"That's not the word I'd use to describe him, so I'll take your word for it," Reese commented. "She's so busy practicing with him that she doesn't have time to practice with me."

Kendall laughed. "You really sound like a jealous fifth grader, you do realize that, right?"

"I'm just saying." Reese smiled. He was glad that Niya was coming out of her shell and meeting friends, but he did feel like he'd been pushed to the side recently. "I'm keeping my eye on him."

"As you should. Well, I guess I'll catch up with Niya another day this week. We're getting down to crunch time, and we want to make sure her gown is a perfect fit. No room for errors whatsoever."

"I'm sure it will fit like a glove. And speaking of gloves, what's the attire for Saturday night? You haven't given me any details," Reese said, remembering he had agreed to attend the party she'd invited him to.

"Oh, I'm glad you reminded me. It's festive casual," Kendall told him.

"What does that even mean?"

"Nothing fancy. Jeans, white button-down shirt, which I'm sure you already have. But, trust me, it'll be fun," Kendall said.

"What time should I plan to pick you up?"

"Actually, I'll already be at the venue, so you can meet me there. I'll make sure you have your party hat."

"Party hat? Why do I get the feeling you're not telling me something?" Reese asked.

"Do you trust me?"

"I do."

"Then you have nothing to worry about. Talk to you later," Kendall told him, then hung up.

Reese sat in his seat and smiled. There was definitely more to this party than she was telling him, but he had gotten to know her well enough to know that whatever it was, they were going to have fun. He was actually looking forward to it.

Tap. Tap. Tap.

The knocking on his driver's window caused him to jump.

"Reese, what the heck are you doing? I've been standing here waiting for five minutes," Lynnette demanded when he opened the door and stepped out of the car.

"My bad. I didn't even notice you were here, sweetie." He kissed her forehead.

"Because you were too busy grinning on the phone, that's why." Lynnette frowned. "Who was that, anyway?"

"It was Rick," Reese told her. Technically, it wasn't a lie, because he had been on the phone with Rick.

"Well, he must've been telling you something really funny, because you were smiling hard."

"Uh, you know how he is. Everything he says is funny," Reese said. "But now I'm smiling because I get to see your beautiful face."

"Mm-hmm, I bet," Lynnette smirked as he took her hand. They went inside the store.

A tall older guy dressed in a tailored suit greeted them. "Welcome to J. York's. Can I help you?"

"Yes, I have an appointment to get fitted for a tuxedo," Reese told him. "Last name . . ."

"Ah yes, Mr. Fine. We've been expecting you. I'm Franklin, and I'll be your tailor." He turned to Lynnette. "How do you do, madam?"

"Wonderful," Lynnette answered.

They followed Franklin toward the back of the store, where he ushered Lynnette to a seating area to wait, then led Reese to a long rack of formal suits.

"Now, what type of tuxedo will you be needing?" Franklin asked.

Just then, Reese's phone chimed, indicating he'd received a text. He looked at his phone and smiled at the photo that Kendall had sent of a cartoon character wearing the exact tuxedo he needed, along with the words "Just in case you need a visual reminder, LOL."

Smiling, he told Franklin, "White dinner jacket, black tuxedo pants, black patent shoes, and white gloves."

"Ah, classic. Let's start with your measurements." After taking the measurements, Franklin selected a jacket and pants and gave them to Reese. "I think these will be suitable to try on. The fitting room is through that curtain and leads to where your fiancée is waiting."

"She's not my fiancée," Reese remarked without hesitation. Upon noticing the look that Franklin gave him, he softened his tone. "I mean, that's my beautiful girlfriend."

"I see. Well, you can go through the other curtain, and I'll meet you in the area where your girlfriend is waiting," Franklin replied.

Reese entered one of the empty fitting rooms and slipped on the pants and jacket. *Not bad. Not bad at all. I'm looking quite debonair*. After briefly admiring his reflection in the mirror, he ventured out through the other curtain to meet Franklin and Lynnette.

"White dinner jacket? Baby, I think you should do all black. I'm not feeling that white at all. You don't want to look like a maître d'," Lynnette said. "And that won't go with my dress at all."

Reese frowned. "It's a requirement, Lynnette. I really don't have a choice. All the fathers are wearing the same attire."

"Oh, your daughter is a part of the cotillion this year?" Franklin asked. "First Noel?"

"His niece," Lynnette answered before Reese had a chance. "Which is why I don't understand why he can't be different." She shrugged. Her attitude was becoming increasingly aggravating, and Reese's already worn patience was quickly fading.

"Oh, that wouldn't be proper at all. If he's standing in as her father, he still must be in the proper attire," Franklin explained, as if he was an expert on debutante ball formalities. He walked over to Reese and checked the fit of the jacket and pants, taking more measurements and making notes on the tiny notepad he kept in the front pocket of his shirt. "How does it feel? Can you move freely?"

Reese moved his arms around. "Yeah, feels okay."

Franklin looked over at Lynnette. "Can we borrow you for a moment?"

Lynnette hesitated a moment, then walked over to where they stood. "Okay."

"I always want to make sure my cotillion customers have what I call a 'waltz fit,'" Franklin told them. "Try it and see."

Reese didn't know what he meant, until Franklin positioned Lynnette directly in front of him, then put Reese's arm on her shoulder. He finally understood and took Lynnette's other hand and lifted her arm, as he'd practiced with both Kendall and Niya.

Lynnette's brows furrowed. "What in the world?"

"Relax. Just follow my lead." Reese smiled, then guided her through a simple box step.

"How does it feel?" Franklin asked again.

Reese and Lynnette stared at each other for a moment. She touched the side of his face. The irritated look that she had had earlier was gone, replaced with a dimpled smile and a hint of desire.

This was the woman he wanted to take to Aruba, not the one who constantly whined and complained or snapped when she didn't get her way.

"It feels perfect," Lynnette answered. Reese knew it wasn't the suit that she was referring to.

"Good. Good to hear," Franklin said. "But the question was more for Mr. Fine, considering he's the one who has to wear the suit."

Lynnette nodded. "I'm sure he feels the same, right?"

He took a moment and thought about Lynnette's answer. Being with Lynnette did feel good, and sometimes great. But it wasn't anywhere near perfect. Over the past few weeks, there had been times when things didn't even feel right between them. Still, he did love her, and now that things were improving for Niya, he hoped his life could get back to normal and he and Lynnette could return to a good place.

Reese stepped back and shook his arms. "Uh, yeah, it feels fine."

"Good. We'll go with this one. I'll place the order and have it shipped ASAP, so we'll get it in time for a final fitting and alterations for the big event," Franklin told him.

"I wouldn't call this the big event," Lynnette sighed. "The big event would be our wedding. But, hopefully, we'll be back soon for that, right, baby?"

Franklin saved him from having to answer her by saying, "I'll meet you out front at the register, Mr. Fine."

"Thanks." Reese gave him a nod. "I'll go and change and be right there."

He was changing when his phone rang again; this time it was his mother. The only time she called was when there was an emergency. He anxiously answered the phone, thinking something must've happened to Niya.

"Hello."

"Reese, what time will you be home this evening?" his mother asked.

"Huh? Uh, later. Why?" he answered. She'd never asked him about his schedule before, so he was caught off guard.

"Well, I have a meeting, then plans afterward, so I probably won't be home until late," she told him.

"Okay," Reese responded. He wasn't much interested in her schedule, so her telling him this made him even more confused.

"Are you still at work?"

"No, I'm at J. York's right now, ordering my tux. Mom, what's going on? You do know you don't have to tell me that you won't be home. We're both adults." His concern turned into irritation as he prepared himself for whatever negativity she was about to spout.

"I'm aware of that. But you do know that a minor resides here. She's not home, and I'm about to leave."

Reese exhaled. "Niya is at a community service project, Mom. She's not out roaming the streets or drinking or doing drugs. And she isn't a child. She's a good teenager, and she can stay by herself for a few hours, until one of us gets home. I wish you would just stop trying to make things difficult. We get it. Your house is your castle, and you expect everything to remain in its rightful place, including Niya and me. You don't want her to be a deb, but it's too late. Get over it. It's happening, and in case you haven't noticed, Niya is doing a great job, and I'm proud of how far she's come in a short time.

"With that being said, we have made every effort to stay out of your way, not bother you, or ask you for anything. As a matter of fact, the only thing you have to complain about is the beautiful Christmas tree in the living room. Other than that, I'd appreciate it if you would go your way and let us go ours. You can continue to be bitter by yourself, because we don't want any parts of it."

After he spoke, the phone line was silent. Reese looked down at his cell phone's screen to make sure that his mother hadn't hung up. She hadn't.

"My only concern and reason for calling is that if neither one of us will be home, the door will be locked. I was going to suggest that maybe it's time that we get Niya a key."

Reese realized that his assumption had been incorrect and that the purpose of his mother's call was to offer assistance, not express her usual displeasure. He had misspoken. It was his turn to be silent as he tried to think of how to apologize.

"Mom, I . . ."

"It's fine."

The call ended. Reese tried calling her back, but she didn't answer. His words had cut deep, and she was hurt. He quickly got dressed and bade farewell to Franklin, hoping to get home before his mother left, so that he could apologize in person. As he and Lynnette left the store, he told her he needed to get home.

"Wait, I thought we were going to have dinner, then go to my place for a little while tonight," Lynnette told him.

"I know, and we can. I just need to get home and take care of something first," Reese replied. "It shouldn't take that long."

Lynnette shook her head. "You know what? Take as much time as you need, Reese. I'm done. You can have all the time in the world, as a matter of fact. I've been patient enough and willing to compromise, but not anymore."

"What are you saying?" Reese frowned.

"I'm saying it's over. I'm sick of being pushed to the side and placed on the back burner. I took time out of my busy schedule this afternoon to come with you because you asked me. Now, once again, I'm being told that you don't have time for me," she snapped. "Plans canceled, as usual."

"That's not true. I didn't cancel them. I said I had to go home first."

"Well, let me help you out. I'm canceling them." Lynnette stormed off toward her car.

Reese decided the best thing to do was let her go and give her time to cool off. Instead of chasing after her, he got in his car and headed home.

Chapter 13

Kendall

"The hardest-working woman at Diablo's, and the prettiest."

Kendall hadn't even realized she'd fallen asleep until she heard Simon's voice as he entered the room. It took a few seconds for her to gather herself and turn around. She smiled and pointed. "Is that a part of your company-issued uniform?"

Simon touched the flashing Santa hat he wore in place of his usual baseball cap. "This is the holiday flair I opted to wear. You like it?"

Kendall nodded. "I do."

"I mean, it's not as fly as yours, but it's still festive," he said, referring to the red-sequined beret on her head. "I see yours has a little more international appeal, mademoiselle."

"Oui," Kendall said with a French accent as she posed in her chair.

"A little birdie told me you and Amber are in charge of the Diablo Christmas Soiree this year. I can only imagine what the two of you have planned," he said as he unloaded the cart.

"We are," was the best response Kendall could give because Amber had been pretty much giving her the cold shoulder for the past week. She had tried explaining and apologizing for not being available on the day they had designated to finalize the party plans, but Amber hadn't been receptive. The party was just days away, and her friend had barely spoken to her in days.

As if she could sense that they were talking about her, Amber appeared in the doorway. "Kendall, Mrs. Brooks is here for her dress. It's not on the rack. Do you have it?"

"It's right here." Kendall reached for the gown she'd finished hours earlier.

"Is it ready?" Amber asked.

"It is. I just haven't had a chance to bring it out," Kendall replied.

"I'm sure." Amber took the gown and exited just as quickly as she'd entered.

Simon gave Kendall a concerned look. "She okay? Normally, she got jokes for days."

"She's fine. Everyone is kinda on edge around here. You know how stressful the holidays can be," Kendall told him.

"I work for FedEx. You ain't gotta tell me. I get cussed out daily for stuff that ain't even my fault. But I just wear my hat and continue making spirits bright."

Kendall laughed. "You definitely do that."

"Glad I can put a smile on your pretty face." Simon winked. "Maybe one day you'll give me a chance to do it outside of this place."

Kendall's eyes widened. She couldn't tell if he was joking or not. "Are you asking me out on a date?"

"Are you saying you'd go out on a date with me if I asked you?" Simon countered.

"I guess you're gonna have to ask and find out," Kendall told him.

"Okay." He grinned.

Kendall waited for what she thought was going to be some sort of invitation, but instead, before leaving the room, Simon said, "Au revoir, Mademoiselle Kendall."

Confused, Kendall went back to working. It didn't matter how fine he was; she didn't have time to play whatever kind of game Simon was playing. Her plate wasn't just full it was overflowing. She had a debutante gown to finish, a rack of alterations to complete for customers, Christmas shopping to do, and a party to plan with a best friend who wasn't speaking to her.

Amber returned a few minutes later and asked, "Are all of these finished?"

Kendall looked at the rack of gowns and nodded. "Yeah, they are."

"I can bag them and take them out for you," she offered. "Things are kind of slow on the floor right now."

Kendall accepted the olive branch being offered. "Thanks. I appreciate it."

"No problem." Amber picked up a stack of Diablo garment bags and began placing the gowns inside them. "You got a lot done."

"Yeah, I've been grinding all week." Kendall decided to extend a peace offering of her own. "If you want, we can go and take care of the party stuff after work."

Amber hesitated before responding. "I mean, that's cool. If you have time."

"I have time, Amber," Kendall sighed, then snapped her fingers. "As a matter of fact, we are both about to have even more time. I got an idea."

"What?"

"I'll be right back," Kendall said as she marched past her friend. She returned a few minutes later, just as Amber was placing the last gown in a bag. "As soon as we get these out, we can leave for the day."

"Stop playing. How?" Amber shrieked.

"Deena's orders. I told her we needed to meet with the owner of the party venue to take care of some last-minute details, or she would have to host the party at her house. She had no problem telling us to take the rest of the day off." Kendall laughed.

They gathered the gowns and took them to the designated rack near the fitting rooms, then wasted no time leaving the boutique. Kendall didn't even bother cleaning up her work space or turning off her machine.

For the next three hours, she and Amber worked their magic, and before she knew it, they had everything taken care of for the event they were hosting in a few days. Luckily, despite not having talked to her, Amber had secured the deejay and had paid the deposit for the venue and the caterer. After a quick lunch, they finalized the food menu, ordered a cake, and headed to the arts and crafts supply store to grab the last-minute items they'd need.

"Well, I must say, we accomplished a lot today," Amber told her as they walked down the fabric aisle of the store.

"Because we work well together. We always have." Kendall paused. "But thank you, because you did most of the footwork. I dropped the ball, and I'm sorry," she admitted.

"You didn't drop the ball, Kendall. You just fumbled it a little."

Kendall frowned. "Isn't that the same as dropping the ball?"

"Is it? Girl, I don't know. I don't watch sports. I just date ballers." Amber laughed. "Speaking of ballers—"

Amber was interrupted by the ringing of Kendall's phone. "One sec. Lemme get this. Hey, you."

"Hey, yourself," Reese said. "How's your day going?"

"Going good. I'm out with Amber, getting some last-minute goodies for this weekend. How's your day?"

"It's cool. Last-minute goodies, huh? What kind of goodies?" he said.

"A little bit of this and a little of that." Kendall took out her AirPods and put them in her ears so she could multitask while on the phone. Once they were secure, she began combing through the bolts of fabric, searching for what she needed.

"You know, you've been really vague about this little shindig you invited me to. I'm starting to get nervous."

"Nervous? You? I doubt that." Kendall laughed. "There's no need to be nervous. The party starts at eight. I'll text you the address and make sure you have everything you need before then."

"That's why I'm nervous. What could I possibly need?" Reese asked.

"You'll see when you get it. You said you trust me, so you'll be fine." She glanced over at Amber, who was holding up a bolt of holly-patterned cotton. "Now I have to go and finish prepping. Tell Niya I'll call her later."

"Why are you calling her? Does she know any information about this party?"

"Bye, Reese." Kendall ended the call.

Amber held up another bolt for her to look at. It was a bright shade of green, one that was almost shocking.

"That's horrible. I'll take it," Kendall said.

"So, wait, you invited Reese to the party? Why didn't you say something?" Amber put the fabric into the cart Kendall was pushing.

"About what?" Kendall shrugged.

"About his being your date, that's what."

"First of all, he's not my date. He's just my friend. I kinda invited him to prove a point to Niya," Kendall informed her. "And when was I supposed to tell you? You weren't talking to me, remember?"

"Still, don't you think you should've said something? At least mentioned it?"

"Not really, because I didn't think it was a big deal. And I'm mentioning it now." Kendall shrugged. "Is something wrong?"

"No. I guess I'm just surprised because I didn't know y'all were that cool. I mean, I know y'all were helping Niya, but . . ."

"Amber, we're just friends, that's all. Now, I can't front. He's funny and smart and easy to talk to. And he loves Niya. The brother is fine too. But I don't like him like that. Besides, Reese has a girlfriend." Kendall stopped the cart and turned around. "She's a mess. And you know her."

"I know her? Who is she? Is she a customer?" Amber gasped.

"Well, maybe *know* isn't the right word, but you've interacted with her." Kendall giggled and explained what she was referring to.

"Stop lying! Oh, hell no! Not the mighty, mad midget." Amber cackled. "That is hilarious."

"It is." Kendall nodded.

Amber gave her a strange look. "Just cool, huh? Are you sure?"

"Yeah, just cool, and yes, I'm sure. Why are you looking at me like that?"

"Because I know you, that's why. I didn't ask you if you liked him. You volunteered that information and gave a list of reasons why you should. And if you ain't feeling him, then it wouldn't matter if he had a girlfriend or not. You may be fooling yourself, but you ain't fooling me." Amber nudged Kendall to the side and took over pushing the cart.

Kendall stood in the aisle, thinking about what Amber had said. Was she fooling herself? *No, that's just Amber talking. Reese and I are just cool. Aren't we?* Granted, their phone and text conversations had become more and more frequent. But that was only because they were getting closer to the ball and needed to make sure things were in place.

Not all the conversations had been about Niya, though. Some of them had been late-night chats about favorite movies, music, and childhood memories. He had told her about finishing at the top of his class in both high school and college, then getting accepted into his father's alma mater, Meharry Medical College. He'd planned to become the second surgeon in the family, until one day he was at a park when a woman began screaming because her baby had stopped breathing. Reese had gone into action and performed CPR and had revived the child before the paramedics arrived. Saving a life had done something to him, and he'd changed directions, deciding to pursue a career as an EMT instead. His father and sister had supported his decision. But his mother had called him an adrenaline junkie and a disappointment. She'd had high hopes for him, and he'd let her down, the same way his sister had years earlier, after sneaking off to get married to a man their family never met, then getting pregnant.

"I get it in a way, though. My mom raised us in a way that we had no choice but to be great. She poured her energy into us consistently, and we kind of let her down. She and my father had two children, and instead of continuing the family tradition of affluence and plenitude, we chose the path of least resistance," Reese had told her during one of their late-night conversations. He'd been home in bed, and she had still been working on Niya's gown.

"Plenitude? Really? And from what I know, you and your sister still became great," Kendall said. "Your lives could have turned out way worse."

"Maybe *great* is a somewhat subjective word. Let's just say we failed to live up to her expectations. My mom lived her own difficult life and wanted better for her children and gave us better. I just wish she didn't look at our decisions to do things differently as a slap in the face sometimes." He sighed. "Example, the First Noel Ball and Niya's decision to participate. She doesn't agree with it, and because I do, she acts as if I'm public enemy number one in the house."

"Have you tried talking to her and maybe expressing how you feel?" Kendall suggested. "Sometimes having honest conversation helps, especially an adult one. Parents have a tendency to always look at us as children, and we have to help them see that we are grown-ups. It took a while for my mother to accept what I wanted to do in life. She thought I wanted to play dress-up for a living, until I had a real conversation. After that, she began to see me and respect me as an adult. I was still her child, but there was a shift in our relationship, like an added layer."

"We definitely don't talk. She criticizes or commands, and I listen, then do my best to avoid her. Makes things easier on everyone. Even Niya's learning this strategy." Reese laughed. "When we see her, we stop, listen, leave."

"Sir, that is not a healthy way of communicating. I'm going to need you to do better, ASAP," Kendall scolded. "Listen, just try while you have time. You understand loss the same way I do. My mother, your father and sister aren't with us anymore, but your mother still is."

"You're right, and maybe that's what I need to do. I'm going to have an honest conversation. I appreciate the advice, Kendall. Thanks." He paused for a moment. "And I appreciate everything you've done for Niya. I love her more than life itself, and I gotta admit, I couldn't ask for a better teammate than you to make this happen for her."

His words made her heart full, and she almost cried. In the short amount of time that they'd known one another, she'd come to care for him and Niya too.

That doesn't mean I like him, she thought now. *At least not in the way Amber is talking about. And even if I did, it wouldn't mean that he likes me. More importantly, even though he really doesn't talk about her a lot, he has a girlfriend.*

Her phone chimed again. This time, there was a text from Reese. She opened it and smiled at the Christmas meme he had sent from an old episode of *Martin*, her favorite TV show. As she typed the response, which she knew would make him laugh, she reminded herself that they were just cool.

Chapter 14

Niya

"Niya, guess what?" Jada squealed.

"What? No, wait, don't tell me. Let me guess. Khalil asked you to the winter formal," Niya blurted out, hoping she was right.

Jada had been crushing on Khalil since eighth grade, and Niya had given her best friend the same advice that Kendall gave her, and had told her to just ask Khalil out. Jada didn't ask him out on a date, but she did ask him to be her partner for the science fair, since Niya had moved away, and he agreed. It was a baby step, but it was in the right direction.

"Uh, no, he hasn't," Jada replied, her voice deflating a bit. But then she added, "But he hasn't asked anyone else, either, so fingers crossed."

"Okay, good. There's still time, anyway. He'll ask you, and if he doesn't, you can ask him," Niya told her.

"I could never do that." Jada giggled. "I told you I would be too scared."

"And I told you there's no reason to be scared."

"Who are you, and what have you done with my best friend? You know, the quiet, funny one who loves to stay home and binge watch reality TV while eating frozen cookie dough," Jada quipped.

"I'm still here, and as a matter of fact, I'm making treats to enjoy while I watch all the shows I've been missing."

"Missing them because you've been hanging out with your new friends and having fun. I'm getting a little jealous." Jada sighed. "You're living in your fancy new house with your cool uncle and being a debutante with the popular kids at your new school. Your life is totally different."

In a way, Jada was right. Her life was different, and she was enjoying doing all those things. Not only had she gotten to know Jira and all the other debs, but she and Gavin had become great friends too. The more time she spent with him, the more she liked him. Between school and the cotillion schedule, they spent plenty of time together. Not to mention the time they spent on the phone. However, there was one major catalyst that had caused this major life change that Jada seemed to have forgotten, so Niya reminded her. "Don't be jealous. None of this would be happening if my mother was still alive. And I would give it all back to be back there in our tiny house, just me and her."

Jada quickly apologized. "Niya, I'm sorry. That's not what I meant at all. I was just saying . . . I miss you, but I'm glad things are getting better for you."

"I know you didn't mean anything by it. I just don't want you to think my life is all happy and perfect, because it's not," Niya told her. Hoping to change the heavy pall that had fallen over the conversation, she perked up and said, "Now, since I guessed wrong, what did you have to tell me?"

"Huh? Oh, Mommy and I got tickets to the ball. We are coming!" Jada squealed.

Niya became so excited that she nearly dropped the large bowl of batter she was preparing. "Oh my God, Jada!"

That her best friend would be at the cotillion was the absolute best news she could have ever gotten. Niya truly missed Jada, and despite their constant communication by phone, text, and FaceTime, she needed to spend some quality time in person with her. Now she was even more elated about her huge upcoming night.

"I know, I know. I can't wait. Mommy and I are going dress shopping tomorrow. I wish you could come. But I'm gonna FaceTime you so you can help me pick one out," Jada told her.

"I'll try. I wish you guys could come and let Kendall help you pick one out at the boutique. She's amazing."

"A Diablo Designs dress is definitely not in the budget, girl. But I can't wait to meet her and Gavin when we come to the ball. It's going to be so much fun," Jada told her.

"Yesss. I have the final fitting for my gown next week, and it's gorgeous. I told—"

The sound of the side door opening caused Niya to stop in mid-sentence. Her uncle Reese was upstairs, getting ready to go to a Christmas party, which meant there was only one other person who could be entering the house. *Uncle Reese said she wouldn't be home until later. This is* not *later.* She ended the call without saying goodbye and looked at the cluttered counter in front of her. There was no way she was going to be able to clean it up in the fifteen seconds she knew it would take for her grandmother to walk from the mudroom into the kitchen. The only thing she could do was wait and pray.

Dear God, please don't let her be too mad. There's already enough tension around here between her and Uncle Reese. I don't want to make it worse.

Her grandmother walked in. "What's going on in here?" she asked as she looked around. She was dressed in a simple black pantsuit and heels, and she carried a small clutch. A beautiful broach in the shape of a Christmas wreath was on her lapel. If anyone else had been wearing it, Niya would've wondered if it was real or not. But she knew better: the jewels in the broach were as authentic as the diamonds her grandmother had in her ears.

Niya blinked, tearing her eyes from the sparkling stones. "I . . . uh . . . I was just making something. Uncle Reese gave me permission. He said it was okay."

"And what exactly are you making?"

Niya moved swiftly to the sizzling pot on the stove and looked inside. Using the slotted spoon that was laid out, she set about removing the perfectly golden deep-fried pastries from the hot oil and placing them on a baking pan that she'd already lined with paper towels. A sweet aroma filled the air, and for a second, she imagined being in the kitchen with her mother. Once all the pastries were out of the pot, and the stove was off, Niya picked up the baking pan and turned to her grandmother. "Beignets."

"What?" Claudia seemed surprised by Niya's answer, even though she was holding a pan of beignets as proof.

Reese walked into the kitchen and saw the beignets. "Good They're ready." Before Niya could stop him, he grabbed one off the baking pan and bit into it. "H-ho—"

"Yeah, they're hot, and I haven't put the powdered sugar on top yet, either." Niya laughed at her uncle fanning his mouth. She looked over and noticed that the corner of her grandmother's mouth was slightly turned up. It wasn't a smile—it was more like a sneer—but Niya could tell she was amused by Reese's reaction.

"You could've warned me," Reese mumbled.

"You could've waited." Niya snickered as she placed the pan on the island, then proceeded to dust the beignets with powdered sugar. "That's what you get for being greedy."

"A brother is starving, and you got the house smelling like Cafe Du Mont in New Orleans."

"Cafe Du Monde," Claudia and Niya chorused, correcting him.

"Sorry. Café Du Monde," Reese told them. "Excuse me."

"Uncle Reese—" Niya began, then stopped speaking and stared at him, taking notice of what he was wearing. "What in the world?"

Reese shook his head and smoothed the front of what had to be the craziest Christmas vest Niya had ever seen. "I know. Don't ask, okay? This is what I was given to wear for the evening."

Niya tried not to laugh. "Did she make that for you?"

Reese nodded. "Of course she did. And there's a hat, too, that lights up."

A strange sound caused both Niya and her uncle to turn and look. This time there was no doubt about it. Not only was her grandmother smiling, but she was also laughing uncontrollably as she stared at Reese. Niya gave in and released the giggles she'd been trying to hold in.

Reese looked at them like they were crazy. "Oh, so y'all both got jokes, huh?"

"No, but whoever has you wearing that certainly does." Claudia smiled. "You're wearing it, so obviously, you must like her."

Reese grabbed another beignet and bit into it; this one was cooler, and he didn't waste any time finishing it. "I swear, Niya, these taste just like Grandma Noonie's. The exact same."

"It's Grandma Noonie's recipe." Niya beamed with pride.

"Try one, Mother," Reese said.

Niya looked at her uncle as if he'd lost his mind. He knew as well as she did that Claudia wouldn't dare taste the beignets. *This woman thinks sugar is Satan's reward. Ain't no way she's gonna try one.* To Niya's surprise, her grandmother walked over, took a piece of a beignet, then ate it.

"It does taste like my mother's," Claudia told her. "How did you learn to make these?"

"My mom. She taught me the way her grandmother taught her. She taught me a lot of Grandma Noonie's recipes. We made all kinds of stuff during the holidays the way my mom used to when she was little," Niya explained.

Reese nodded. "I forgot about Nina and Grandma Noonie baking stuff. Cookies, cakes, beignets, pralines."

"Yeah, I know how to make all of those," Niya told him.

Claudia turned away quickly. Niya could see her fumbling with her purse. She looked over at Reese, and he shrugged.

"Here." After placing something on the counter beside the beignets, Claudia headed toward the kitchen door, then paused long enough to say in a trembling voice, "Make sure you clean everything up and leave this kitchen exactly as you found it."

When she was gone, Niya looked at what had been placed on the counter. It was a key ring with her initial and what appeared to be a house key.

Reese walked over and gave her a hug. "You okay?"

"Yeah, but what was that all about?" Niya asked. "Did I do something to make her cry?"

"Yeah, kiddo. I think you're melting the ice from her heart," he told her.

"Wow," Niya said.

"Well, let me grab my hat and get ready to get out of here."

"Wait, I've got to get a picture of this. Meet me by the tree please," Niya told him.

A few minutes later, Reese was posing by the Christmas tree in his very festive and somehow outrageously cute matching vest and cowboy hat. What made it even more comical was when he turned both of the items on and they lit up. Niya kept laughing and was tempted to summon her grandmother so that she could see this sight.

"Okay, enough pictures, and you'd better not post them anywhere," he warned.

"I won't, I promise. You gotta give it to Kendall, though, Uncle Reese. Your outfit is kinda fly," Niya told him. "But Grandma might be right."

"About what?" he asked.

"You must like Kendall if you agreed to wear it."

"Good night, Niya. Don't forget to clean that kitchen."

"I won't. Have fun at the party and please take lots of pictures. Tell Kendall I said hello." Niya grinned.

"I will." He turned to leave the room.

"Quick question, though, Uncle Reese," Niya said as she scrolled through the pictures she'd just taken. "How did you finally get the angel on top of the tree?"

Reese stopped in his tracks and turned back. "What?" He glanced up at the tree and frowned, then looked back at Niya. "I didn't."

Chapter 15

Reese

As he drove to the party, Reese got several strange looks from other drivers. He was too busy thinking about his mother to be concerned with the attention his somewhat ridiculous party attire was receiving. They hadn't spoken for a few days, not since the awkward phone conversation that had gone awry. He had planned to apologize in person and to tell her that he agreed that Niya having a house key was a good idea, but he hadn't had the opportunity. It had seemed as if each time he went to talk to her, she was either on the phone or heading out of the house. And wherever she'd gone, she'd be there for hours. One night she hadn't returned until almost eleven at night. He'd never known her to stay out that late.

Until tonight he had assumed that she'd changed her mind about the key. Giving Niya that house key was a huge moment for his mother, and although he'd been surprised, Reese had known not to react and negate the step in the right direction that she'd taken. The thing that was most odd was the mystery of the tree topper. Neither he nor Niya had placed it on the tree, so that left only one possibility. But at only five feet, five inches, his mother would've needed a tall ladder to reach the top of the tree, and they didn't have such a ladder in the house. It made absolutely no sense. Lost in thought, Reese was surprised when he found himself at his destination.

Kendall grinned when he stepped out of the car. "You look amazing!" she exclaimed.

She had given him strict instructions on where to park and had told him to wait for her to meet him and not to go inside alone. As he stared at her, he understood why. She looked just as festive and outrageous as he did. Her outfit consisted of a bright green tulle skirt covered in twinkling lights, a white blouse, black cowboy boots, and a vest exactly like the one he wore. Her thick, curly hair was pulled on top of her head and held in place by what looked like a set of flashing Christmas bulbs.

Reese laughed, tickled by the fact that they matched perfectly, resulting in a high-fashion, avant-garde black Mr. and Mrs. Claus. "Yo, this is crazy. You know that, right?"

"I do. But what can I say? I'm an artist, and I like to see how far I can go with my creativity,"

Kendall told him. "I was a little pressed for time and couldn't really go all out, so I kept it simple."

Reese turned on the flashing lights of his cowboy hat and put it on his head. "Oh, you definitely went far. This is *not* simple at all."

"Believe me, it's simple. If I had had a little more time, you'd have an awesome lighted belt."

"Oh wow, I guess this is simple." Reese held his arm out for her to hold. "Shall we?"

Kendall slipped her arm in his, and they entered the doors of Woody's Tavern. A roaring country rendition of the song "Sleigh Ride" welcomed them, along with screams and applause from the crowd of people already inside. Most of the attendees were dressed in western attire: there were plenty of cowboy hats, red and green plaid shirts, overalls, bandannas, and boots. Some outfits were creative, but none could compare to those of the couple who'd just walked in.

"Oh my God, Kendall!"

"What in the world! That's crazy!"

"You look so freaking amazing!"

"We knew you were gonna show out!"

When everyone began snapping pictures of him and Kendall, Reese wondered if this was how models on the red carpet felt. He looked around and was amazed at how incredible everything looked. He'd been inside Woody's Tavern, a honky-tonk dive, a couple of times during emergency calls, and it had looked totally different then. Now the tables were draped in white tablecloths, which were topped with centerpieces made of tiny red and green cowboy hats, boots, and spurs. A few couples had lined up to have their picture taken in an antique wagon decorated with lights and garland. An array of hors d'oeuvres stations had been set up throughout the large space, and two Santas were serving drinks behind the bar. People were already dancing. He'd been inside the tavern for less than five minutes, but Reese already knew by the vibe he was getting that Kendall was right: it was going to be a fun night.

"We can grab a table over there," Kendall said, and then she led him to a table near the dance floor. Reese pulled out a chair so she could sit, then sat beside her.

Moments later a woman dressed in a red fringed-denim outfit, white cowboy boots, and a white cowboy hat walked over. "My, my, my, Kendall. You never cease to amaze me," she said. "Everything looks phenomenal, and your and your guest's ensembles are fantastic. How did I miss the memo?"

"Uh, I didn't send one." Kendall made the introductions. "Deena, this is Reese. Deena is my boss."

"Nice to meet you." Reese extended his hand to the woman.

"Likewise," she said, then looked back at Kendall. "I can't wait to see what else you and Amber have in store for us."

"The night is young." Kendall smiled. "We have an entire evening of festivities for everyone to enjoy."

"I'm sure," Deena said. "Reese, welcome and enjoy."

"Thank you." Reese nodded.

He looked at Kendall. "Wow. Wait, so you put all of this together?"

"Amber and I did," Kendall said.

"How? I mean, we can barely get the Secret Santa potluck at the station pulled together every year, and there's way less people than this. This is incredible." Reese was even more impressed with Kendall now.

"It's not that hard if it's something you enjoy doing. It's not work for me. It's art," Kendall explained.

"But you work full-time, and yet you planned a company Christmas party, taught Niya and me how to waltz, designed a debutante gown, and created these wonderful . . . What did your boss call them? Ensembles?" Reese touched his vest. "When do you sleep?"

"I rest when I can," she answered. "You want a drink?"

"Sure," Reese said. "I'll grab us something."

"No, you stay. I'll get it. I have to check on something, anyway," Kendall told him. "It won't take long."

"You sure?"

"I'm positive. Be right back," she assured him.

She wasn't gone long when the cutest Afrocentric elf arrived at their table, wearing a dress made of red and green kente cloth. She looked at him and said, "You must be Reese."

He nodded. "I am. What gave it away? Was it the hat?"

"Actually, it was the vest." She smiled. "I'm Amber."

"Oh, you're Amber. Nice to meet you," Reese said. "Kendall went to check on something and grab some drinks."

"Okay, cool." Amber sat down across from him. She was cute and bubbly, much like Kendall, and very pretty. "I've heard so much about you. It's nice to put a face with the name."

Reese raised an eyebrow. "I hope it was all good."

"Mostly good. Everything except your dance skills," Amber teased.

"Wow. I thought Kendall was going to keep that between us. I guess not." He laughed.

"You thought wrong. But I'm sure you'll get the chance to redeem yourself soon," Amber told him as she stood. "You're wearing one of Kendall's designs. They have a way of bringing out the best in everyone."

Reese had no idea what she meant, but he had a feeling he was going to find out. He glanced over at the bar and was surprised to see Kendall talking to a tall, muscular guy, who seemed to be a little closer to her than he needed to be. He carefully watched her and the guy as they laughed and chatted until Santa handed Kendall two drinks. Reese quickly turned away when he saw her leave the bar.

"I wasn't sure what you like, but we have two signature drinks of the night. One is Jingle Juice. And if you don't like that, we have a Cranberry Cowboy Kamikaze. Which one would you like to try first?" Kendall placed both drinks on the table and took a seat.

"I'll start with Jingle Juice," he said, instead of asking who old boy in her face at the bar was.

Chill, Reese. Why do you care? She's not your woman. Lynnette is, or was. He wasn't even sure, because the last time he'd spoken to her was the day she told him they were over. He had tried calling, but she hadn't answered any of his calls or responded to any of his text messages. This wasn't the first time that she'd decided they were over. Usually, he'd have gone by her place by now and made things right. But this time, he hadn't. Truthfully, he hadn't really thought about her until now.

"Cheers." Kendall held up her glass, and they shared a toast. "To teamwork."

"To teamwork," Reese said and took a sip. The drink was strong and tasty. He began to relax. The music lowered, and everyone's attention went to the stage, where Kendall's boss stood, holding a microphone.

"I'd like to welcome everyone to Diablo's annual holiday get-together. We're so glad to have you all here with us tonight. I'm going to turn it over to the two special people in charge of tonight's festivities. Amber and Kendall, two of our favorite Diablo employees," Deena announced.

Applause erupted, and Reese helped Kendall out of her seat. He clapped loudly and whistled as she made her way to the stage, where she met Amber. Then he heard someone calling Kendall's name even louder than he was. He looked over and saw the guy she'd been with at the bar.

Kendall took the microphone. "Thank you. I want to start by saying how amazing you all look. We have a full night planned, so we aren't gonna waste any time. I hope everyone is ready, because Diablo's Holiday Hoedown has officially started! Yeehaw! Ho ho!" Kendall tossed the cowboy hat she'd been holding into the crowd, and the music kicked in. Reese, who was no longer looking at the guy, laughed as he watched Kendall and Amber do a simple country line dance to "This Christmas." Then they announced the first of what turned out to be many games of the night.

Throughout his life, Reese had attended plenty of holiday parties, but none compared to this one. The food, drinks, music, and laughter were non-stop. They played musical chairs, holiday movie trivia, and Christmas karaoke, and before he knew it, he and Kendall were on the floor, in the center of the crowd, performing a swagged-out waltz that was so good they were named the winners of the dance contest. He had a blast. Just as everyone anticipated, they were also awarded the trophy for "Best Dressed."

"You really know how to throw a party," he told Kendall as he held her close in his arms while they danced. Luther was serenading them with "Every Year, Every Christmas." The lights were dim, and the night was winding down.

"Thank you. I'm glad you're having a good time," she said.

"I'm having a great time," he replied. She put her head on his shoulder, and he pressed his chin against the top of her head. He enjoyed the feel of her next to him.

"Excuse me. Can I cut in?" a voice said, interrupting them.

Reese looked over and saw the guy from the bar smiling at Kendall. He waited for her to tell him no, but she didn't.

"Oh, Simon," she said.

"You don't mind do you, man? I've been waiting on a dance all night, and I think this might be the last song," Simon explained.

Reese quickly released his hold. "Yeah, cool. As a matter of fact, I'm gonna go ahead and cut out."

"Really? You don't have to go yet," Kendall told him.

"Nah, it's kinda late. I had a good time, though. Thanks for the invite." Reese began backing toward the door. "We'll talk soon."

Simon putting his arm around Kendall was the signal for Reese to turn and rush out the door. He made his way to his car and unlocked the doors. Just as he was about to get in, he heard Kendall calling his name.

"Reese, wait!"

He turned and waited until she reached him. His eyes drifted, and he saw his hat in her hand.

"You forgot this," she told him, handing him the hat.

"Aw, man, thanks," he said.

"Reese." Kendall's eyes met his.

"Yeah?" he asked.

She opened her mouth to say something, but no words came out. Reese turned his head and saw Simon waiting at the door to the club.

"Thanks for my hat. You'd better get back in there. It's getting cold out here," he told her. "And your boy is waiting."

She gave him a strange look before turning and walking away. He got in his car and drove off. The last thing he saw in his rearview mirror was Simon putting his arm around her as they went through the door.

Reese didn't understand why he was so upset. He tried to put any thoughts of Kendall out of his head. *She's not even my type. I don't even like her like that. Instead of worrying about her, I need to try to figure out how to get my girlfriend back.*

It was almost two in the morning, but he didn't care. He dialed Lynnette's number, hoping that she'd answer. She didn't. He dialed it again, but she didn't answer. The third time he dialed, his call went straight to voicemail. It was obvious she didn't want to speak to him. It really was over. Reese contemplated driving over to her house but decided not to. One thing he knew was once Lynnette made up her mind about something, there was no changing it. He drove home. As he turned into his driveway, he thought he was seeing things when a pair of headlights pulled in behind him. He parked, turned off his engine, and waited. The driver parked and emerged. As the shadowed figure stepped into view, Reese smiled and stepped out of his car.

"What are you doing here?" he asked.

"Waiting on you," Lynnette said with an innocent shrug.

Reese didn't hesitate to pull her into a hug that was so strong, it lifted her off the ground. Lynnette giggled, and he eased her down, then kissed her passionately. His hands circled her tiny waist, and she wrapped her arms around his neck. Seeing her was unexpected, and the kiss was exactly what he needed.

"I missed you," Lynnette whispered.

"I missed you too," Reese responded. He took her hand and pulled her up the front steps.

"Where are we going?" she asked.

"Inside. Where do you think?" he said as he unlocked the front door. "I know you didn't drive all the way here for a kiss."

"I guess not," Lynnette said and followed him inside. Once they were in the foyer, he turned on the light, and she stared at him like he was crazy.

"Why are you looking at me like that?" he asked.

"What the heck do you have on?" Lynnette's eyes widened.

Reese looked down at his vest and realized why she was so confused. "Oh, I went to a Christmas party tonight."

"I was wondering where you were. I felt like I was waiting forever. What kind of Christmas party has you dressed like that? You look like a Christmas jester." Lynnette shook her head.

"It was Kendall's company party." Reese slipped the vest off and tossed it on the credenza.

Lynnette became serious. "Oh gosh, Kendall again? I should've known. I'm starting to wonder about her. Now you're taking her to her company functions, Reese? What's up with the two of you? And don't lie."

"There's nothing up with the two of us. You know how ridiculous you asking that is? She needed a plus one, that's all. I felt bad for her when she asked me, and decided to go. It's the least I could do after everything she's done for Niya. Come on, Lynnette. You know better." Reese shook his head, as if he was offended by her insinuation.

"I'm just checking. I mean, you've been acting real distant. Then I drive all the way here and wait for hours so we can make up, and then I find out you were with her."

"I wasn't *with her* with her," Reese said.

"So there's nothing going on? You don't like her?"

"No, I don't like her. Why would I like her when I've got you?" Reese reached for her.

Lynnette shrugged. "I don't know. Maybe you're an undercover chubby chaser who's suddenly got a thing for thick thighs."

Reese laughed hard, making his eyes water. "The only person I wanna chase is you. And your thighs are perfect and the ones I want. Kendall isn't even on my radar," Reese stated, trying to convince himself now, not Lynnette. The truth of the matter was that Kendall was very much on his radar, and that was the last place he needed her to be.

Chapter 16

Kendall

Everyone raved about how much they had enjoyed the company party. Deena could not stop talking about how great everything had been and how impressed the guests had been. A few of the vendors who attended had even asked if Kendall and Amber would consider event planning. For Kendall, it was just another testament to her creative skills and talents, and more proof that together, she and Amber really could conquer anything. The celebratory moment was short lived, though: even though the party was finally over, she still had a lot of work to complete. Christmas was only a week away, which meant there were only two weeks remaining until the First Noel Ball. The boutique was a madhouse, and Kendall was running on fumes.

Deena walked in and fumbled through the rack of gowns. "Kendall, I need Mrs. Dixon's dress finished by tomorrow morning."

Kendall turned and frowned. "Tomorrow morning? It's not supposed to be done until Thursday."

"I know, but she called and said they have decided to leave for their vacation a few days early, and I told her it was no problem." Deena pulled out the blue-sequined floor-length gown, which Kendall had yet to start working on.

"Deena, that dress is gonna take a while to finish," Kendall pointed out as she walked over to where her boss was standing. Deena handed her the gown. She looked at the tag that listed all the changes that needed to be made to the gown: the sleeves and the bottom had to be hemmed, the shoulders needed to be taken in, and padding had to be added. It was an all-day job, and Kendall didn't have all day.

"I know, and I'm sorry. But she's one of our best customers, and I need you to do whatever it takes to make sure it's ready." Deena peered at her. "I don't understand what's going on with you, Kendall. I know planning the party took some time—and you did a marvelous job—but I gave you time to take care of the last-minute details. Normally, you're ahead of schedule, and not behind. You came in late twice last week. Is something going on with you that I need to know about?"

Deena mentioning this caught Kendall by surprise. She had thought the mornings she arrived ten minutes late had gone unnoticed, and she hadn't thought it was a big deal, considering the fact that she could count on one hand the number of times she'd left the boutique on time at the end of the day. Usually, she came in early and left well after her scheduled time to get off. There was also the fact that the other employees were constantly tardy.

Disheartened, Kendall shook her head. "No, there's nothing."

"You are the most skilled person on this team, Kendall. That's why I hired you. And I have mentored you because I believe in you and your abilities. Being successful in this business means learning how to balance work. And sometimes balancing means reprioritizing at the drop of a dime and figuring out how to make time for everything you have going on." Deena paused for a long moment. "Don't let me down. If nothing else, consider doing this as one of your angel assignments for the season. It would mean a lot and would make Mrs. Dixon happy. Isn't that what it's about?"

Kendall held the gown in her hands and tried not to cry. She was exhausted physically and emotionally and was trying hard to hold it together. There wasn't time to have a breakdown.

As soon as Deena left the room, Kendall began working on Mrs. Dixon's alterations, hoping to get them finished and to leave work at a decent time, because she planned to go and check on Niya. For the past three days, she'd tried reaching her but hadn't been able to. She also hadn't heard from Reese. It was obvious from his abrupt exit from the party that he wasn't happy about Simon's attentiveness, and their daily phone conversations were now nonexistent.

"You really think he's in his feelings?" Amber asked as they sat in the food court at the mall during lunchtime.

Feeling overworked and overwhelmed, Kendall had decided to take a much-needed break and go out for her allotted sixty minutes instead of working through lunch, like she'd been doing for the past month. The mall was crowded and noisy, but to Kendall, the change of scenery felt like paradise.

"I don't know about all that, but he did have a little bit of an attitude, and it's been a couple of days since we talked." Kendall dipped one of her waffle fries into the tiny container of Chick-fil-A sauce.

"Yeah, he's definitely in his feelings. Typical male mind games. He has a girl and doesn't want you, but he doesn't want to see you with anyone else. Forget him. Focus your attention on the one who's focusing on you. Simon," Amber suggested. "Who, by the way, couldn't keep his eyes off you all night."

"I guess. I still can't believe he was there, either. Are you sure you didn't invite him?"

"Nope, I didn't. I mentioned it to him, but I definitely didn't extend an invitation."

"Maybe it was Deena," Kendall mused. But then she thought about the odd reaction her boss had had when she saw Reese.

"I doubt it. You know she is very selective about who attends company parties. Employees, family, select VIP customers, vendors, and whatever friends she's trying to impress. She definitely ain't gonna invite the random FedEx guy." Amber laughed.

"True. It's just weird, though," Kendall sighed. "He did look good in those jeans and that shirt, though."

"Yes, he did. That man is beyond fine, literally. Reese is cute, but he needs to go ahead and give that last name to Simon." Amber fanned herself. "I can see why he could be a little jealous. No man wants to see his woman with a dude finer than he is. It's an ego thing."

Kendall laughed. "Uh, I'm not his woman, fool, and I promise, jealous is the last thing Reese Fine is right now. And we gotta hurry and get back to the boutique. We have only ten minutes left."

"I say we don't go back. The hell with Diablo Designs. At this point, Kendall, your work is as good as Deena's, if not better. You're reconstructing and re-creating gowns so much that it's your designs with her label. Can't you see the reason you have so much work piled up at this point is that almost every dress we sell, the clients want you to 'fix'? You're doing so much more than simple alterations. That's why you're the only seamstress we have. Deena knows that I can sew as well as she can. But she won't put me in front of a machine. You know why?"

Kendall replied, "Why?"

"Because I can't do what *you* do. No one can." Amber reached across the table and grabbed Kendall's hand. "Look at everything you've created in the past few weeks—the things for Niya, the outfits for you and Reese, hell, the fly Wakanda elf you helped me create and put together. That's all you."

"I get what you're saying, Amber, but I'm not ready. I'm getting there, but not yet." Kendall thought back to the criticism she had received earlier from Deena. "I still have to figure out how to balance it all out."

"You balance it out by putting you first," Amber told her. "I got your back."

"I appreciate it, Amber. Just give me a little more time. And I've already decided to talk to Deena about possibly bringing a couple of my own designs to the spring collection."

As much as she appreciated Amber's undying support, there was no way she could quit her job. Since she worked for a high-end boutique and fashion house, Kendall's salary was much greater than that of other seamstresses in her field. She brought home nearly triple what she'd get anywhere else. There was also the honor of being mentored by Deena, and that in and of itself was something she could not give up easily. She just needed to get through the next two weeks, that was all.

The two cleared the table and returned to work, five minutes late. Luckily, Deena was gone for the day. Without their boss there, Amber broke the unwritten rule and assisted Kendall, taking care of the basic sewing tasks that she was more than qualified to handle but was not allowed to perform. Kendall focused on Mrs. Dixon's gown, and by the time the boutique closed, not only was it finished, but so too were a lot of the other alterations for the week. Amber was a lifesaver, and Kendall was relieved.

"You'd better hope no one on the floor says anything to Deena about your being back here today," Kendall said as they cleaned the work space.

"Trust me, they know better. I have enough blackmail pics of almost every single person we work with, including you. Folks know not to try me." Amber winked.

"I don't know whether to be relieved or afraid." Kendall laughed.

"If I were you, I'd be both." Amber hugged her as they both laughed some more.

When their laughter had subsided, Kendall announced, "Well, I think we've cleaned up enough. I'm heading out."

"I hope everything is okay with Niya."

"Me too," Kendall said. "I'll call you later."

Once she arrived at the Fine mansion, Kendall tried calling Niya. When there was no answer, she hung up before the voicemail picked up. Neither Reese's car nor his bike was in the driveway or in his usual spot, parked on the side of the house. She glanced past the holiday lights on the outside, checking to see if any indoor lights were visible. It was hard to tell, mainly because heavy curtains covered the windows. She decided it was easier just to get out and ring the doorbell. She climbed out of her car, trekked up the walkway and onto the wraparound porch, then rang the bell twice. And waited and waited. She was about to leave when the lock clicked and the front door opened.

"Mrs. Fine," Kendall said. Even though they'd been in one another's presence several times over the past few weeks, Kendall still felt as if she was talking to a stranger every time. "Uh, hello. Merry Christmas. I know you aren't fond of unexpected guests, and I apologize. It's just that I've been trying to call Niya, and she hasn't answered. So, I'm here . . . to, uh, check on her."

"Niya is fine. I'll let her know you stopped by," Claudia said and placed her hand on the door, indicating that as far as she was concerned, that was all that needed to be said and the conversation was over.

Kendall wasn't satisfied with what she'd been told and felt as if something was off. She hesitated, then after taking a deep breath, said, "Can I come in for just a moment?"

Claudia pursed her lips and looked at Kendall as if she were a persistent salesman whom she wanted to leave, but then she reluctantly opened the door and allowed her inside. As usual, the beautiful woman looked stunning in her attire, this time a red silk blouse, houndstooth pants, and black heels. Her long tresses fell past her shoulders in perfect waves, and her hands clutched a pair of reading glasses.

"Thank you." Kendall stepped inside. Claudia didn't go any farther, and they both stood face-to-face in the foyer. "Is Niya here?"

Claudia nodded. "She is."

Kendall blinked a few times and reminded herself to remain composed. Despite wanting to ask the obvious questions in her head, she smiled and said, "Oh, okay, great. Would you mind if I spoke with her?"

"Niya really isn't feeling well. She's been in bed for the past few days. I assumed my son had updated you and let you know. I apologize for his failure to keep you informed," Claudia stated.

Kendall immediately became concerned. "Oh, no, I had no idea she wasn't feeling well. Is she okay? Is there anything I can do? I hate that she's sick so close to the holidays and the ball."

"Kendall."

Claudia addressing her by her first name caught Kendall off guard. She tried not to seem taken aback, even though she was. "Yes, ma'am?"

"I don't think Niya will be participating in the ball. She's not well and says she no longer wants to do it," Claudia informed her matter-of-factly.

Kendall's heart dropped, and she inhaled sharply. *She's lying*, she thought. She refused to believe what Claudia had just told her. Niya had been so happy, so excited, and had worked so hard over the past few weeks. There was no way Niya would quit. Not now, unless there was a real reason, like someone was forcing her. Someone who didn't want her to attend the ball in the first place.

"You're telling me she's quitting?" Kendall shook her head in disbelief and gave Claudia a defiant stare. "I just . . . I don't believe she'd do that."

"I admit I was concerned about her decision when she told me this afternoon, but I was not surprised. I told you at the beginning that Niya is a fragile young lady and that this was a lot for her to undertake." Claudia exhaled. "And you."

Kendall's glare softened, but not much.

"You've put in a lot of time and work with Niya. I admire your tenacity. But as a former debutante, as am I, you know as well as I do that it's not for everyone. Your efforts were noble in trying to assist her."

Claudia sounded somewhat sincere, but Kendall remained suspicious. If what she was saying was true, why hadn't Reese said anything about this? Was this why he'd gone ghost all of a sudden? But why the disappearing act? Why wouldn't he have had me speak to Niya instead? Together we could've helped. Weren't we supposed to be a team? None of it was making sense.

"I am not the only one who put in time and effort," Kendall mumbled.

Claudia gave her a sympathetic look. "But you are the only one who was sincere about why you were doing it. My son was doing it to be defiant and to prove something to me."

Kendall didn't believe that, either. If she knew nothing else, she knew Reese wasn't being supportive to prove a point to his mother. He did it out of love for his niece.

"What did he say when she told him?" Kendall asked.

"She hasn't. As I said, she informed me only this afternoon, and that was after she emailed the committee chair herself. She hasn't been to school all week and barely comes out of her room."

Reese not knowing what was going on made Kendall feel a bit better, but she was still concerned about Niya. "Something had to have happened. Did something happen between her and Gavin or one of the other debs? This doesn't make sense."

"I will let Niya know you stopped by," Claudia said and gestured toward the front door.

"Can I talk to her? Just for a minute? I won't upset her, and I won't be long at all, I promise. I just want to make sure she's okay," Kendall pleaded, praying that some miracle would take place that caused Claudia to have just a twinge of compassion and allow her to speak to Niya.

Claudia didn't say anything as she walked away. After taking a few steps, she turned back and said, "Are you coming?"

Kendall quickly fell into step behind her and followed her down the hallway and up the massive spiral staircase. When they arrived at the top landing, Kendall took in the view of the foyer below. Claudia's heels clicked on the marble floor as she continued down another hallway, and Kendall raced to catch up to her. They entered one of the wings of the house and finally stopped at a closed door.

"This is her suite. She's inside." Claudia nodded, then proceeded farther down the hallway, leaving Kendall alone.

Kendall tapped lightly on the door and waited for a few seconds before opening it and entering. The bedroom was dim, illuminated by a single lamp on the nightstand next to a canopied bed, where a shadowy figure lay. The room was massive, and she imagined that she could probably fit her entire apartment inside it. In addition to the king-size bed and the nightstand, there was a desk, a bookshelf, and a mounted television. A small sitting area with a couple of beanbag chairs was nestled in front of a window, and there was still plenty of space left over. She spotted the jacket she'd given Niya. It had been tossed on the floor in a corner.

"Niya?" she whispered as she slowly eased toward the bed. Niya shifted a little. Kendall moved close enough to touch her and softly rubbed her back. "Niya, sweetie, are you okay?"

Niya rolled over and opened her eyes. She looked shocked for a moment and stared at Kendall for several more moments, then whispered, "Kendall?"

Kendall smiled. "Hey there."

"Uh, hey." Niya sat up. A pillow and something else that she'd been clutching landed on the bed, and Kendall saw that it was a picture of her and her mother. She picked it up and smiled. Although

Niya's mother was several shades lighter, the resemblance between the two was strong. They had the same bright smile, deep-set eyes, and perfectly shaped brows.

"Nice pic." Kendall handed it to her.

"Thanks." Niya put it on the nightstand. "What are you doing here?"

"I came to check on you. You've been kinda MIA, and we gotta get these fittings done. We are down to the wire," Kendall replied, nudging her. She decided not to mention what her grandmother had told her. If Niya had made the decision to quit the cotillion, Kendall wanted to hear it from her directly.

Niya lowered her eyes. "I was gonna call you tomorrow so I could tell you."

Kendall sat down beside her on the bed. "Well, I'm here now, so what do you have to tell me? Fill me in."

"I . . . I can just tell you tomorrow." Niya's voice was barely above a whisper.

"Nope. Tell me now." Kendall slid closer, so that their shoulders were touching. "This better be good too. You've had me on ice for three long days, chick. And don't lie to me, either, because you know I know you."

Kendall could see the pain in Niya's eyes, the same pain that she'd seen when they first met. The mixture of fear, loneliness, and sadness in her had faded as she became more social, vocal, and confident, but now it had returned. Something or someone had caused a regression, and Kendall was determined to find out what it was.

"Okay." Niya sat up straight and pressed her back against the headboard. She looked directly at Kendall and told her, "I quit being a debutante. I'm not going to be at the ball."

Kendall remained calm. "Why? Did something happen, or did someone say something to you?"

"No, not to me. I just don't want to do it anymore." Niya shrugged nonchalantly and added, "It's all fake. All of it. And I don't want to do it."

"What do you mean? What's fake?" Kendall asked, even more confused by Niya's reason for bowing out.

"Everything people say about you, me, us. They're all lying, including Uncle Reese," Niya told her. "He's a fake and a liar."

"Niya, what did he lie about?" Kendall remembered Claudia's doubt about Reese and wondered if he'd changed his mind about the ball, like he'd done before. If so, she was going to have some choice words with him and possibly some physical contact.

"He's been pretending to like you this whole time. Acting like he thinks you're cool, smiling in your face, calling and texting you, saying you're pretty. But the only reason he's been being nice to you is that he feels sorry for you." Niya sniffled.

"Why would he feel sorry for me?" Kendall frowned.

"Because he thinks you're a big girl who can't get a man. That's the only reason he went with you to your Christmas party. He pities you." Niya shook her head. "And I don't want to be a part of it. This whole thing is a lie. He says size doesn't matter and it's what's on the inside that counts, but he doesn't believe it. I heard him laughing and joking about fat girls with his girlfriend."

Kendall took a moment to process this. The fact that Reese had even said those things was one thing, but knowing Niya had overheard him was another. That was what was causing her pain. Reese's disrespect of big girls was a reflection of who Niya was. Kendall was not about to allow his ignorance to take away all that she'd helped Niya become.

"So what?" Kendall smiled.

Niya gave her a confused look. "Huh? He said guys that like big women are chubby chasers and that he'd never be one of those. And only desperate guys go after big girls. The two of them laughed. No matter what, I'll always be a joke to people, especially guys. Don't you get it?"

"Nope, I don't," Kendall replied. "Your uncle Reese was wrong about desperate guys and about my not being able to get a man. That's not true, sweetie. Not true at all. But he was absolutely right about me being a big girl. I mean, I am. So what?"

"Huh?"

"He's entitled to say that if that's how he feels. What he can't and won't do is make me feel less than or bad about being who I am. Just because your uncle Reese feels that way doesn't mean I'm unlovable. That's his loss, not mine. If no one else loves me, I do. And another thing, Uncle Reese is not the last man on earth or the finest. Besides, he can't even dance for real."

Niya smiled. "True."

"Girl, I'm not mad, and you shouldn't be, either. Listen, if you want to quit the ball, that's fine. But you can't allow what other people say or feel to dictate the way you live your life, whether you're big, small, or in between," Kendall explained. "The right people will love you no matter what size you are. And those who don't love or appreciate you aren't the right people for you, and you don't need them, anyway."

"But Uncle Reese said that you—"

"That was about *me*, Niya. It had nothing to do with you," Kendall interrupted. "You've gotta stop doubting who you are and love yourself. You are beautiful, amazing, and important, but the reality is not everyone is going to recognize this, and that's okay. Just because your uncle and his girlfriend said those things about me doesn't mean I have to accept and internalize them, and neither do you."

"I don't know," Niya whispered. "But what if he's right? What if I'm not what guys are looking for?"

"Niya, you may be a little too young to understand this, but think of it this way. Some guys like baked potatoes, and some guys like french fries. Why focus on french-fry guys when there are so many men out there who enjoy a good baked potato? Trust me, they're out there." Kendall hugged her tight. "You have grown so much and worked so hard to get through all of this. You deserve to be at that ball. Think about your decision. Don't give away your power to anyone."

"I'll think about it," Niya promised.

"Okay, good." Kendall stood and walked out of the room. She kept walking until she was out the front door, fearing that the tears that she'd been holding back would fall. There was no way she was going to let Niya see her cry. It was too important to be strong in that moment. She'd almost made it to her car when someone called her name.

"Kendall, hold up."

She turned and glanced briefly at Reese, who was jogging toward her. She rushed to her car and quickly climbed behind the wheel.

He reached her just as she was getting in. "Wait! Don't leave yet!" He took a second to catch his breath. "What's up? I guess you came to check on Niya. That's what's up."

Her anger rose higher. *I should slam the door on his hand*, she thought when he grabbed the door before she could close it.

"Yeah, I did," she told him.

"She's been sick the past couple of days. I've been meaning to call you, but I've been kinda busy . . . last-minute Christmas shopping and stuff. How've you been?" He had the nerve to smile and sound sincere, as if he and his stick of a girlfriend hadn't just had plenty of laughs at her expense.

"I'm cool. I'm pretty busy myself, so I need to take off." Kendall's voice was as icy as the look she gave him.

"I feel ya. Well, hopefully, Niya will feel better in the next day or so. I know you need her for her final fitting this week. Time is winding down," Reese said. "I know she's as excited as I am."

"She's not," Kendall said.

"Well, I mean not right now, because she's sick. But once she gets over this bug, she has—"

"She doesn't have a bug. She's not sick, and she's not gonna participate in the ball. As a matter of fact, she quit." The words tumbled from Kendall's mouth.

Reese blinked a few times. "What? No she didn't. When?"

"She told your mother today. She doesn't want to do it anymore."

"Why not?" He shook his head back and forth, as if he was trying to comprehend what she had told him.

"You should ask her yourself." Kendall turned the ignition and started the engine, hoping he would realize that whether he moved or not, she would be pulling off.

"Kendall, I don't—"

"It's funny, because as much as you complain about your mother, you're more like her than you realize," Kendall said, interrupting him. Maybe that's the problem between the two of you."

"What are you talking about?"

"You're shallow, superficial, and judgmental. And for the record, you didn't do me any favor by coming to the party the other night. I did that for you." She grabbed the door handle and pulled, barely giving him enough time to move out of the way before the car door closed.

As she drove off, there was no stopping the tears that fell—both from anger and disappointment—not just for herself, but for Niya as well. They both had expected more from Reese, and he'd done just what his mother had said he'd do—let them down.

Chapter 17

Niya

"She's right."

Startled by her grandmother's voice, Niya gasped. Not wanting her to see that she'd been crying, she quickly wiped the tears from her face before getting up out of bed. The last thing she needed was to be accused of being lazy or disrespectful for not standing while she was being addressed.

"Who?" Niya asked.

"Kendall. What she told you is absolutely right. If participating in the cotillion is something you truly believe in and want to do, then quitting shouldn't be an option. You must never allow the thoughts or opinions of others to control how you view yourself," her grandmother said. "It leads to doubt and despair."

"Including you? You have an opinion about me," Niya pointed out. "Isn't that why you didn't want me to do this in the first place? Because I wasn't good enough?"

It was a question that she had been wanting to ask for weeks, but she hadn't had the courage until now. Niya had concluded that there wouldn't be any harm now, especially since she'd already quit, anyway.

"I never said you weren't good enough. What I said was that you were fragile and not strong enough. There's a difference."

"You were against it from the start. You said yourself I didn't possess the je ne sais quoi needed. That's why I didn't come to you. You don't even like me." Niya almost laughed.

"But I do love you. I haven't spent enough time with you to know you well. You have barely talked to me while you've been here."

"Because all you do is criticize me and point out things I do wrong."

"Because I love you, and that's my job as your grandmother," she said. "I want the best for you. Always have. The same way that I wanted the best for your mother and uncle. But, very much like them, you chose to exclude me, even in your decision to become a debutante. So, I allowed you to do it your way, thinking that one of two things would happen. Either you'd prove me wrong and succeed because you're stronger than I thought or you'd prove me right and fail."

Niya didn't know what to say. Her grandmother verbally acknowledging that she loved her was a surprise. She hadn't expected to hear that at all. Niya's mother had always said her own mother, Niya's grandma Claudia, gave her tough love while she was growing up, which had been hard to bear but had made her strong. Learning about it was one thing; experiencing it firsthand was another.

"I didn't know . . . ," Niya began.

At that very moment, Reese rushed into her bedroom, disrupting the conversation she was having with her grandmother. "Niya, you quit the cotillion? Why?"

Niya looked at him. "I . . ."

Reese turned to his mother. "What did you say to her? Just because she's sick doesn't mean she has to quit."

"Excuse me? You need to correct your tone, Reese, I won't have you speaking to me this way," Claudia snapped at him.

The tension in the room increased. Niya had been emotionally overwhelmed and was trying to process everything. She had already been dealing with having Christmas without her mom and managing her anxiety about Gavin and the upcoming ball. Reese and the conversation she'd overheard were too much.

She'd waited up for him the night of Kendall's company party. She'd been excited to hear the details and to learn if he'd made his move and asked her out, like she had suggested. When she heard the front door open, she raced to meet him and was surprised when she looked down into the foyer and saw him with Lynnette, a woman she'd met only once. Curious, she listened to their conversation. Not only did she feel personally attacked by what the woman was saying, but the mean things she said about Kendall made it worse. Niya shut down, claiming to be sick and avoiding everyone.

"It wasn't her. She didn't do anything," Niya told him now. "You did."

Reese's mouth fell open. "Me? What did I do?"

"I heard you. I heard everything you said about Kendall and feeling sorry for her. You said you'd never be a chubby chaser and big women were unattractive and unhealthy, Niya revealed, fighting back tears of anger. "You think that's funny?"

"Niya, no . . ." He shook his head.

"Really? Because you were laughing really hard," Niya said.

"It's not what you think, Niya, I promise." He reached for her.

Niya pulled away. "You know what? I'm glad Kendall doesn't like you and doesn't even care that you said those nasty things about her. She deserves someone way better than you. Someone who loves and appreciates her."

"Niya, come on," Reese pleaded. "Let me explain."

Niya ignored him and ran into her bathroom, then closed the door. Her heart was pounding as she leaned against the counter. There was complete silence at first, and she wondered if her grandmother and uncle had left the room. Then she heard their muffled voices, and she moved closer to the door to listen.

"I didn't say all of that. I promise. Those are things that Lynnette said, and I did laugh . . . at first. But then I stopped her, because I realized she was wrong."

"You were both wrong." Her grandmother's voice was stern.

"We *both* were wrong," Reese stated, correcting himself. "Lynnette was wrong for the things she said, and I was wrong for laughing. It was disrespectful, and honestly, I didn't agree with any of it. That's why I called her later that night and told her that I didn't want to see her anymore."

Niya frowned, unaware that her uncle had done that. "You owe both Niya and Kendall an apology, Reese."

"I know, I know, Ma," Reese sighed.

"And I owe you one, as well."

As she pressed her ear against the door to hear better, Niya imagined that her uncle probably had the same stunned expression on his face as she had had just a little while ago. Claudia Fine apologizing? That was unheard of. What was she apologizing for?

"I haven't been fair to you or Niya. This is partially my fault, because I could've been more supportive, and for that, I'm sorry. I acknowledge my part. Losing Nina . . . it . . . This hasn't been easy for me. You and Niya have always been close, and I told myself that it was what Nina would've wanted. So, I removed myself and focused on my own grief, instead of taking into consideration this hasn't been easy for any of us."

"Mom . . ."

"No, I'm fine. There's no need for that."

Niya carefully opened the bathroom door and peeked out. Her grandmother was cringing as Reese tried to hug her tight. It was so funny, and she couldn't help smiling. Then she burst into laughter.

Reese looked over at her. "What are you laughing at? You can get some of this to."

Niya squealed as her uncle released her grandmother, then rushed over and pulled her into a bear hug. There was no way to resist, and Niya giggled as she hugged him back.

"I'm sorry, Ni-Ni. I never should've allowed that conversation to continue. I should've shut Lynnette down the moment she was disrespectful. But I don't feel that way at all," Reese told her. "I know the inside of a person is more important than the outside. You are beautiful inside and out."

"So is Kendall," Niya reminded him.

"She very much is," he agreed.

"It's like our house. The outside looked perfect, but Kendall made the inside just as great. She helped us bring laughter and warmth and the spirit of Christmas to the inside," Niya said.

"Kendall definitely did that," her grandmother commented. "She's quite impressive. I can see why you like her, Reese."

This was definitely a side of her grandmother that she'd never seen before. Her demeanor was still stern, but she seemed a bit more pleasant. It felt strange hearing her speak so positively about someone, especially Kendall. Niya had always assumed that her grandmother disliked her. Now she realized that she may have been wrong.

"I do, but I don't think she feels the same about me." He glanced over at his niece. "Niya, you said yourself that she doesn't like me, remember?" he reminded her.

"I know, but she needs to know. You should call and tell her, Uncle Reese. You've gotta explain what happened," Niya pleaded.

"Maybe. We'll see." Reese put his hands on her shoulders and faced her directly. "I'm more concerned about you understanding how valuable you are, and how proud I am of you. Which is why I need for you to be at the ball. You can't quit, Niya."

"Thank you, and I'm not going to," Niya told him.

"You're not?" Reese smiled.

Niya turned and walked over to a corner of the room and picked up the jacket lying on the floor. She held it close as she said, "No, I'm not. But not because you don't want me to. It's my choice, and I choose to see it to the end, no matter what."

"I'm glad you're choosing to do that, Niya," he told her.

Niya turned to her grandmother and said, "Guess you'll be wrong, after all, huh?"

Her grandmother smiled and gave her a wink. "First time for everything."

The following day Niya went back to school. She'd made up her mind that even though she'd been hurt by both Jira and Gavin, she wouldn't give them the satisfaction of seeing that she cared. *All I have to do is remember to keep it calm, cool, collected, and to remain cute.*

"Niya, you're back," Jira called as she rushed to Niya's locker. "I was so worried about you. I've been calling and texting you, girl."

"Yeah, I was a little under the weather, but I'm good now." Niya's eyes remained fixed on the metal shelf that held her books.

"I'm glad. Gavin's been worried sick too. When you didn't make rehearsal the other night, Mrs.

Sinclaire stood in, and Gavin was not happy at all. It was all over his face. I should've taken a picture so you could see." Jira laughed. Even in her letterman's jacket and Mom jeans, she looked cuter than the other girls, who had probably spent hours in the morning trying to find the perfect outfit to wear, Niya included.

Niya wanted to tell her that she'd seen enough pics of Gavin, including the one where they were hugged up. Instead, she simply said, "I bet."

"Well, I'm glad you're feeling better. I'll see you in class. Oh, and don't forget we're supposed to go shoe shopping, because we gotta wear them for final rehearsals. I'll text you about that, though." Jira gave her a brief hug before disappearing into the crowd of students in the hallway. Then she turned around and yelled, "You look really cute today, Niya. I love the fit."

Niya couldn't believe the nerve of Jira. She had to know that she'd seen the picture on Instagram. Everyone in school had. But she acted as if nothing had happened: spewing fake compliments and pretending they were still buddies and expecting Niya to feel the same way. Then again, technically Gavin wasn't her boyfriend, so maybe that was what it was. She closed her locker door.

"Hey there. Welcome back."

Niya stared blankly at Gavin, who was smiling beside her. Remaining calm, cool, and collected with Jira was one thing, but with Gavin, it was quite another. Clearly, God wanted to test her ability to do so first thing in the morning. She hadn't expected to see him until AP English in the afternoon.

She finally spoke. "Hey."

"How are you?" Gavin asked. "You good?"

"Yep," Niya told him. "I'm great."

"You look great too. I'm happy to see you. I missed you."

The statement was so comical that Niya giggled. Gavin couldn't possibly think she was that gullible; then again, he probably did because she was a big girl. But he was about to find out that he was wrong.

"What's funny?" he asked.

"You are," Niya told him.

"I am? How?"

Niya slipped her backpack on her shoulder and folded her arms. "Because you're really standing here telling me you missed me and how great I look. You're hilarious."

"I mean, I'm glad I can make you laugh, but I wasn't trying to. I did miss you, and you do look great," Gavin said with a confused look.

"You're right. I do. But I don't need you to tell me that. You want to offend somebody, then make jokes about them. You and your girlfriend can go and find someone else, because I'm not the one. I'm not now and never will be a *duff*," Niya snapped and then walked off.

"Niya, wait. Come back," Gavin called after her.

Niya was too busy holding her head high and enjoying the pride she felt as she walked to class.

And that's how you remain cool, calm, and collected while keeping it cute.

Chapter 18

Reese

"Merry Christmas, Uncle Reese," Niya said as she entered the living room, wearing a pair of footed pajamas covered in dancing reindeer.

Reese, who'd been up for a few hours, smiled. "Merry Christmas, Ni-Ni. Cute pajamas."

Niya scrunched her nose at him. "Thanks. They're a gift from my favorite uncle."

Gifts were piled under the tree. Most of them had been purchased by his mother, but he'd somehow managed to grab a few surprises to add to the pile. His recent breakup had allowed his Christmas budget to increase significantly, and the money he'd planned to spend on Lynnette had gone to the most important women in his life: his mother and his niece. There was another gift that he'd purchased, but he wasn't sure it would be received by the intended recipient.

He put his arm around Niya after she plopped down beside him on the sofa. "How are you?"

"I'm okay. I do miss my mom, though. Christmas Eve was the only night she would let me sleep in her bed. When I was little, she told me it was because she wanted us to wake up together on Christmas morning. But then I realized it was to keep me from sneaking and opening the gifts. She wanted to make sure she kept her eye on me." Niya's voice was soft, and although there was a semi-smile on her face, he could see the sadness in her eyes. "Last night I slept by myself. It was weird."

"I know, Niya. I remember the first Christmas without my dad. It was like something was missing. Still feels like it today. But then I remember the good memories of when he was here, and how he would fuss about the tree looking crooked, even though to everyone else, it looked straight. And there never seemed to be enough ornaments or lights on it, despite there not being any room to hang anything else. I used to be so scared that the doggone thing would fall over." Reese laughed. "And Grandma would just shake her head and stand back while saying, 'Reginald, I know you mean well, but you've got so much going on with that god-awful tree that you can't see the beauty of the angel on top.'"

"I can definitely hear her saying that." Niya laughed.

"So, my dad, your mom, and I would put all these decorations on the tree at night. Then, when he'd go to work the next day, Grandma would have us take some of them off. And he'd come home and say, 'That tree is looking crooked, and I think it needs more lights,' and we would decorate the tree all over again."

"Wait, he never knew you were taking them off?" Niya asked.

Reese shrugged. "I think he did, but I honestly can't say."

Just then, his mother walked into the living room. "He didn't care. He loved listening to those Christmas records while decorating the tree with you and your sister. So it gave him a reason to do it every night."

"What? Are you serious?" Reese couldn't believe he had never known that was what they were doing, but it made complete sense. His father had never questioned why they were putting the exact same bulbs and lights back on the tree, and they were so busy having fun redecorating that it hadn't mattered.

"I am," she told him. "Merry Christmas."

While he and Niya were dressed in loungewear, his mother wore a chic off-white pantsuit, a silk pashmina, and a diamond brooch. She looked like she was headed to Christmas brunch with the Fine Foundation board members.

"Merry Christmas, Mom." He stood and hugged her.

Niya followed suit. "Merry Christmas, Grandma."

It seemed awkward at first, and his mother was a bit tense. But after a few seconds, she relaxed and enjoyed the heartfelt moment. Reese could see that she really was trying, and he appreciated it.

"Well, shall we begin opening the gifts?" she asked.

"Yes!" Niya yelled and clapped, then abruptly stopped. Her face became serious, and after composing herself, she spoke in a proper voice as she looked at them. "My apologies. Yes, we shall."

His mother took a deep breath, then began laughing so hard that tears formed in her eyes. Reese and Niya were just as tickled by her reaction. While he and Niya settled back on the sofa, his mother reached under the tree and proceeded to give Niya her presents.

"Wow! Thanks, Grandma." Niya grinned as what seemed like an endless number of boxes were handed to her.

It didn't take long for her to open them. Reese was surprised that in addition to giving Niya the practical, traditional gifts he had expected, such as a new coat, socks, and books, his mother had also bought her things she would enjoy, such as a new laptop, a Bluetooth speaker, and gift cards. She also gave her a gift certificate for a driving class.

Niya clutched the paper to her chest and gasped with excitement. “Does this mean I can get a car?”

“It means you will be properly taught how to drive and prepared to take the test for your license,” his mother told her.

“But Uncle Reese has already taught me how to drive. He lets me . . .” Reese shot Niya a warning look, and she quickly corrected herself. “I mean, thank you, Grandma.”

“You’re welcome.” Reese’s mother shook her head at him as she handed him several foil-wrapped boxes. “For you.”

In that brief moment, Reese felt like a kid again, and his heart beat with anticipation. “Thanks, and thank you for my other gift as well.”

“What other gift?” she asked with a puzzled look.

“My tuxedo for the ball.” He grinned.

“What about it?” She shrugged and quickly turned her attention back to the tree.

He’d been pleasantly surprised when Franklin told him his tuxedo had already been paid for in full when he went to pick it up. Whoever paid had also purchased gloves, socks, shoes, and a monogrammed handkerchief, which Franklin had ready for him, along with the suit. Franklin had said he was sworn to secrecy and wouldn’t confirm the identity of the mystery person, but Reese knew that his mother had to be the generous benefactor.

"Nothing. Just thanks." He decided to open the smallest box first. Upon seeing what was inside, he nearly dropped the box. "Mom."

"He would've wanted you to have them. They'll be perfect to wear for the cotillion as well."

Reese stared at his father's white gold and diamond cuff links. After he had passed, his mother had given Reese the opportunity to go through his father's things. Reese had been so emotionally overwhelmed at the time that the only things he took were a couple of his watches and neckties. Over time, he had come to wish that he had been a little more acquisitive, regretting that he had not chosen certain things when he had the chance. Now he realized that his mother had saved those things for him. In addition to the cuff links, she gave him another precious memento.

"And this?" Reese held up his father's stethoscope. "Are you trying to hint at something else?"

"Not at all. Isn't that something that you use at work daily?"

"It is," he admitted.

"Then, there you have it," she said innocently. Then she added, "Now, if you should happen to be inspired to continue your education and further your career in another capacity, such as the one your father used it for, then I have nothing to do with that."

Once again, he was subjected to her feeble attempt to coerce him into returning to medical school. But, for some reason, instead of being insulted, he felt a twinge of possibility. Losing his sister, being back at home, and spending less time at work had given him a chance to see things differently, including his mother. As much as he hated to admit it, she was right: he'd forgone medical school because he didn't want to face the challenge. But now he didn't need his father's stethoscope for inspiration; Niya had shown him how to confront things head on. The difference was that she hadn't had a choice of challenges she'd faced and overcome. He did. So her resilience over the past few weeks was motivation enough.

"I'll keep that in mind," he told his mother as he stood. "In the meantime, there are more gifts to be given."

Reese proceeded to give the two ladies the gifts that he'd purchased. His mother was pleased with the donation he had made to the homeless shelter in both her and Nina's name and with the gift certificate to her favorite day spa. Niya was equally satisfied with the items he'd purchased from her Amazon wish list, which he'd stumbled upon, and with the karaoke machine he'd got her.

"Oh my goodness, Uncle Reese. This is awesome." She jumped up and gave him a hug. "I love to sing."

"I know. I've heard you in the shower," Reese told her. "Well, if that's what you call it."

"I probably should've gotten you voice lessons and driving ones." His mother's joke caught them off guard. "What, so you all can tease, but I can't?"

"The only way you can join in the teasing is if you take that fancy scarf and blazer off, ma'am. It's Christmas morning. You should not be in here dressed like Olivia Pope at a campaign meeting." Niya giggled.

"Fine." His mother removed the brooch from the scarf, then slipped out of the jacket. "It's handled."

Reese had never imagined Christmas morning being this enjoyable. He'd planned on spending most of the day comforting his niece and being pleasant to his mother. Something had changed between all of them. *We're all we've got. The only thing we have to hold on to is each other. This is love. This is family.*

"Grandma, do you mind if I invite a couple of friends over later to use this thing?" Niya asked, pointing to the karaoke machine.

"Friends?" his mother repeated.

"Just Gavin and Jira, and maybe a couple of the other debs and escorts. Not a lot. And I promise we won't be rowdy or disrespectful," Niya explained.

"I suppose, but it will have to be much later. I figured the three of us would cook breakfast together. It's time you taught your uncle and me how to make Grandma Noonie's beignets," she told her.

"Deal." Niya nodded. "But you might wanna change out of those fancy clothes first."

Claudia nodded and walked out of the room.

Reese looked over at Niya. "I thought you weren't cool with Jira and Gavin anymore. What about the disrespectful picture and comment?"

"It was all a misunderstanding. They weren't referring to me when they made the comment. Jira was at a party for her dad's job, and Gavin was making a poinsettia delivery for his grandfather. They saw each other and a few other kids from Duff High School, which apparently is one of our rival schools. That's what the comment meant. I was wrong. We talked it out and cleared things up." Niya reached under the tree and handed him the box containing the gift he'd bought Kendall. "That's what mature people do, Uncle Reese. They talk things out and clear up misunderstandings. They don't avoid one another."

Reese had made plenty of effort to try talking to Kendall, but she had refused his calls, had ignored his texts, and hadn't even responded to an email he sent. It was useless. He figured the best thing to do was to give her some space. They would have to talk to one another at some point, and when the time came, he would apologize and clear the air. Until then, he would deal with the misery of missing her. The irony was that while Kendall was ignoring him, he was ignoring Lynette.

"I'm not avoiding her, Niya. I can't make someone talk to me that doesn't want to talk," he said. "I tried."

"Try harder," she insisted.

"I will after the cotillion. Maybe it'll be better then."

"Or it'll be too late," Niya told him.

Chapter 19

Kendall

You did it, Kendall thought as she stood back and fought her tears as she stared at the beautiful white gown that she had miraculously designed and completed. It was stunning and had come out better than she could have ever imagined. She'd seen the gowns that some of the debutantes had bought from the boutique. And, in fact, she'd altered many of them so that they fit perfectly. One of her main concerns during the entire process had been to make sure Niya had a gown that not only fit well and complimented her in every way, but also looked comparable to the gowns of the other debs. She had also wanted Niya to feel as comfortable as possible. It had been a challenge in every way possible, but it was done.

Kendall had taken the day off, thinking she was going to attend the ball, but she had changed her mind. Her plan now was to make sure the gown was delivered to Niya at the hotel and to spend the remainder of the day relaxing. The past month had been a whirlwind, and she needed to decompress.

"Wow, Kendall. It's beautiful," Amber gasped as she walked into the extra bedroom that served as Kendall's home work space. It wasn't as equipped as the one at the boutique, but it served its purpose.

"It is, isn't it?" Kendall nodded. The dress was a visual dream come true. The white satin bodice, which had taken the most time for Kendall to finish, was hand beaded, covered in pearls and Swarovski crystals. The floor-length skirt, which she had made from organza, was full and elaborate.

"It's . . . couture . . . and honestly better than the Diablo Designs number. It's literally breathtaking, Kendall." Amber carefully ran her fingers along the sweetheart neckline. "Girl, brides would pay top dollar for this, and don't get me started on girls going to prom. You'd have a line of customers out the door. I have always told you, you have a gift. I can't wait to get married, because I know my dress is gonna be the bomb. I don't care about Deena and her stupid noncompete agreement. My gown will be a Kendall Freeman original design. She's gonna have to get over it."

Kendall laughed. "If you say so."

"I do say so. Don't worry. I'll pay you, with my substantial BFF discount you'll be giving me, of course. But I know you're gonna hook me up when the time comes." Amber shrugged.

"Your time will probably come way before mine, so I gotcha." Kendall began searching for the bridal garment bag she'd purchased and embroidered with Niya's initials.

"Maybe not. Who knows what will happen with you and Simon?" Amber shrugged again. "I mean, he did ask you out, right?"

Kendall nodded. "He did. And I accepted. I told him I just needed to get through the holidays and finish this."

"Well, Christmas was last weekend, and the ball is tonight, so looks like we need to get these plans in motion." Amber nudged Kendall's arm.

"I guess," Kendall responded.

"Oh my God, Kendall. I'm gonna need you to at least pretend like you're a little excited. You've had your eye on this guy for months, and now it's happening. Come on."

"It's just a date, Amber. How do you want me to act?" Kendall sighed. A date with Simon was the last thing she'd been thinking about. Truth was, she hadn't even responded to his efforts since the night of the party, even though he had tried to connect. For some reason, she just wasn't interested. "Can you help me out here?"

Amber held the garment bag open as Kendall carefully folded the bottom of the gown and maneuvered it inside the bag. It took a few minutes, but the precious cargo finally was covered, zipped in, and securely protected. Kendall placed the garment bag on one of the clothing racks and stood back and stared again. *I know Niya's gonna love it. And she's gonna look so beautiful in it. If nothing else, she's going to be the belle of the ball. Tonight is going to be everything she's hoped for. I can see her and Reese now. Reese. No, this isn't about him. Forget about him.* She was so caught up in trying to get him out of her head that she didn't realize that Amber had said something else until she called her name.

"Huh?" Kendall asked as she turned around.

"I asked if you'd at least talked to him," Amber said.

"Heck no. I told you I blocked him and have no plans to talk to him again. I have nothing to say to him," Kendall exclaimed. "Reese Fine no longer exists to me."

Amber sighed. "Not talking about Reese, friend."

Kendall frowned. "Yes you are. You asked me if I would talk to Reese."

"Nope. We were talking about Simon. At least I was." Amber shook her head.

"Oh."

"I know this is gonna sound crazy, considering the circumstances, but I think maybe you should really talk to Reese."

"Are you crazy? Why in the world would I do that? Did I not just say I had nothing to say to him?"

"You've been saying that for a while now. So much that I'm starting to wonder if you're trying to convince yourself as much as you're trying to convince me," Amber said, as if she were a therapist and Kendall were her difficult patient. "I'm just suggesting that a closing conversation might be helpful for both of you. For Niya's sake, at least maybe. She's kinda the common denominator that brought you together. Even she said there was a misunderstanding . . ."

"Niya is fine, and I'm quite capable of continuing my relationship with her without dealing with Reese. It's been working so far," Kendall pointed out. Each time Niya brought her uncle up in conversation, Kendall made sure to change the subject, and when that didn't work, she would end the conversation altogether. Eventually, Niya got the hint and stopped trying to resolve the issue. "And another thing, Reese and I were never together."

"You know what I meant." Amber gave her a knowing look.

"I know what you said. Now, are you gonna go drop this off for me, like you promised? I told her it would be there by noon." Kendall looked at her watch. "It's already after eleven."

Amber shook her head. "I promised I'd ride with you. I didn't say anything about dropping it off."

"Fine." Kendall struggled a little to pick up the bulky garment bag, and Amber had to step in and help her lift it and carry it out to her car. Amber tried to make small talk during the ride over to the hotel, but Kendall wasn't paying attention. She was too busy hoping and praying that she wouldn't run into Reese once they arrived. By the time she pulled up to the hotel entrance, she was sweating and her anxiety was elevated.

"Oh good. There's a bellhop with a luggage cart already waiting," Amber noted. They hopped out and carefully loaded the gown on the gold metal cart just in time. A minute later a few young ladies and gentlemen and their parents, carrying garment bags and suitcases and flashing smiles galore, appeared at the entrance. The excitement of the event was evident.

"It's going to the presidential suite. But can you wait one moment?" Kendall asked the bellhop.

"Yes, ma'am," he agreed.

"You want me to move the car while I wait for you?" Amber offered.

"No," Kendall told her. "Amber, can you please take the gown upstairs for me? I'm begging."

"What?" Amber's eyes widened.

"I really don't want to go up there. First of all, I look a mess." Kendall rubbed her hands along the favorite leggings she had on and pulled the draw-strings of her hoodie. "I didn't even put on a hat."

Amber shook her head in disbelief. Kendall, you . . . you should at least help her put the gown on. You deserve at least that."

"I'll see pictures. That's good enough. Amber, please," Kendall said, trying to sound convincing. "All you have to do is escort the gown upstairs. You don't have to stay until she gets dressed. Her grandmother should be the one to help her, anyway. Just . . . just tell Niya to FaceTime me if she needs me." Kendall's eyes pleaded with Amber. "Please."

"Okay, Ken. I got you," Amber finally said.

Relieved, Kendall hurried back to the car. She got behind the wheel and drove to the other side of the hotel, determined not to be anywhere near where there was the slightest chance she'd run into her adversary and the woman she was sure he'd bring as his date. After pulling into a space at the far end of the parking lot, she leaned back and closed her eyes. An image of her mother smiling appeared in her mind, bringing her a feeling of peace.

Mommy, I know you're proud. My angel assignment is complete.

"Why in the world did you park all the way back here?"

Kendall's eyes opened. She didn't realize she'd drifted to sleep until Amber spoke and woke her. The overwhelming anxiety she'd felt all morning was gone. She felt much lighter, happier, and somehow, she knew that everything was going to be okay.

Amber opened the car door and climbed into the front passenger seat.

"How did it go? Was everything okay?" Kendall asked.

"Everything is great. That presidential suite is everything. Mrs. Fine has all kinds of snacks . . ."

"I don't care about that, Amber. How is Niya? Is she nervous?" Kendall turned in her seat to face her friend.

"She looks beautiful. I swear, Kendall, I almost didn't recognize her. Her hair is perfect, and my goodness, her face is flawless. Kudos to the makeup artist you sent. I wish you could've seen her," Amber said.

"I'm glad. I knew she'd be beautiful." Kendall smiled.

"And before you ask, there was no sign of Reese."

"I wasn't going to ask about him," Kendall lied.

"However, Mrs. Fine wanted me to tell you how much she appreciates everything. And this is for you." Amber took out an envelope and handed it to her.

"What is this?" Kendall looked at the red envelope for a moment.

"Looks like a Christmas card." Amber shrugged. "Oh, and I peeked into the ballroom, and, Kendall, it's gorgeous. The tables and centerpieces are exquisite. I can't lie. I wish we could go to the ball." Amber sighed. "We should come."

"The ball has been sold out for months, Amber. At this point, even if we wanted to go, we can't. I told you, those tables are over a thousand dollars apiece," Kendall said.

"Wow. I guess it would take a miracle for it to happen."

"A big one." Kendall carefully opened the envelope. "Oh my God!"

"What?"

Kendall held up the two tickets that had fallen out of the card when she opened it. "Look."

"It's a miracle!" Amber squealed. "We're going to the ball."

"No, I'm not, but you can," Kendall said. "My assignment as Niya's angel is over."

"Kendall, what if this whole assignment isn't just about Niya? I mean, Mrs. Fine didn't say it, but I could see that she was sad when it was me that brought the gown and not you. She wanted to share this moment with you," Amber told her.

Kendall didn't respond. She began reading the card she was holding.

Dear Kendall:

There are no words to express the gratitude I have in my heart for you. Since the moment you entered our home, our lives have changed immensely. Without reservation, you demonstrated joy, compassion, and support during the time when we needed it most. Your determined spirit and infectious laugh were a breath of fresh air, and we are better for it. I am aware of your decision not to attend tonight, but I am offering these tickets in an effort to have you join me at my table. This moment is yours as much as Niya's. Know that the entire *Fine family loves you because* you *are family.*

With love,

Claudia Fine

Kendall wiped away the tears that fell from her eyes. *Family. That's what this is.* The Fines had somehow become her family without her realizing it. Not just Niya, but Claudia, and even Reese, despite the current state of their friendship. *They are my family.* Could it be that the hardest angel assignment she'd ever been given had brought her to the one thing she needed the most?

Amber's right. This wasn't just for Niya. It's for me too.

Chapter 20

Niya

The First Noel Ball . . .

"My God, Niya!" Reese gasped when Niya emerged from the bedroom of the hotel suite. "You're beautiful."

"Yeah, Kendall did her thing with this dress." Niya looked down at the masterpiece, which her grandmother had helped her into moments before.

"No, sweetheart, that's not what he's talking about," Claudia whispered. "Yes, Kendall did a phenomenal job on your gown, but he's referring to you. You are beautiful."

"Thanks, Uncle Reese." Niya beamed at her uncle, who was looking quite handsome in his tuxedo. He'd gotten a fresh haircut and shave, and she could tell by the way he kept fidgeting with the white gloves in his hand that he was just as nervous as she was. The butterflies had been in her stomach all morning, so much so that she hadn't been able to eat, despite all the food available in the suite. But her grandmother had intervened.

"The last thing you want to be is one of those young ladies who become the highlight of the ball because they fainted, Niya." Claudia's warning had been enough to compel Niya to finish half the bagel she'd been nibbling on and drink a glass of juice.

By the time she'd finished, her whirlwind of a morning had begun. While waiting on her gown to arrive, the glam squad for the day had made sure that Niya and her grandmother were picture perfect. The hair stylist and makeup artist, both selected by Kendall, had worked tirelessly for what felt like hours, but it had been worth the time, because when they'd finished, Niya had barely recognized herself in the mirror.

"I look like Mommy," Niya said to Reese now.

"You've always looked like her." He nodded. "But you're right. The hair makes you look like her twin . . . well, triplet."

Niya glanced at her grandmother, to whom he was referring. She was amazed that she could see the strong resemblance she bore to the two women she had always desired to look like and had always thought were the most beautiful in the world.

"Niya, do you have your gloves?" Claudia asked.

"Yes, ma'am." Niya eased over to the nearby table to pick up her gloves. The gown was a little heavier than she had expected, and she wondered if she'd be able to walk gracefully, let alone dance. She pulled the elbow-length gloves onto her hands and smiled as Reese began snapping pictures with his phone.

Claudia exhaled. "Now for the final details, so that we can head downstairs." She picked up a sparkling tiara and placed it on Niya's head, then reached for a black velvet box. Niya held her breath as Claudia removed a strand of pearls from the box and placed them around her neck. "They were your great-grandmother's, mine, and your mother's, and now they're yours."

"I . . . they . . ." Niya began to get choked up.

"Uh-uh. No tears. You'll ruin your makeup, and there's no time to fix it. We have to go," Claudia whispered.

"Can I call Kendall? I want her to see me . . . I need her," Niya pleaded while she searched for her phone.

"There's no time, Niya. I'll make sure to send her some photos," Claudia promised.

"But . . ." Niya started to panic. It was hard enough not having her mother there. Kendall was at least a phone call away.

"Hey, look at me." Reese held his arm toward her. "It's okay, Niya. You make a fine Fine debutante, and I'm proud of you. Now, what is it you said that Kendall taught you?"

"Head up, shoulders back, eyes forward. Smile from the heart, and don't forget to breathe," Niya reminded herself, following each step, as she put her arm through his. Her grandmother took Reese's other arm, and he escorted them out of the room.

While the guests assembled in the hotel's grand ballroom, the debutantes and their escorts were tucked away in a smaller room, where they could be distressed together and remain unseen until they made their grand entrance for all the world to see.

"OMG, *Niya*!" Jira squealed when Niya walked into the designated room. It didn't take long for all the other debs to rush over and bombard her with compliments, as she was sure they had with one another, and deservedly so. They all looked amazing, including Niya, and she basked in the sincerity of their words. She took out her phone and joined in the impromptu photo shoot that was already taking place.

Niya glanced over and nearly gasped when she spotted Gavin staring at her. *He looks like a movie star. No, a model. Better yet, a professional ballplayer. Never mind any of that. He looks* foine*! And I am going to be on his arm.*

Niya swallowed hard as he smiled while he walked over to her. It was as if she was in a movie and everything was in slow motion. As they stood face-to-face, neither one said anything for a moment.

She finally spoke. "Gavin."

"Niya," he responded.

"Okay, ladies and gentlemen, take your places. Line up in order, and for God's sake, please put those phones away. I have told you time and time again that there will be no selfies allowed during the cotillion. This is not the time or the place." Mrs. Knight, who was usually quite calm, said anxiously.

"You look incredible, Niya," Gavin said as he led her to their place in line.

"Thank you, Gavin. You look amazing," Niya told him. "I'm so nervous."

"You don't have to be. I got you." He moved his arm and gave her hand a squeeze. "I'm glad you asked me to do this with you."

"I'm glad you said yes." She laughed.

"And I'm glad we made up after that stupid IG post. I still can't believe you thought I would say anything like that about you. I would never do that." Gavin looked her in the eye. "There's something I've been meaning to ask you."

"What is it?" Niya's eyebrows furrowed.

"All talking needs to cease. And if you have gum in your mouth, you need to remove it," Mrs. Knight instructed.

"Well, I've really gotten to know you over the past few weeks," he said.

"Caleb, where are your gloves? Jira, put that phone away." Mrs. Knight's voice seemed distant, even though she was only a few feet away. "I'm not gonna tell you again."

"Yes, ma'am, Mrs. Knight. But can I at least get a pic with you?" Jira said sweetly.

"Fine. Then put it away."

Niya blocked out everything else, and her eyes remained glued on Gavin as he leaned closer so she could hear.

"Niya, will you be my girlfriend?"

"And we are walking!" Mrs. Knight yelled before Niya could answer.

The doors opened, and the processional began its march out of the room and into the grand ballroom. Gavin looked horrified, but he and Niya had no choice but to walk. The line seemed to go on forever, until they finally stopped a few feet away from the door they were to walk through. Reese and the fathers were waiting in their places. Niya saw him and waved.

His girlfriend. Gavin has asked me to be his girlfriend. Niya was so excited that she felt as if she would explode. She couldn't wait to tell Jada, who was already inside the grand ballroom. *And Kendall. I need to tell Kendall.*

"Niya?" Gavin whispered her name.

"Huh?" She turned and looked at him.

"You didn't answer," he said. "I mean, if you need time to think . . ."

"I have to ask you something," Niya said quickly.

"Okay. Ask."

"Which do you prefer? French fries or baked potatoes?" she asked.

"Fathers, to your debs." Mrs. Knight snapped her fingers.

Niya held her breath as she watched her uncle approach. They were running out of time. "Which one?"

"Uh, I mean, I like both," Gavin said. Then he added, "But I prefer baked potatoes."

Niya smiled and whispered, "Yes, Gavin, I'd love to be your girlfriend."

Gavin nodded and gave her a quick hug before moving so Reese could take his place beside her.

"Ready, Ni-Ni?" Reese asked.

"I am," Niya told him.

Reese

The tension in the hotel's grand ballroom was so thick, one would've thought that the people inside were waiting to hear the name of the politician who'd won the presidential election, not the name of the debutante who would be crowned queen of the ball. Two young ladies, Jira and Niya, stood beside the emcee, waiting with anticipation. Reese gave Niya a reassuring smile as she stood center stage, wearing the "Miss Congeniality" sash she'd been presented with moments before. In a perfect world, her name would be called again. She'd told him time and time again that there was no way she'd be crowned and that her friend Jira was a sure winner, but he still held out hope that a small miracle would happen and she'd win.

"The queen of this year's First Noel Ball is Miss Jira Phillips," the emcee announced.

Applause erupted, and everyone stood. Niya didn't win, but based on the way she was celebrating her friend's achievement, she wasn't disappointed at all. The two young ladies hugged and smiled at one another. Reese took out his phone to capture the moment to send to Kendall. Though she hadn't responded at all when he'd reached out, he'd continually sent her photos throughout the evening. He glanced at one of the two empty chairs at the VIP table his mother had secured. One of those empty chairs was reserved for Kendall.

"This was amazing. I'm so glad we're here," said Emmi, who looked stunning in her formfitting gown.

"Man, me too. I thought this was gonna be a chance to witness my boy here embarrassing himself in a tux." Rick playfully hit Reese's shoulder. "That didn't happen, but it was still great."

"Thanks, Mrs. Fine, for the invitation." Captain Yates nodded at Reese's mother.

Having his boss and Emmi and Rick at the event was a welcome surprise. He had thought Rick was kidding when he mentioned coming to the ball, but his mother had personally invited his boss and his two coworkers and given them three tickets to be Reese's guests. She had also reached out to Niya's best friend, Jada, and invited her family. Typically, those seats at the Fine Foundation table were reserved for board members and endowment donors, who requested tickets months in advance and were lucky enough to be deemed worthy by Claudia, who rarely attended the event herself. This year, however, that table was full of those who truly meant something to the family.

Now that the formal program of the cotillion was over, the fun part began. Reese quickly made his way through the thick crowd toward Niya.

"Can you believe this?" Niya pointed to her red sash.

"I can." He nodded and hugged her. "Who else is more congenious than you, Ni-Ni?"

Niya laughed. "Is that even a word, Uncle Reese?"

Claudia stepped out from behind her son and faced Niya. "I don't believe it is."

"I'm sorry I didn't continue the family legacy." Niya's gaze fell to the floor. "I wasn't crowned queen."

"Of course you did." Claudia smiled. "You, my dear, are the ultimate queen. I'm so proud of you."

"Me too, Niya!" Jada exclaimed as she ran over. She hugged Niya tight.

"Excuse me, Mrs. Fine?"

They all turned and stared at the man standing behind Claudia. It took a second for Reese to realize that it was Gavin's grandfather. Every other time Reese had seen him, he'd been in coveralls and a hat. Although they were at a formal event, and all the other men wore tuxedos, it was still an odd sight to see him so dressed up.

"Hey there, Mr. Carmichael." Reese shook his hand. "You're looking sharp, sir."

"You as well." Mr. Carmichael nodded. "And, Niya, you are an absolute dream. My grandson is one lucky young man."

"Thank you." Niya grinned.

Mr. Carmichael turned and asked, "Claudia, would you do me the honor?"

"Why, Vernon, I'd be honored." Claudia beamed and held her hand out. He took her hand, and the two headed toward the dance floor.

Niya shrugged at Reese. "Claudia?"

Reese glanced back at her. "Vernon?"

The two stood there laughing until Niya's eyes widened and she rushed past him and screamed, "Kendall!"

Reese turned and watched Niya rush over to Kendall, who was a few feet away, standing beside Amber. Both ladies were gorgeous, but Kendall was stunning. Her black beaded gown was form-fitting, flawlessly hugged her luscious curves, and made her ample cleavage even more inviting than it already was. Her hair was pulled back into a smooth ponytail on one side and hung over her shoulder. He didn't even care about the makeup on her face, because in his mind, she was already beautiful without it.

Damn. She's here. His heart leapt, and there was no denying the sensation that charged through his body, letting him know that he wanted her in more ways than one. Everything within him wanted to run behind Niya and grab Kendall into his arms. But he remained in place, watching and waiting.

Rick strolled over just then. "Yo, *that's* Kendall?" he asked. "Shorty got face *and* body, man. I see why you ain't wanna put me on. You was blocking."

"Oh, he definitely was," Emmi agreed. "But she's here now for you to pull up on, Rick. She's gorgeous. Go for it."

"Bet." Rick straightened his tie. "I think I will."

Reese watched in horror as his best friend walked off, and then he glared at Emmi. "Why would you do that?"

"Do what? Certainly, you're not interested in her, are you? Because if you truly were, you wouldn't be standing here looking dumb and letting Rick shoot his shot." Emmi sighed. "You've been moping for days about this woman. You're miserable without her."

"You're right, but she won't talk to me. I've tried, and Niya's tried, but it's pointless." Reese shook his head.

"Here's an idea." Emmi grabbed Reese's shoulders. "We're at a ball. Instead of trying to get her to talk, you ask her to dance."

Reese raised an eyebrow. "I mean . . . you think that'll work?"

"I don't know, but if I were you, I'd at least try." Emmi gave him a push.

Try. Try harder. Keep trying. He couldn't seem to escape those words. He took a deep breath and decided that he was done trying and failing. It was time for him to start succeeding.

Kendall

"I can't believe you're here. Oh my goodness! Thank you so much." Niya threw her arms around Kendall so hard that she nearly knocked her over.

After holding her for a few seconds, Kendall heard the soft sobs and realized Niya was crying. "Niya, sweetie, don't cry."

"You're here," Niya repeated over and over.

Kendall, now fighting back tears, looked over at Amber and saw that she, too, was crying and thus wasn't going to be much help other than rubbing Niya's back. It was evident that her decision to attend the ball was a good one. Being in her feelings about Reese had been selfish, and Kendall felt bad about that. She should've been by Niya's side all day for support.

"I'm here," Kendall whispered, and Niya finally released her hold.

"I have so much to tell you. My best friend, Jada, is here. You've gotta meet her . . . oh, and Gavin. I've gotta tell you about him too. Wait, everyone loves my dress and keeps asking who made it. So many people want your information. And I won Miss Congeniality," Niya exclaimed.

"I was here when you won." Kendall laughed.

"Attention. We need all debutantes to the lobby for photos," a woman announced. *"Now."*

"Ugh. I have to go. Mrs. Knight will spaz if I don't show up." Niya looked frantically at Kendall. "Please don't leave," she begged.

"Girl, the ball just started. I'm not going anywhere, I promise," Kendall said. Niya hugged her once more, then rushed off.

"I'm glad to hear that."

Kendall turned around. Reese was standing so close that she had no choice but to look at him, something she'd avoided doing all night. During the father-daughter waltz, she'd forced herself to focus only on Niya and pretend she didn't see how incredible he looked. It had been a struggle, and after the dance had ended and he returned to his seat, she'd found herself biting her bottom lip. *He looks good. Real good,* she'd thought. She'd been surprised that she hadn't spotted his girlfriend, not that she'd looked for her.

"Hello, Reese." Kendall's body shifted nervously, and she suddenly felt hot. Thankfully, Amber had agreed not to leave her side, so that she wouldn't risk being alone with Reese.

At that very moment, a handsome guy walked over and asked, "And who are these lovely ladies?"

"Uh, this is Kendall, and this is Amber," Reese replied, introducing them. "This is Rick, my best friend."

"Nice to meet you," Amber replied and extended her hand, and Rick immediately kissed it, instead of shaking it. Kendall knew her friend was instantly charmed. Within seconds, the two of them were heading to the bar.

Clearly, she has forgotten the plan for the night, Kendall thought.

"I . . . it's . . . ," Reese stammered. "Kendall, would you like to dance?"

Kendall was caught off guard by his request. She'd expected uncomfortable small talk and an awkward silence between them. "Huh?"

Instead of repeating himself, Reese took her by the hand and guided her to the dance floor. She placed her arms around his neck and continued to avoid his eyes as his hands rested on her hips. Her head turned, and she saw Claudia dancing and laughing with a handsome man. Claudia looked over at Kendall and smiled.

Reese leaned in and spoke into her ear so he could be heard over Anita Baker singing about sweet love. "So, you're going to avoid looking at me all night?" The scent of his cologne wafted into her nose as his arms pulled her closer, inviting her into a space she was trying not to enter.

"I'm not avoiding you, Reese," Kendall lied and lifted her eyes toward his handsome face.

"We both know better than that." He gave her a knowing glance. "You've been avoiding me since the night of the party, and we both know why."

"It's okay, Reese. We're cool."

"We're not cool. Niya overheard part of a conversation, and . . . "

"Reese, Niya already told me everything, and so did you in your texts, voicemails, and emails. I get it." Kendall sighed.

"So, you *did* get my messages." He smiled.

"I did. All of them. And I appreciate the effort. Like I said, we're cool."

"Then why the cold shoulder? Why have you refused to talk to me?" he asked, a sincere look on his face.

"Because we were getting too close, and the last thing I want to do is fall for someone who is unavailable and can't give me everything I need emotionally, physically, mentally. I deserve someone that's confident in who they are and knows what they want, and that's not you, Reese. And that's fine," Kendall explained.

"But I am available, and I know what I want, Kendall."

"Yeah, now you do. It shouldn't have taken your girl at the time disrespecting me for you to realize that. That's something you should've figured out long before then. You didn't," Kendall said. "But, again, it's cool. There's really nothing more to say."

"You're wrong. There is a lot for me to say." Reese stopped moving, even though the music was still playing. His stare was so intense that Kendall almost became lost in it and forgot where they were. "I have to say how miserable I've been because I couldn't talk to you. I could barely function at work, and that's dangerous, considering I save lives for a living. You are right. I had no idea how much I needed you until I lost you. But I have known that I wanted you from the day I met you. And I'm confident about how much I'm in love with you, Kendall Freeman."

"Reese—" Kendall whispered.

She couldn't say anything else, because Reese cupped her face with his hands, then leaned in and kissed her. Her eyes closed, and she savored the taste of his mouth on hers, enjoyed the softness of his lips. Her heart was so full that she felt as if she was dreaming, but as the kiss ended and her eyes fluttered open, she was relieved that the moment was real. They smiled at one another. Then Kendall looked around and saw the bubbles that floated in the air about them and the stares of the people around them.

"Did you plan this?" she asked.

Reese laughed. "I couldn't have planned something as perfect as this." He kissed her again, this time playfully, before they walked off the dance floor.

Deena stopped them. "Well, Kendall, you look lovely tonight. I didn't know you'd be attending the ball."

Kendall smiled. "Hey, Deena. It was a last-minute decision. You look nice."

Deena's eyes went to Reese. "Oh, you were at the party. Nice to see you again. Kendall, may I speak to you for a moment?"

"Sure." Kendall nodded, then glanced at Reese. "I'll be right back."

She and Deena made their way outside the ballroom. Kendall decided she'd let her boss talk and she'd listen, in order for the conversation to be brief as possible, so she could go back inside.

"Can you please explain what's going on?" Deena crossed her long, lean arms. The only thing modest about her dress was the long sleeves. The formfitting mermaid design with the plunging neckline left little to the imagination. The bright floral print was bold, daring, and achieved her goal to stand out in the crowd, as if she needed any help doing so. "I'm . . . just lost about all of this."

"There's nothing to explain, really," Kendall declared. "It's my angel assignment, that's all."

"*Your* angel assignment? How so? Do you know how much effort I put into *my* angel assignment? Had I known you had all of this going on, I definitely wouldn't have gotten involved." Deena shook her head in disbelief. "When I asked you if something was going on, you said no. The entire time, you were lying."

"I wasn't lying, Deena. I just . . . didn't think it was a big deal," Kendall told her.

"Oh, it's a big deal. And now I'm caught in the middle of this conundrum. Do you know how this is going to make me look?"

"Deena, I swear, I didn't think anyone would say anything to you about it." Kendall began to regret not being honest and telling Deena about designing Niya's gown. Now that the word was out, there was no telling how many people had asked her about it.

"Why would they not? I was the one who went to Simon in the first place." Deena exhaled. "This is a mess."

Kendall was confused. "Simon? What does he have to do with any of this?"

"He's the one I chose for you."

"Chose for *what*?" Kendall was even more baffled now.

"For you to be with. That was my angel assignment this year, to help you find love. Luigi mentioned you had had a crush on Simon for a while, so I spoke with him and encouraged him to pursue you." Deena delivered this news as if it was no big deal.

"You what?" Kendall didn't know whether to laugh or cuss. It all made sense—Simon expressing a sudden interest and then showing up at the company holiday party. It was Deena's doing.

"I told him that you'd been single for a while, and I thought that maybe . . ."

"Oh, Kendall, there you are," Mrs. Tucker called, then rushed over to where they were talking. Her gown, the one Kendall had reconstructed, now fit perfectly. "Hello, Deena. This is Mrs. Knight, the First Noel Society's director and the coordinator of this year's cotillion."

"Nice to meet you, Mrs. Knight. Everything has been wonderful. You did a phenomenal job," Deena said.

"I need to get back inside. Excuse me," Kendall announced, then turned to walk away.

Mrs. Tucker touched Kendall's arm. "No, Kendall, don't go. Mrs. Knight wanted to meet you."

"Meet me?" Kendall asked as she turned back.

"Yes. You designed Niya's gown, right?" Mrs. Knight said. "Your work is incredible. Do you have a card? I have several clients that I know would love you."

"Kendall is the seamstress at Diablo's," Mrs. Tucker boasted. "She did my alterations."

"Seamstress? Young lady, that gown is far beyond the work of a seamstress. You have a gift." Mrs. Knight smiled.

"Yes, she does." Deena put her arm around Kendall's shoulder. "And we would love to assist your clients at the boutique. Feel free to send them in, and I assure you they'll be well taken care of, right, Kendall?"

"Yes." Kendall nodded.

"Well, that's the thing. They've visited your boutique, but unfortunately, you don't offer any items in their size range. Not everyone is a size six, you know, including myself." Mrs. Knight moved her hands along both sides of her body, which Kendall estimated was a solid size fourteen.

"Oh, see, that's the thing . . . Kendall and I were just discussing the possibility of adding designs of hers that a few above average–size clients could choose from," Deena lied.

"I don't think that's gonna be possible," Claudia Fine declared as she strolled over and joined them. Her dance partner remained a few feet away.

"Claudia, wonderful to see you." Deena's voice was as fake as her smile. "What exactly are you referring to?"

"You weren't aware that Kendall was starting her own line after the beginning of the year? I was sure you'd heard," Claudia revealed. "One of the endeavors that the Fine Foundation will be undertaking this upcoming year is to partner with Carmichael Inc. to provide a grant for minority women–owned start-ups. Kendall Freeman Designs is one of our recipients."

Kendall nearly fainted. She wondered if someone was pulling a practical joke and if there was a hidden camera recording her reaction.

"Oh really?" Deena looked as if she smelled something sour. "I wasn't aware. Congratulations, Kendall."

"Thank you, Deena." Kendall was still somewhat in shock.

"Kendall, dear, can you let my son, Reese, and the other guests at our table know I stepped out and I'll be back shortly?" She winked.

"Yes, ma'am." Kendall nodded. "Ladies."

Reese stood from his chair as soon as he spotted Kendall. "Everything okay?" he asked when she reached the VIP table.

She looked at him. "Everything is great. Your mom just told me I won a Fine Foundation grant. Did you know anything about this?"

"No, I didn't. But congratulations." He hugged her. "You deserve it and so much more."

Kendall looked around the ballroom. It all seemed so magical. Niya was across the room, laughing with Gavin and her friends. Amber was on the dance floor, having the time of her life with Rick. And then there was her, standing beside the man of her dreams, who held her close.

"I have more than I ever hoped for," Kendall told him. "Kendall Freeman Bridal Designs. How does that sound?"

"Bridal designs?" He grinned.

"Big girls get married too, you know." She nudged him.

"Oh, I know, and I already know you'd make a perfectly *fine* bride." He kissed her forehead.

Kendall could only hope and pray his words were as true as she felt.

Epilogue

Claudia

"Someone's having too much fun."

"Oh really? Who?" Claudia asked as Vernon led her back into the ballroom and straight to the dance floor.

"You know who. But I'm enjoying watching you enjoy yourself." Vernon put his arms around her waist, and they began swaying to the music. "It's nice to see the old Claudia."

"Old Claudia?" She frowned.

"The Claudia I met in Mr. Graham's history class all those years ago, the one with the long hair and short skirts." He grinned. "And beautiful eyes."

"My skirts were never short, Vernon Carmichael. You need to stop lying." She playfully tapped his shoulder. He was still tall and handsome. That had never changed over the years, but so many other things had.

"Well, I wanted them to be short. Then again, I wanted a lot of things back then," Vernon said with a sentimental look in his eyes. "This has been a long time coming."

"What has?" Claudia asked.

"Me, you, dancing together at the First Noel Ball. It took only fifty years. But here we are." He put his cheek against hers.

"Indeed, we are." She closed her eyes.

He was right; this had been a long time coming. It was fifty years ago that she'd been selected to be a debutante of the ball being hosted by the first black society club in the city. She had been ecstatic and had known exactly who she wanted to invite: Vernon Carmichael, the handsome classmate who carried her books to class every day. She'd asked him, and he'd said yes. But her mother objected and insisted that Claudia choose someone else instead. Reginald Fine attended their church. He was a college boy and was slightly older and from a prominent family. He was a better choice than Vernon, whose only claim to fame was being the dependable guy who cut yards in the neighborhoods. It broke Claudia's heart when she told Vernon that she had another escort. It also broke his. The heartbreak continued over the years: when she married Reginald, had his babies, and became a socialite. They became distant strangers, and yet something between them remained, for decades.

Niya being escorted by Vernon's grandson wasn't ironic. It was fate.

"When do you want me to come take the angel off the tree?" Vernon whispered, bringing her out of her revery.

"Whenever you can make time," she told him, smiling at the memory of him nearly falling from the ladder he brought inside the house after she called him and asked for his help with the angel. That favor had resulted in her agreeing to join him for lunch, then meet him for dinner. Soon, there were long phone calls and walks around the tree lot. With Vernon, she had found a trusted friend and confidant, and someone who pointed out her shortcomings as a mother and grandmother.

"I always have time for you. I don't put those lights around your house for free every year for nothing, you know." He leaned back and said, "And speaking of time, how much longer until you give me my answer?"

Claudia pretended she had no idea what he was talking about. "About?"

"About marrying me," Vernon reminded her.

Claudia stared into the eyes of the man she'd loved for five decades. "Yes, Vernon Carmichael. I will marry you."

Vernon's eyes widened, and she saw the tears form.

It had been a long time since she'd been this happy. At one time, she had thought she'd never find joy again. She'd been wrong. She experienced joy with her son and her granddaughter, whom she loved dearly. And now she would also share all the love, joy, and happiness she had with Vernon. Life was finally perfectly fine.

The end . . . maybe. LOL.

Also from La Jill Hunt

Large and In Charge

Prologue

Devyn

"You look beautiful, sweetheart."

Devyn looked at her mother, who'd just placed the lacy, cathedral-length veil into her hair. "Mom, please don't cry. You promised."

"I can't help it. You're breathtaking," her mother sniffed.

"She's right. You are, Dev." Asha, her best friend of over twenty years, passed Devyn's mother a tissue. "That dress is absolutely perfect—everything is. The church, the bridesmaids . . ."

"Thanks to you." Devyn reached over and grabbed Asha's hand.

"Can't say I wish you had a different groom, but . . ." Asha smirked.

"Ash." Devyn gave her a warning look. "Not today."

Despite their decades of friendship, Asha not only declined Devyn's invitation to be her maid of honor, but she also refused even to be a brides-maid. Her reason? Because she believed that when people accept their positions as members of the bridal party, they stand in solidarity with the bride and groom. And in doing so, they are declaring in front of God and the world that they support the marriage, which Asha absolutely did not. She'd voiced her opinion on more than one occasion about how she disliked Devyn's fiancé, Tremell Simmons, even before he put a ring on her finger.

Devyn and Tremell had dated less than a year before he popped the question on the biggest night of her career. She'd just walked the runway of her first designer show at New York Fashion Week and exited the stage where he was waiting for her on bended knee with a ring in hand and a photographer and videographer to capture it all. Asha felt that Tremell was using Devyn, who was known professionally as D'Morgan, and who was making waves in the modeling world, as a come-up. Tremell believed Asha was jealous of their whirlwind romance that was often displayed in the blogs and on social media. Devyn's followers and fans soon became his. Tremell was head over heels in love with Devyn and would accompany her when she traveled for work, despite his own schedule being full as he pursued his music career.

"She's right, you know." Scorpio, Devyn's matron of honor, turned toward the bride. The legendary cover model who mentored Devyn looked stunning in her chartreuse gown, custom-made by the same designer she'd commissioned to design Devyn's dress for both the ceremony and reception. "But so are you. Now is not the time for that conversation."

"I agree." Devyn's mother looked a little uncomfortable by the discussion the bridal party members were having.

"Well, considering he's about to be her husband, we probably shouldn't be having this conversation ever again. She has made her decision, and all we can do is support our girl." Chastity, also known as Chase, was the maid of honor who looked equally as beautiful as the other ladies. She put her arm around Devyn. "We got you, Dev."

Devyn looked at her small, two-person bridal party and sighed. "I get it. Tremell isn't anyone's favorite choice for me to marry. But he's my choice. He's not perfect, and neither am I, and for the record, none of y'all are either, but I love the shit out of y'all. Sorry, Mom." Devyn glanced at her mother.

"It's okay, sweetie." Her mother nodded. "Your foul mouth is excused this one time."

"Like I was saying, I love Tremell, he loves me, and despite the arguing sometimes—"

"Sometimes?" Asha groaned.

"Yes, occasionally." Devyn shrugged. "We make a good team. He's going to win a Grammy one day, and I'm gonna be right by his side when he does."

"Damn, he really is getting a good one," Scorpio whispered to Asha. "I hate to say this, but it'll be a miracle if he even gets signed to a major label."

"I have faith in him." Devyn reached for the bottle of Voss water on the dresser and took a long sip. She'd tried to minimize how much she drank all day so she wouldn't spend her entire wedding running to pee. Constant thirst was something she'd had all her life, but it had been even worse over the past few months, along with dizzy spells. The stress of her rising career and planning a wedding in a short time were wreaking havoc on her. *At least I'll be able to relax on our honeymoon. The beaches of Belize are only hours away.*

"You don't need his faith, boo. You're about to sign with one of the biggest modeling agencies in the world and be walking alongside me." Scorpio winked. Devyn was grateful because she'd been the one to put everything in motion for the contract she was signing as soon as they returned from their trip.

Someone knocked on the door. Asha opened it, and Devyn's uncle, who had agreed to escort her down the aisle, stuck his head inside.

"I'm supposed to pick up a package and deliver it to the sanctuary," he said.

"Julian, you look so nice." Devyn's mother told him.

"You do, Uncle Julian." Devyn agreed.

"Thank you. I do clean up nice, don't I?" Uncle Julian grinned as he displayed the diamond cuff links Devyn had given him as a gift.

"Ladies, I guess we need to get in place. Devyn, are you ready?" Asha asked one final time.

"I am." Devyn nodded.

Scorpio looked over at Asha and asked, "You guys made sure no outside press is here, right?"

Tremell wasn't thrilled about that but finally agreed when Devyn told him that she would not permit any press at the event, and Scorpio's security detail would be on deck to make sure.

"Of course," Asha nodded. "Security is in place and knows that only photographers and videographers that have been signed off on are allowed. Thc guests have been instructed that there's to be no cell phone recording during the ceremony."

"Good." Scorpio nodded and headed out the door with Asha and Chase behind her.

Before Devyn's mother walked out, she paused, taking another long look at her daughter. "You are the best thing God blessed me with. Today is a day I prayed I'd see happen. Thank you."

"Mom, you're really being extra." Devyn wiped a tear from her eye. "And thank you because you are the best thing God blessed me with."

"Well, I'm glad he blessed me with both of you, but we kinda gotta get going," Uncle Julian walked in and said.

"I love you." Devyn's mom kissed her cheek, then pressed her forehead against hers for an extended moment, as she'd done so many times before.

"I love you too." Devyn smiled, fighting back the tears as she watched her mother walk out the door.

This is it. I'm getting married. This is really happening, Devyn thought as she stood beside her uncle in the vestibule of the church. The sound of the saxophonist playing "All of Me" faded, and the first chords of the "Wedding March" began. Devyn's heart raced, and the slight pain in her chest that she'd been ignoring for the past few days started to increase, along with slight dizziness. *Damn it. I should've grabbed my water.*

"You all right?" Uncle Julian gave her a concerned look.

"I'm fine. Just runway jitters." Devyn nodded. "I get them all the time before I walk."

Asha's nod signaled that it was time. The doors opened, and Devyn took a deep breath as she took her first step. The sanctuary pews were full of invited guests, most of whom Devyn didn't know. Unlike herself, Tremell came from a large family. She smiled under her veil at the sound of the *ooohs* and *aaahs* as she walked. Standing at the altar was her groom, looking handsome in his white tuxedo. Devyn could already picture in her mind how gorgeous their wedding photos would be. She glanced around, making sure she knew exactly where the photographer was located and was surprised that she saw three instead of two. But she continued. When she got to the front, she smiled at Tremell, who looked more nervous than she did.

"Who gives this woman to be wed?" the minister asked.

"I do," Uncle Julian proudly announced, then meticulously lifted Devyn's veil, kissed her, and whispered, "I love you."

He took his seat next to her mother on the front row. Devyn took Tremell's hand, and they faced each other. The sweat on his forehead was visible. He shifted his weight from one leg to the other.

"You're beautiful, Dev," he whispered. "Oh my God."

"Thanks, boo." Devyn gave him a quick, reassuring wink in an effort to comfort him.

"Dearly beloved, we are gathered here today to join together in holy matrimony Devyn Morgan Douglass and Tremell Devaughn Simmons. Tremell, please repeat after me. I, Tremell."

Tremell swallowed and didn't say anything. Devyn frowned.

The minister repeated the vow, this time a little louder. "I, Tremell."

Devyn's heart pounded as she waited for Tremell to repeat the words.

Finally, he spoke, "I-I'm sorry, D."

Devyn lightly cleared her throat and leaned closer. "What?"

"I . . . I can't do this. I'm sorry." Tremell shook his head. The unison gasps from everyone were so loud that they seemed to bounce off the church walls and echo, followed by mumbling.

The reality of what was happening finally registered in her head. She refused to look away from Tremell, even though he no longer looked at her as he rubbed the back of his head nervously. *This fool is trying to jilt me. He's trying to leave me at the altar. Wait. No, the fuck he ain't.* She closed her eyes for a second, and before the cascading bouquet of dusty rose and ivory cottage roses in her hand fell to the ground, her fingers had formed a fist and connected with his jaw so hard, it nearly knocked him backward. His best man caught him, and as he regained his balance, she used the elbow of the same arm to strike again, then charged at him.

"Noooo!" the pastor yelled.

Devyn couldn't tell who was screaming and didn't care. She was too busy trying to tear off Tremell's head while maneuvering in the fitted gown. A pair of strong arms managed to pull her from the floor.

"Are you crazy?" Tremell screamed and scrambled to his feet. Blood oozed from the scratches on his face and fell on his white tuxedo jacket, creating what looked like crimson polka dots.

"Get off me! Let me go!" Devyn shrieked and continued to try to reach him. She was breathing so hard that she panted. Her chest was on fire. Tremell's groomsmen pulled him up and sheltered him while the minister quickly jumped in front of them.

"She's crazy! She's crazy!" Tremell yelled as he reached toward Devyn while his boys prevented him from doing so and guided him toward the side door. Total chaos erupted with people leaping out of their seats, shocked at what they witnessed and not knowing how to react.

Devyn lurched toward Tremell once more. This time, she was stopped by the pulling of her hair with the veil still attached. Enraged and determined to get free, Devyn turned and struck her captor with as much strength as she had struck Tremell moments before. Scorpio, the recipient of Devyn's blow, instinctively grabbed her to keep from falling, and they both tumbled to the ground. Within seconds, Scorpio's security guard yanked Devyn off and scooped Scorpio into his arms, carrying her out.

Finally, Devyn stopped. She turned toward the guests. The church was so quiet. The only thing heard was her heavy breathing. Her mother's eyes met hers, and despite wanting to rush into her arms and cry, Devyn decided to stand and handle this situation. She picked her crumpled veil off the floor, along with the tattered remnants of her bouquet.

After adjusting the lace on her head and straightening her dress, she proudly said, "There will not be a wedding today. Thank you for coming." Devyn then proceeded with the signature walk that she usually reserved for the runway shows, with her head held high, until she walked out the door. Asha and Chase were by her side within seconds, along with her mother and uncle.

"Devyn, oh my God! Someone call an ambulance!" Those were the last words Devyn heard as she crumpled to the floor in the church foyer and experienced a loss of consciousness.

Chapter 1

Devyn

Two Years Later

Devyn looked down at her Apple Watch for what seemed like the hundredth time in the past hour. This was her last class for the day, and she was beyond ready to go. Usually, the afternoon would quickly pass after lunch, but that wasn't the case today, most likely because the students were more rowdy than usual and because the classroom they were in was hot as hell, which didn't help.

"All right, settle down," Devyn said, her tone indicating that her level of patience was running low. "There is no need for all of these discussions. You've been given your assignment. Now, complete it quietly."

"This is too much work," one of the students groaned.

"And we haven't even gone over this stuff, Ms. Douglass. How are we supposed to know how to do this?" another one asked.

Hell, I don't know, Devyn thought as she looked down at the instructions that went along with the assignment she'd just given. Instead of saying the words she was thinking, she gave an empathetic shrug and said, "Just do the best you can. I'm sure Mrs. Hughes will go over the information when she returns next week."

"Next week? I heard she wasn't coming back until after Spring Break," a cute girl with a short bob and braces informed her.

"That's what I heard too." The girl sitting next to her nodded as she confirmed the information.

Within seconds, the complaints about the assignment quickly changed to a discussion about their teacher's absence. Devyn didn't know whether the rumors about why Mrs. Hughes was out were true, and she didn't really care. All she wanted was for the students to settle down for the remainder of the class, and somehow, someway, she needed to get some air.

"Enough! Now, settle down, do your work, and for God's sake, someone open the windows," Devyn pleaded. "It's burning up in here."

Nathan, one of the male students sitting closest to the windows, quickly jumped to his feet and honored her request. The slight breeze that entered the room was barely noticeable, but it was enough to bring a little coolness to the swelter that was the source of Devyn's growing perspiration. The class began to settle as quickly as the air did. She reached into the desk drawer where her purse was located and fumbled until she found a small pack of Kleenex and a compact. She removed some tissue and stared into the mirror as she dabbed along her forehead, nose, and the top of her lip.

"Stop, Nathan!"

Devyn put the mirror down and frowned as she tried to locate the voice. "What's the problem now?"

"He keeps leaning over and singing something about 'come and feel him.'" Clarissa glared at Nathan, sitting at the desk beside her.

Nathan innocently shook his head. "I wasn't singing."

"Well, he was rapping in my ear," Clarissa clarified.

"Nathan, why are you being disruptive?" Devyn sighed.

"I wasn't tryin'a be disruptive, Ms. Douglass. I was just tryin'a let her know *'I been wit' supermodels even before I was signed, and she tall and beautiful and beyond hella fine. But I had to let her go. I couldn't be tied down because chasing money was more important than me staying around. You tryin'a be wit' me, you betta show me just how much you wanna be by my side because it takes a whole lot for you to get on this ride. Now come and feel me.'"*

"That's my jam."

"You did that, Nate."

"He snapped on that jank."

While Nathan's classmates clapped and showed their enthusiasm, Devyn remained stoic, unmoved by his impromptu performance. She wasn't amused or entertained.

"Apologize to her. Now," Devyn told him.

"Awww, Miss Douglass, I ain't do nothing. I was just playin'." Nathan shrugged. "She just trippin'. It's just a song by this rapper named Touché. It's called 'Come and Feel Me.'"

"I don't care if it's a song. It's disrespectful. Apologize," Devyn repeated.

Nathan stared at Devyn for a moment, then cut his eyes toward Clarissa. "I'm sorry that you're so sensitive that you can't take a joke. That's why nobody wanna come and feel you."

Once again, the class erupted in laughter. Devyn closed her eyes and tried to count backward from ten, hoping that by the time she got to one, the profanity-filled tirade she was on the brink of releasing would be gone.

"Aye, what's going on in here?"

The noise in the class subsided as Officer Jeff Baker, the school security officer, walked in. Devyn slowly released the breath she hadn't realized she was holding as he approached the center of the classroom. He was good-natured and friendly, but the students knew not to play with him.

"I can hear y'all all the way down the hallway. I know you wouldn't be acting up like this if Mrs. Hughes was up in here, now, would you?" He looked around at the students. When no one answered, he repeated his question, "Would you?"

"No, sir," a few students murmured.

"That's what I thought." He nodded. Just as he was about to say something else, the ringing of the bell stopped him, and the class began shuffling and moving as they grabbed their belongings and got up to leave. "Wait, I ain't hear Miss Douglass say anyone was dismissed."

All eyes were on Devyn, including Jeff's. Devyn exhaled and told them, "Class dismissed."

"You good?" Jeff asked when the last student was out the door.

"Yeah, I'm fine. It's just hot in here, and they were a little out of pocket," Devyn explained. "I really could have handled it. But thanks for assisting. I appreciate it."

"I know you could handle it. You're one of the best subs we got around here. But you're right. This classroom is a furnace. Mrs. Hughes got low iron, so she keeps it warm in here. Not to mention, she's the only one with a key to the thermostat."

Jeff pointed to the small case on the wall secured with a lock. "I'm surprised the windows weren't locked too. That's probably why the class was off the chain. They ain't used to getting fresh air in here."

"Well, if they plan on having me cover for her while she's out, they'd better hurry up and find another key," Devyn smiled. "You don't know how close I was to cussing them kids out today."

"Oh, I could tell. When I got to the door, I heard that li'l rap performance, and as soon as I saw your face, I knew you were not happy at all," Jeff teased.

"I was not," Devyn agreed as she gathered her belongings and stood. "I almost ran out of the room with them."

"I feel ya. Well, at least the day is over. You got plans for the weekend?" Jeff smiled.

"What? Isn't today just Tuesday?" Devyn asked, confused by his question and wondering why he was concerned about the weekend already. She barely knew what she was doing the next day, let alone the weekend. *Girl, don't even trip. You know the only weekend plans you have are the same ones you have every weekend: watch Lifetime movies, make herbal tea blends, and sleep.*

"Yeah, it is. But if you aren't busy, I was gonna invite you to a card party at the crib. It's gonna be fun. You should come," Jeff suggested. "I got someone for you to meet."

"I'm not really a card player, but thanks," Devyn shrugged as they walked toward the door.

"Fine. You don't have to play cards. Just come, have a few drinks, get a plate, and meet new people. My boy is a chef, and he's about to open his own spot." Jeff remained by her side as she walked down the hallway toward the school's front office to sign out.

"I'm good."

"I know. That's why I'm inviting you. I only invite good people to my crib, feel me? So, you should consider yourself special." Jeff winked at her. "And I'm not just saying that because you're gorgeous, and my boys would be impressed that you showed up and give me mad props. I really think you're cool people, Dev."

Devyn laughed. Jeff was one of the few people at the school that she liked. And it wasn't just because he also happened to be Black, another anomaly at their place of employment. He always checked in on the classes she worked in and made sure she had lunch. He always tried to set her up with a cousin, classmate, or homeboy that he just knew would be "perfect" for her. Devyn kindly declined each one. Jeff was an all-around nice guy, but she didn't know him well enough to trust him with her love life.

"Thanks, Jeff. You're good people too." Devyn reached for the door handle of the office but stopped upon hearing the haunting, familiar words.

"You tryin'a be wit' me ya betta show how much you wanna be by my side because it takes a whole lot for you to get on this ride. Now come and feel me."

Devyn looked down the hallway to see Nathan once again rapping. A couple of his friends bobbed their heads to the beat and served as his backup crew, laughing as they strolled away.

"You okay, Dev?" Jeff's voice came from over her shoulder. She'd been so caught up in her mind that she'd forgotten that he was there.

"Yeah, I'm fine," Devyn finally said. "I hate that fucking song."

Chapter 2

Asha

"I'm sure they didn't mean anything by it, Dev. It's just a popular song right now, that's all." Asha pulled into the parking lot of the Convention Center. "But I get it. You know I do."

"I'm not going to be able to do this much longer, Ash, I promise. Those kids are terrible, and it's hot as hell in that classroom. You know how bad I sweat now that I'm fat." Devyn reminded her just in case she forgot all about the extra twenty-three pounds Devyn's body now contained.

"Girl, shut the hell up. You're not fat." Asha shook her head even though they were on the phone, and Devyn couldn't see her reaction. She only had a few minutes to spare before she had to be inside for a meeting, and there was no way she was going to spend them trying to convince Devyn that there was nothing wrong with her weight. It would be a waste of time anyway. Her best friend was convinced that because she no longer weighed one hundred and twenty-three pounds, she was obese. Of course, this was far from the truth, but Devyn refused to think otherwise. As far as Asha and anyone else with good sense could tell, there was nothing wrong with her body. Devyn was still beautiful, and though she was slightly larger than the average woman, mainly due to her stature, she still had a gorgeous, modelesque body that most women, including Asha, would love to have.

"I am, and we both know it. Look, I understand that Mrs. Hughes is going through a tough time with her divorce and all, but—"

"Wait, who the hell is Mrs. Hughes?"

"The chemistry teacher I'm subbing for."

"Chemistry? Oh hell, those kids gonna fail. You can't calculate how to tip 15 percent properly, and they expect you to teach them children formulas with chemicals? That's dangerous," Asha sighed. "Wait, she's going through a divorce? How do you know all of this?"

"Whatever. I'm a good tipper, and you know it. And I know because the kids told me all about it. She found out her husband was sleeping with her sister's hairstylist," Devyn explained. "She went to the salon and tore shit up when she found out."

"Oh snap, was she arrested?"

"If she was, they didn't mention it. So I think she wasn't."

"Probably not because Lord knows they would've spilled *that* tea right along with the rest of it," Asha laughed.

"Girl, they probably would've pulled up her mug shot and tried to show it to me. I kept telling them to stop talking and do their work."

"Whatever, Dev. You know your nosy ass was probably all ears while they were talking."

"Only for a second before they started with the dumbness and disrespect. They'd better be glad Jeff walked in when he did," Devyn commented. "He set them straight."

"Oh Lord, not the stalker."

"He's not a stalker, Ash. He just has perfect timing," Devyn told her.

"Because he's stalking you," Asha murmured as she looked toward the entrance of the building. Several young ladies were walking in carrying folders and portfolios. "Oh snap, looks like they're having a casting call."

"Who?" Devyn asked.

"I don't know. You want me to find out so you can come?" Asha asked jokingly but slightly hopeful that Devyn would be curious. She'd been subtly trying to encourage her friend to get back into her passion but hadn't been successful yet. Still, Asha wasn't going to give up.

"Hell no. I'm good." Devyn gave the same answer she always had when Asha mentioned modeling.

"I'm just asking because you were the one who said you needed to find something else other than substitute teaching."

"Well, that ain't the something I wanna do, and you know it."

Asha looked at her watch and saw that it was almost time for her appointment. "I gotta get inside to meet this client. We still meeting up for Taco Tuesdays at Pablo's?"

"See? You're such a bad influence. I just told you I was fat, and here you go inviting me to eat tacos and drink margaritas," Devyn teased.

"Who said anything about margaritas, heffa?" Asha laughed. "I'll see you at seven."

Asha ended the call and grabbed her laptop bag before hopping out of her Acura SUV. Her long strides across the parking lot allowed her to make it to the front of the glass door within moments. Being nearly six feet tall did have its benefits. Once inside, she looked around, expecting to find the client she was meeting but didn't see anyone. She ventured further down the corridor toward the ballrooms of the Convention Center.

"Miss Bailey, what brings you to our fine establishment today?"

Asha turned around to see Gail, one of the sales managers, walking toward her.

"Hey, Gail. I'm supposed to be meeting a client, well, a potential client, this afternoon. But I don't think they're here yet," Asha said.

"Oh, okay," Gail nodded.

Asha motioned toward the row of ladies sitting outside one of the ballrooms. "Casting call for an agency?"

"No, they're candidates for a beauty pageant," Gail told her.

"Beauty pageant?" Asha was surprised to hear that, especially in her line of work. Usually, her firm was the first to know about large-scale events in the area, and no one had mentioned anything about it.

"Yeah, it's a big deal, and the first time it's being hosted here this year. Miss Teen Elite." Gail imitated a sophisticated pose. She was an older woman in her late fifties who reminded Asha of Rose from the TV show *Golden Girls*.

"Miss Teen Elite," Asha repeated, glancing at the beautiful but nervous-looking young ladies waiting to be called inside.

"They've been lining up all day, I can tell you that much," Gail said as they went back toward the front of the building. "The woman in charge, Marcia Thompkins, is a piece of work. She has everyone around here stressed."

"I'm sure you say the same thing about me," Asha laughed. She'd worked with Gail on several occasions, and they'd bumped heads a time or two.

"We've had our moments, but working with you is always enjoyable. This woman isn't pleasant at all, and knowing that I have to deal with her for the next six weeks is giving me anxiety," Gail sighed.

"Yikes. Maybe it won't be as bad as you think," Asha suggested.

"Let's pray that it's not." Gail shrugged. "Do you need anything while you wait? Water or coffee? I have some snacks in my office."

"No, thank you. I'm fine," Asha told her.

"Grace!" a stern voice called.

Asha and Gail both turned around. A slender, blond woman dressed in a dark business suit walked toward them with precision and intensity. One look at her blouse tied at the neck in a perfect bow, long, blond tresses, a glammed face, bleach-white teeth, and the word "pageant queen" instantly popped into Asha's head. The only thing missing was a crown and sash announcing the title she probably held in her glory days.

"Oh Christ," Gail murmured, "Here comes Satan."

"I told you we'd need more chairs outside the room. I would hope you wouldn't expect my ladies to stand while waiting," the woman said, her voice as crisp as her blouse.

"Of course not, Mrs. Fisher. My apologies. I was just over near that area, and there were a few empty seats," Gail told her. "And it's Gail."

"Well, there aren't any now," the woman responded, then added, ". . . Gail."

"I'll call maintenance and have them bring some right away," Gail nodded.

"I need them now," the woman said before turning back around and walking away.

"Five weeks, four days, three hours." Gail closed her eyes and inhaled when she was gone.

"Damn, she is a handful." Asha gave a sympathetic look.

"It was nice seeing you again. Let me get these chairs before Cruella returns." Gail rushed off, and Asha took out her phone and dialed her office.

"Great Expectation Events, this is Libby," the administrative assistant answered in her bubbly voice.

"What's up, Libby? It's Asha. Did my four o'clock call?"

"No, I haven't heard anything. Sorry," Libby answered.

"Okay, thanks. I was just checking to be sure before I left." Asha exhaled. This was her last appointment for the day, and she wanted to get home in time to shower and change before meeting Devyn. She wanted to be comfortable while eating her tacos and drinking tequila.

"That's odd. When he scheduled the appointment, he was the one who specifically asked if you could meet him at the Convention Center instead of here at the office. Are you sure he's not there, and you didn't miss him?"

Asha went back to the front of the building. She looked around the lobby and then toward the front doors. The only person she saw was a maintenance man in grimy coveralls near the entrance along with a couple of other women, who, she assumed, were there for the pageant. "Yeah, I'm sure."

"You want his number?"

Asha checked her watch once more. It was almost four thirty. At this point, she was ready to go. By him not showing up, she had a chance to beat traffic and get home early. Knowing she had no intention of calling, she told Libby, "Sure, send it to me."

"Sending it over," Libby said.

"Thanks, Libby. See you in the morning." By the time the text came through with the name Max Transportation and the phone number, she was already out of the parking lot.

Almost forty-five minutes later, she pulled into the driveway of her town house directly beside a late-model pickup truck that she hadn't expected to be there. She stepped out of her SUV and called out for the owner of the truck.

"Sully? Are you here?"

A few seconds later, the gate leading to her backyard swung open, and Sully emerged, pushing her garbage can. "Yeah, I'm here. I thought you had a meeting?"

"I was supposed to, but it didn't happen. What are you doing here?" she asked as she watched him push the large plastic can with her address painted on the side to the edge of the driveway. When he finished, he walked over and kissed her cheek.

"I came to take the can to the street. And I wanted to make sure I put out those bags of leaves I raked this weekend to be picked up." Sully smiled.

"Oh, I forgot about those," Asha said.

"I figured you would. That's why I came to do it for you," he winked.

"Thank you, handsome. I appreciate it."

Calvin Sullivan wasn't someone Asha would've ever considered dating. He was attractive, hard-working, dependable, and the man could fix damn near anything. They'd met at the hardware store one Saturday afternoon. Not only did he help her find the tool she needed to fix her faucet, but he also repaired it, in addition to mounting her television, installing her ceiling fan, and painting the accent wall of her living room. He'd retired from the army, owned his own business, and was a deacon at his church. He was the most consistent man she'd ever met. She enjoyed spending time with him, and he was everything most women look for in a man. There was just one minor detail: at 51 years of age, Calvin Sullivan was a whopping twenty-three years older than she was. But for the most part, their age difference didn't matter to her, and he didn't seem worried about it either. They liked the same movies and restaurants. Asha wasn't a party girl like she'd been in her younger days and spent most of her time working. The only person she hung out with was Devyn, who was just as much of a homebody as she was these days. Unlike guys her age, Sully didn't require much.

"Well, since you're home, why don't you show your appreciation by letting me take you to dinner?" He grabbed her hand.

"Aw, I would, but I'm meeting Devyn for Taco Tuesdays," she replied. "I gotta get inside, shower, and change so that I won't be late."

"You look fine to me. Why you gotta change?" Sully asked, looking her up and down.

"Because as comfortable as this blouse and these slacks are, I need to put on something a little less boardroom and a lot more booyah," she laughed.

"I don't know what that means, but whatever. You and Devyn have fun. I'll talk to you tomorrow." Sully gave her a look of disappointment.

"Don't be like that. It's just tacos. We won't be out long. I'll call you when I get home. I promise." Asha put her arms around his neck. Because she wore flats, they were about the same height and stood eye to eye. She wanted him to see that he had nothing to worry about. He wasn't a jealous guy, but he seemed a bit bothered whenever she hung out with Devyn.

Sully nodded. “All right, just be careful. I’ll try to wait up for your call.”

“Good.” She gave him a reassuring kiss.

Chapter 3

Devyn

Pablo's Mexican Bistro was packed. Since a gentle breeze was blowing and a decent amount of sunlight was still out, Devyn and Asha had opted to sit out on the restaurant's patio and feast on tacos, tortilla chips with white sauce and salsa, and a round of half-off happy-hour double-shot margaritas. The last thing Devyn needed was the enormous amount of calories she was consuming. Not only was she starving, but she also definitely needed a drink, in addition to a face-to-face girl chat.

"I'm telling you, he's into you," Asha said.

"He's not into me. First of all, he has a girl. Second, he keeps trying to hook me up with one of his boys. If he wanted me, he wouldn't be tryin'a do all that," Devyn said.

"It's a front. He's just saying that. He's not trying to hook you up for real. But then again, he might be. What does his friend look like?" Asha asked.

"Hell, I don't know. I ain't even ask. It doesn't matter because I ain't interested."

"In the friend or Jeff?" Asha raised an eyebrow.

Devyn reached across the table and took her glass. "Gimme this."

"What are you doing?" Asha gasped.

"Clearly, you're drunk," Devyn laughed.

Asha snatched her glass back and finished the last of her drink. "Now, you know I'm not drunk. I've only had one drink."

"I'm honestly surprised you even had that one. Hell, I'm surprised you even *wanted* to hang out tonight. You know how the deacon doesn't like for you to hang out with me," Devyn said, referring to Asha's boyfriend, Sully. Since they'd become a little more serious, Asha had become less and less available to hang out. Devyn knew it was because he didn't really care for her. "He must not know you're out. You're dressed cute too. And curled your hair?"

"You're trying to be funny." Asha gave her a snarky look.

"I'm not. I'm just saying that you're looking cute," Devyn commented. In addition to being surprised by Asha's suggestion earlier that they indulge in Taco Tuesday, she was equally shocked to see her best friend dressed in jeans and a cute top. Asha always dressed as if she were about to go into a corporate meeting: business suits, blazers, slacks, and heels. She also kept her shoulder-length locs pulled back. Tonight, they were hanging freely, framing her gorgeous face.

"You know Sully doesn't have a problem with you. And I figured you needed a night out after the day you had. You've been quite grumpy these days," Asha said, tucking a loc behind her ear.

"Grumpy? What the hell? Am I one of the Seven Dwarfs?" Devyn frowned.

"Maybe that was the wrong word. But I didn't want to use the word 'bitchy.'"

"Wow, I think I like grumpy better." Devyn's eyes became small as she looked across the table.

"Dev, you're my best friend. I know you better than anyone else on this earth." Asha picked up a chip and dipped it into the white sauce.

"Oh God, here we go . . ." Devyn groaned.

"The reason why you're in such a mood these days . . ." Asha continued.

"Please don't say it." Devyn pleaded.

"Is because you need some dick," Asha stated.

"I knew it." Devyn shook her head.

"It's been almost two years since your back has been blown out properly, Dev. That's a long time. And I know you've been through a lot. But you need—"

"What I need is another drink. And I'm gonna go get one." Devyn stood up, smoothing the front of her floral jumpsuit. She planned only to have one drink, but Asha was on one, and it was going to take more alcohol than usual to get through the evening.

"Señora, did you need something?" Miguel, their server, rushed over and asked.

"I was just gonna go get another drink from the bar," Devyn told him.

"Sí, I'll get it for you. It's no problem." Miguel nodded, then turned to Asha, "Another for you as well?"

Asha shook her head, "Oh no, I'm fine."

Devyn teased. "She's a lightweight."

"Whatever. I may be many things, but I ain't never been light nothing: light-skinned, lightweight, lighthearted. Besides, I came for the tacos, not the tequila." Asha pointed to the food in the middle of the table. "Now, stop trying to be cute and sit down and eat. People are staring."

Devyn glanced in the direction Asha was motioning, and sure enough, a guy was looking at her. She politely smiled back, then sat down and picked up a taco, taking a bite.

"So, about your dating dilemma," Asha continued.

"How can I have a dilemma when I ain't dating?" Devyn pointed out.

"That's my point. We're gonna fix that."

"But it's not broken. If I wanted to date, I would—but I don't. And it has nothing to do with what I went through. I'm over that. I just haven't met anyone I vibe with enough even to be interested in," Devyn explained. "Dating is the last thing I'm even thinking about right now. I have more important stuff to worry about than penis and the drama that comes with it."

"Really? Like what?" Asha asked.

"Like figuring out what it is that I'm supposed to be doing with my life. Something that's less stressful and gonna make me more money than this bullshit I'm doing now." Devyn immediately regretted her words as soon as she said them. She didn't have to look at Asha's face to know that they had probably stung a little, which she didn't mean to do. "I mean, don't get me wrong, Asha, I'm grateful for my job. But . . ."

"It's cool, Dev. I understand, and you don't have to apologize."

Asha's flat tone confirmed that Devyn had struck a nerve. Devyn hadn't meant to sound unappreciative. She wouldn't even be working if Asha hadn't heard about the job from a client and suggested that she apply since she complained about being bored. At the time, the savings she'd been living off of were dwindling fast, and she was still trying to figure out her next career move. Being a substitute teacher seemed to be a good idea and a way to put a little money in her pocket while figuring it out. But it definitely wasn't what Devyn enjoyed doing, and it was becoming harder and harder to go to work each day. Not only that, but she also wasn't any closer to discovering what it was she wanted or needed to be doing next.

"I do, and I'm really sorry. I'm not trying to be a bitch, but I'm just so . . ." Devyn tried to think of a word to describe her current state of mind.

"Unfulfilled." Asha found the word Devyn had been searching for.

"Exactly." Devyn nodded. She wasn't used to being in a rut. She'd spent her entire life maneuvering and positioning herself for success. Years of hard work, determination, discipline, and ambition had paid off—until she lost everything within a matter of days. Asha had been by her side through it all. Devyn couldn't ask for a better best friend.

"You went through a season of loss. We all go through that. Yours was longer and harder than most." Asha sighed. "But you've gained some things too. Like Fantasia says, sometimes you gotta lose to win."

Devyn thought about all the things she'd lost: her relationship, her dream job, her mother, and her health, all within a matter of months. The only thing she'd gained in the process was the house that her uncle allowed her to live in and thirty pounds that she didn't want.

"What exactly did I win? Remind me," Devyn said.

"It's all going to come together, Dev. I promise. It just takes time, that's all." Asha gave her a reassuring smile.

"I've given it enough time. I'm tired of being lost. It's like I'm searching for something, but I don't even know what I'm looking for." Devyn shook her head. "I don't even know what direction I'm supposed to face. I used to look in the mirror and know exactly who I was. Now, I don't even recognize the person on the other side."

"Devyn, you're still the same person. You're still beautiful, you're still smart, you're still talented, and God still has a plan for your life."

Devyn looked down at Asha's hand touching her arm. "I know. I just wish he'd give me a sign because right now, I feel like I'm all alone, stuck in a fog and can't see anything."

"You're not alone, Dev. You know I'm right here with you tryin'a help you figure it out. And God is gonna direct both of us to exactly where we're supposed to be."

"You think so?"

"I know so." Asha nodded. "You just gotta be open and willing to receive."

Devyn closed her eyes and lifted her hands, pretending to pray. "God, I'm open. Send me a sign."

"Compliments of the gentleman in the corner." Miguel reappeared and set her margarita on the table moments later.

"Well, that was nice," Devyn said. "Please tell him I said thank you."

"You can tell him yourself. He's standing behind you," Asha whispered.

Devyn turned around, expecting to see the guy she smiled at moments earlier, but it wasn't him. Instead, she found a lanky guy who looked like he wasn't much older than the students in Mrs. Hughes's chemistry class. "Oh, uh, hi."

"Hey, there, beautiful. I wanted to come over and make sure you got your drink," he said. "I'm RayQuan."

"I did. Thanks." Devyn hoped her dry tone would be a deterrent, but he remained where he stood.

"You are more than welcome. You've gotta be the most beautiful chick I've ever seen. May I ask you a question?"

After cringing at the word "chick," Devyn sighed and gave him the answer she knew he wanted to know. "Five-eleven."

"Damn, that's tall as fuck, ma. I love me an Amazonian woman." He nodded. "I guess you already knew what I was gonna ask, huh?"

"Yep."

"So, you think I could get your number?"

"I would, but I'm engaged." Devyn shrugged.

"Damn, that's too bad," RayQuan said, then turned his attention to Asha. "What about you? How tall are you, ma?"

"Six feet, but I'm going to have to decline that delightful offer as well," Asha said, looking quite amused. Devyn knew her friend was suppressing her laughter.

"Well, enjoy the rest of y'all night," RayQuan said, then walked off.

When he was gone, Devyn looked across the table at Asha's face, which was now red. "Go ahead. Let it out."

"You asked for a sign," Asha giggled.

Unable to keep her own straight face, Devyn joined in her friend's laughter. Within seconds, they were both shaking and dabbing at the tears that were streaming. Devyn was so caught up in the moment with her best friend that she didn't even think to turn around and make sure their young suitor was no longer in earshot until seconds later. She turned around in her seat and scanned the area nearby, relieved when she didn't see any sign of him. Just as she was about to turn back around, she noticed the guy who'd caught her eye earlier exiting the patio area. As she watched him, he turned around, and their eyes met. He smiled at her again.

"Do you know that guy?" Devyn turned to Asha. "I think I know him from somewhere, but I don't know where."

"What guy? Where?" Asha leaned over and looked past Devyn.

"The guy smiling at us. He's right by the door in the jacket."

Asha shrugged. "I don't see anybody by the door, Dev."

Devyn turned back and saw that he was gone. "That's crazy. He was right there."

For a second, Devyn considered getting up and going to see if she could find him. He seemed so familiar. But it was too late. He was probably long gone, and her free frozen margarita was melting.

Later that night, Devyn stepped out of her shower and stood in front of the full-length mirror behind the bathroom door. Instead of using her bath towel to wrap around her wet body, she used it to wipe the moisture from the mirror, then stared at her reflection. It was like looking at a stranger. Her face was the same, but the abdomen, which was once flat, now puffed out, and she could pinch mounds of skin on the sides. The once-perfect B-cup breasts were a full C cup, closer to a D, now. Countless hours of cardio that she'd been putting in lately had only resulted in her hips widening, buttocks tightening, and legs toning. No matter how hard she worked out, she couldn't get back to the perfect bikini body she used to have. The body that had made her almost famous was forever gone.

No longer able to tolerate what she saw, Devyn turned around and stared at the bathroom counter, which held the source of her contorted, fuller figure that also enabled her to live: her meds. The pills, prescribed by her physician, kept her alive, but they killed her dreams.

Devyn had never heard of Addison's disease until the doctors finally diagnosed her after she lay in the hospital for damn near two weeks after the wedding disaster. Her frequent nausea, fainting spells, constant thirst, and irritability that she'd been suffering from for a year prior were all a result of her illness. What she thought were panic attacks and chest pains brought on by stress were also symptoms that she ignored. Devyn was faced with the reality of never going back and doing what she loved: modeling. Because she was susceptible to blood clots, traveling on planes every week to get to even meet with design houses, let alone walk in runway shows, was no longer possible. The somber likelihood of having to be on oxygen in the future meant that her career was over.